MW01503854

PRAISE FOR *BLACK MARIA*

"No one leaves the past behind in Boyer's gritty debut—it's an open wound to the heart. The shocking murder of a child is the final nail in a wider American tragedy engulfing the dried-up coal town. More than ever regional writing is defining crime fiction and *Black Maria* marks out Boyer as a voice you want to hear."

—Paul Burke, Crime Time

"*Black Maria* is a feat of literary muscle and grace. Boyer's electric rust-belt mystery probes the deep sub-territories of geography and psyche, always alive to the dissolving present and to time's dizzying sweep. The era is the '70s, the place a moribund Pennsylvania mining town vampired and poisoned by greed, where a young, ambitious cop and a worn-out one must solve the horrifying murder of a child. But the place where everything in *Black Maria* really happens is the deep, vast, coal-dark chambered maze that is the human heart."

—Jo Perry, author of *The World Entire*

"*Black Maria* is a blue-collar procedural narrated in the poetry of the damned. Boyer's debut depicts, unguarded, that we live in a damn mean world...and even the offspring of 'captains of industry' carry no immunity to wrath. If justice is a human right—all evidence to the contrary thus far—then it mandates that regular people, imperfect and salt-of-the-earth, serve as guarantors of said right. But Boyer reveals how justice is a shape-shifter and takes the form of the vessel by which it is delivered—and sometimes that cup runneth over."

—Matt Phillips, Thriller Award finalist
and author of *A Good Rush of Blood*

Editor: Krysta Winsheimer of Muse Retrospect
Cover photograph and design: Garth Jackson

ISBN: 979-8-9869930-9-6
Run Amok Crime, 2024
First Edition

RunAmok

Printed in the USA

BLACK MARIA

CHRISTINE BOYER

For JD, who gave me his support.
And for Irene, who gave me my first books
and my love of storytelling.

1972

CHAPTER ONE

The dead boy looked like one of the painted angels on the ceiling at St. Callistus: fat cheeks and dark curls, pale skin with the barest hint of warmth. He looked so peaceful, so outwardly asleep, it took Detective Felix Kosmatka a moment to adjust his field of vision and take in the rest of the crime scene.

The boy's slashed throat. The bedding turned black with congealed blood. Felix swallowed hard against the burn of acid that crept up his throat to lay heavy against the back of his tongue. He inhaled deeply through his nose, but that was the wrong thing to do. The iron-heavy scent of blood crawled inside his nostrils, made him taste pennies, made his stomach twist and heave.

He glanced at his captain, standing beside him in the bedroom doorway. That'd be a quick way to end his career, puking in front of his boss like some idiot rookie.

Captain Krause shook his head and turned to face Felix. The old man was tall and stooped, vulturous with his beak of a nose and darting eyes. His uniform hung off his frame like a line of wash on a windless day.

"I've never seen anything like this," Krause said, his stale cigarette breath wafting over Felix in a haze. "Not in all my years here on the force. A kid, for Christ's sake."

Felix said nothing. He didn't parrot any of the empty platitudes people always said when terrible things happened. Krause hated trite shit like that, and he hated small talk as a rule anyway. It'd be smart not to set him off in the middle of a crime scene, especially one like this.

A kid. Who the hell could do such a thing?

It was early Friday morning and still dark outside. Felix guessed the officers trawling the crime scene functioned on little to no sleep, already nursing their payday hangovers from the night before. The captain watched them, made sure they kept it professional, his rheumy grey eyes wary.

1

Krause turned back to Felix. He rubbed his hand along his stubbled jaw. "Take a quick sweep of the scene, then we'll go talk to the boy's family. Just the basics. We can bring them to the station later for formal statements."

"Yes, sir." Felix tipped a nod to Krause, then turned to face the crime scene.

He braced himself. This was a career-defining case. Anyone could see how a high-profile case like this could change his trajectory: from young detective in another dying Pennsylvania town like Mariensburg to up-and-coming star in a larger jurisdiction. There would be better pay, better cases. Maybe a future with promotions, a captain-track role, and all of it happening elsewhere.

The thought flitted through his head, came and went in an instant. This was a goddamned *kid*. Chubby faced, curly haired. Slaughtered in his own bed and laid out like a piece of grotesque art. There was no room for selfishness about future promotions. There was a killer on the loose, and Felix Kosmatka would be the one to catch him.

*

The boy's bedroom didn't look like any kid's room Felix had ever seen.

Felix was one of five boys, right in the middle of the pack, and he'd always shared a bedroom with his brothers. Everything had been handed down, passed around, salvaged and patched-up. The faded bedding threadbare in the middle. None of the furniture had matched, and the room always held the heavy fug of boyhood that could never quite be aired out.

The furniture in this room, ornately carved from dark wood, gleamed richly. A deep-green bedspread covered the bed. It looked like it belonged to some old lord out of a gothic novel. It made the sight of the dead boy and the blood that much more shocking.

Everything was tastefully appointed, the subtle elegance of the very rich. From the textured wallpaper to the few small paintings hung on the walls, it hardly seemed like a child's room. There were no toys, no model airplanes strung from the ceiling. No posters of sports teams or movie stars tacked to the walls.

The only sign the room belonged to a child at all was the small shelf lined with books. Felix knelt down to read the titles. The entire collection of Oz books, first editions from the looks of them. The Hardy Boys, the Boxcar Children. *The Lord of the Rings*, an omnibus as thick as a phone book.

He hoped the boy got to read them all before he died. He hated to think he was murdered halfway through something, the plot unresolved, missing the satisfaction of snapping a book shut when it was finished—

Stop, he admonished himself. *Focus. Work the scene. Examine the body.*

Felix walked toward the bed and steeled his nerves with each step. The iron tang of the spilled blood slunk back into his nose and throat until he could taste it. He swallowed hard against the flood of saliva that filled his mouth.

He would not throw up in the middle of this crime scene. He would *not*. It wasn't professional, though lots of guys puked at the worst scenes: the car crashes that broke open bodies, the house fires that left the occupants as gnarled black lumps that smelled unnervingly like barbecue. He had thrown up on the job exactly once, back in his patrol days, and the memory still made him wince in remembered shame.

Felix would *not* puke now. It would be offensive to the victim. Someone had done a terrible thing to the boy, and Felix would honor him by being a professional. He would not let his roiling emotions—or his roiling gut—taint the scene.

He stood beside the bed, closed his eyes. He took a steadying breath through his mouth.

He opened his eyes. He looked at the dead boy.

The officer standing guard by the front door of the house had already given him the scant details. The victim was Thomas John Farney, named for his grandfather. Everyone called him "Junior" even though the name had skipped a generation. Seven years old but he looked small for his age, likely because he was laid out in the center of the huge bed.

Or maybe he looked smaller because he was dead. Death made people small. Felix had seen enough of it in his personal life—his father, his grandparents—and in his professional one. Death took a person's essential qualities and left behind a husk, as if the spirit or soul had pushed against the edges of the body and filled it a touch beyond capacity.

Alive, the boy had probably seemed bigger, filled to the brim with the endless energy of the young that Felix could just barely remember from his own childhood. That skinned-knee, dirt-under-the-nails exuberance. A vivacity so blinding and bright that death seemed an impossibility.

Now the body was an empty vessel, shucked off and discarded. Whatever made Thomas John Farney *him* was long gone.

The boy was tucked under the bedspread with his hands arranged on top of it. His head was propped against a bank of pillows, pointed chin against his chest. An errant strand of his dark hair curled like a comma against his cheek. His lips were parted, as if he were about to speak.

Felix bent down and examined the slashed throat. The neat, straight line extended across the entire length of the boy's thin neck. The cut was deep. He swallowed thickly, realized without the heap of pillows, the boy's head might detach from the body.

Felix made his mental notes. *Deep, one stroke, no hesitation. No signs of struggle. No apparent defensive wounds.*

He stepped away from the bed. His head swam. A million sparks of light fizzled and popped in his peripherals. Forget puking. He was dangerously close to passing out. He clasped his hands in front of him, and he pinched the webbing of one hand between the thumb and forefinger of his other. He dug his fingernails in until they made crescent-shaped indents that filled with blood and would leave bruises. He focused on the pain until his vision cleared.

Then he turned to survey the room more closely.

Nothing appeared out of place. He walked over to the pair

of windows and studied each. Both locked from the inside. He peered outside, barely able to make out the view in the weak grey light of early morning.

The boy's bedroom was on the second floor on the west side of the house. The property sloped down into a scrub forest, and the boy's bedroom faced that pitched drop. It was steep, but not impossible to navigate, Felix supposed. Someone determined enough wouldn't be stopped by it. He made a note to check outside for prints or indents from a ladder, though it seemed unlikely.

He turned away from the window and scanned the floor. No footprints, no dropped murder weapon. Nothing.

He walked over to the policeman dusting the dresser for prints.

"Got anything?" Felix asked.

"Just a bunch of small prints that probably belong to him." The policeman jerked his head in the direction of the body. "I might have a few partials that look like they belong to an adult, but I wouldn't get your hopes up. They might not be enough to use."

"Keep working it."

Keeping the dead boy carefully in his peripherals, Felix rejoined the captain in the doorway.

"First thoughts?" Krause asked.

"Room's remarkably clean. It's strange the body doesn't show any sign of a struggle. There should be more of a mess, but most of the blood is pooled on the bed. No spatter."

"Prints?"

Felix jerked his thumb over his shoulder in the direction of the policeman dealing deft daubs of powder along the surface of the dresser. "They mostly belong to the kid, but he might have a few partials on an adult."

"Farney has an entire fucking fleet of servants. It's gonna take a while to eliminate everyone who's been in the house."

"Assuming it wasn't one of them."

Krause fixed him with one of his steely stares. His eyes were watery, probably from lack of sleep, and the whites were shot through with fine red lines, probably from his love of bottom-shelf whiskeys. The captain called it his medicine, and he ran a small dispensary out of the bottom drawer of his desk back at the precinct.

"You thinking a disgruntled housekeeper did this?" Krause asked.

"No, but..." He let the conjunction hang heavy in the air.

"Yeah, *but*. But we have to rule them out. We can get a list of people who work in the house and go from there."

The two stood in the doorway and watched the careful cataloguing of the crime scene. Then Krause heaved a sigh, reached up, and straightened his tie. He gave Felix an appraising look.

"Let's go talk to the family, but let me do the talking. Stand there and keep your mouth shut. Thomas Farney is a powerful man, and we gotta play him real careful. Got it?"

Felix nodded. "Got it, Captain."

CHAPTER TWO

Together, they made their way through the enormous mansion to where the family was sequestered. The family, Krause told Felix as they walked, meant Thomas Senior and his wife, Clara. Both of the boy's parents were away, and efforts were being made to reach them.

The hired help was gone for the night. The housekeeper—the one who found the body and called the police—had been in hysterics. She'd been bundled up and sent home. She could give a more detailed statement later in the day.

Felix had grown up working-class on the South Side, where the houses stood in crammed rows, identical company houses from when the town had been owned by the coal mine. They all had the same layout, the same thin walls and windows that rattled in their casings, the same narrow doorways and airless rooms.

After the war, a middle class had sprung up in the town. People were able to afford better, and they moved out of the shitty houses stacked on top of each other for new-build ranches farther out. They spiraled out and away from the center of town into wider spaces with room for driveways and backyard pools, emerald lawns manicured to level perfection.

So while there were nice homes in Mariensburg, Thomas Farney owned the only proper mansion. He had built it apart from the rabble he had employed to work his coal mine, built the stone mansion away from the little patch town of Shale Hollow with its rows of cheap houses and company store and clapboard churches. Back then, the mansion had been surrounded by a copse of black cherry and sugar maple, but as Shale Hollow turned into Mariensburg, the burgeoning town had eventually grown around the Farney mansion and its expansive grounds.

When Felix was a kid, he and his friends used to ride their bikes past to gawp at it. From the outside, it looked like something from the pulp horror books they used to trade on the sly like pornography. They'd ride to the mansion, straddle the frames of their bikes, and gaze up at the imposing stone fortress.

They dared each other to climb the wrought-iron fencing, to break in to prove they were as tough as they pretended to be. Their courage always failed them. They wrote entire sordid histories about the place: ghost stories about workers bricked alive in the foundation or ancient Indian burial mounds razed to make space for the mansion. They speculated about whether it was haunted or not.

If it wasn't haunted then, it surely will be now, he thought. He followed Krause down the staircase, across the slick marble of the foyer, and toward Thomas Farney's study. A pair of uniformed officers stood guard outside of the study, posted to keep the old man inside and away from the crime scene.

Felix peered through the door at the patriarch of the Farney family. Thomas paced behind a massive desk of dark wood polished to a mirror shine. His shirtsleeves were rolled up to his elbows, and his hands curled into fists that flexed with each step he took. His disheveled white hair looked as though he'd been running his hands through it. When they entered the room, he swung his head around to face them. His eyes were bloodshot and swollen.

"What did you find?" he asked without preamble. His voice was hoarse, raw edged.

"We are still processing the scene," Krause replied. He paused, then added, "Let me say again how sorry we are for your loss. We are doing everything—"

Thomas cut him off, stilled his pacing. "I want to know if you found anything in there."

Krause shook his head, once. "We are still working the scene," he repeated.

The older man fixed the captain with a withering glare, then yanked the chair out from under his desk. He dropped into it like a stone and glared at them, his eyes red and baleful.

"Why are you here then? Go work the damned scene."

"We need to ask you a few questions, sir," Krause replied.

"Ask then," Thomas said. "And then get the hell out and find who did this."

Krause glanced at Felix, gave him the barest of nods. Felix slipped his notebook and pen from his coat pocket and nodded back.

"Can you walk us through where you were last night and this morning?" Krause asked.

"I was in my office at the factory all night. I didn't get home until... well, I didn't come home until my housekeeper called. Hysterical..." He scrubbed his face again. Thomas Farney was hale for his seventy-odd years, usually looked an entire decade younger than his age, but in that moment, he looked ancient. Haggard.

"And then?"

"I came straight home to a house full of cops." Thomas paused, shifted his unblinking stare between the two men. "I didn't believe it. Next thing I know, some cop is telling me my grandson, my boy was... was... they wouldn't let me see. They wouldn't let me see what they did to my b-boy." His voice stuttered and broke on the last word, a dry bark of a sob escaping him.

Felix fixed his gaze on the ground to let the man pull himself together. He stared at the toes of his shoes, the intricate pattern of the polished wood floor. Crying made him uncomfortable, though he supposed if there was a time for it, it was now.

Felix had never faced such a tragedy. Life had only ever dealt him common griefs, the everyday tragedies. Grandparents dying of cancer, father dropping dead from an aneurysm, a kinked blood vessel in his head that finally snapped after decades of lying dormant.

Nothing so unthinkable as murder, and certainly not the murder of a child.

When Thomas finally calmed and gave a rough clearing of his throat, Krause asked, "Anyone else in the house last night? Or early morning today?"

"My wife, Clara."

"We'll need to speak with her."

"You can try."

Felix's pen scratched as he wrote, and he looked up at Thomas. His expression turned stony, expressionless save for the bloodshot eyes. The old man caught his glance.

"My wife is senile," he clarified.

"She can't speak?"

"She can, but she's often confused. Much of what she says is nonsense. I can arrange to have her nurse here while you try to question her."

"What about the boy's parents?" Krause asked.

Thomas made a disgusted noise, a *tsk*-ing that spoke of his disapproval. "His mother is off in the city on one of her social visits. She's been contacted and is on her way back now."

"And the father? Your son?"

"I sent my driver out to retrieve Jack."

"Retrieve from where?"

"The country club. He spends his evenings there."

Felix noted it, glanced at Krause who caught his look and arched an eyebrow in reply.

"Your son is at the country club this late?" Krause asked.

"He and his set play cards there damned near every night, often into morning."

"Every night? You're sure on that?"

"Yes, I am. Every night." Thomas's tone turned peevish. "He gets his monthly allowance, and he spends it the same way each month."

Krause nodded. He moved on, but Felix could tell by the two deep furrows between his brows that the captain had tucked that tidbit away for further consideration.

"We'll need a list of everyone who has access to the house. Anyone at all."

"You'll get it."

"That's all we need for now, I think. We'll schedule time for you to come by the precinct to give a formal statement later today." A beat. "You have our condolences."

Felix murmured his own "sorry for your loss." He snapped his notebook shut and tucked it into his coat pocket.

"Save them, your condolences." Thomas stared at them hard, unblinking. "You catch the bastard who did this."

"I've called in help from the state. They're sending someone out of Harrisburg from the Commonwealth's detective bureau."

Felix glanced at his captain in surprise. Krause caught that look, too, and he gave the slightest shake of his head. *Not now*, the gesture said. *Save it for later.*

Thomas waved both of them away with the practiced flick of a man used to ordering others around. They repeated their condolences, then left the man with his grief and anger.

*

Felix followed the captain outside. In silence, they watched the sun rise over the eastern ridge, a shimmer of angry red that cast everything in a ruddy light. The morning air, heavy with dew, held the promising bite of winter. Felix smelled the faint scent of woodsmoke, the earthy aroma of decomposing leaf mold.

A killing frost wasn't far off. It'd finish off the lingering plants in everyone's gardens. His mother would be on his case soon, nagging him to pull up the dead stalks of the summer's tomato plants, to spade in some compost before the ground got too hard.

The thought of impending winter made Felix tired, a bone-deep weariness he always felt when the short days and cold weather loomed. Winter made him feel the press of time, the keen press of another year with him still rooted in place.

He turned his face toward the sun and felt the weak warmth of it. He closed his eyes. The white afterimage of the sun floated behind his eyelids, and then the image of the child on the bed swam into his mind's eye. He tried to push it away—the pale hands curled against the green bedding; the lips parted, already turning blue—

Krause hacked out a phlegmy cough, and Felix snapped his eyes open. He turned and watched the captain reach into his coat pocket and pull out a crumpled pack of cigarettes.

Krause shook one loose, tucked it into the seam of his mouth, lit it. He took a deep drag, the blue-grey smoke pluming out of his nostrils. "What are you thinking?" he asked.

Felix wasn't thinking much at the moment. The shock of seeing a child murdered in his bed forestalled any helpful musing on next steps. If he stayed silent, though, he'd risk Krause's temper. He blurted out the first obvious thought to flit through his mind.

"Why was a little boy left alone at night with just a sick old woman?"

Krause shrugged. "Playing devil's advocate? I left my kids alone all the time once they reached school age. Me and the wife played bridge at the neighbor's. Never thought twice about it."

"I suppose." Felix's parents had done the same. He remembered plenty of unsupervised evenings with just his brothers, a feral gaggle of shifting loyalties that usually left one of them bleeding or lightly bruised.

"Town's safe enough. Most people don't even lock their doors." A beat, then he added, "Most of the crime happens on the South Side. Not here."

A prickle of embarrassment crept up the back of Felix's neck. The South Side was his part of town, though Krause was right. The bulk of the police calls came from there, especially on the weekends. Bar fights that spilled into the streets. Domestics where a husband slapped his old lady around. Vandalism, boosted cars. It was a microcosm of petty crime centered around the working class who lived in Mariensburg.

Even then, it was almost never murder, premeditated or not.

"Devil's advocate," Felix replied, thinking about how he and his friends used to dare each other to break into the mansion as children, "there was no obvious sign of forced entry. How did the perp get in?"

"A question to pose to the hired help when they give their statements." He took another deep inhale, puffed out another rich cloud of smoke. "Another question. If someone brutally murdered your son and your father sent his driver out to retrieve you, why aren't you here yet?"

Jack Farney. The boy's father. Felix played along. "Country club is only fifteen, twenty minutes away."

"Maybe the driver couldn't find him. There's a bunch of buildings in that complex." A beat, another drag on his cigarette. "Or maybe Thomas Farney doesn't know his son as well as he thinks. Gambling, every night? I've known hard-core gamblers. Even they take a break and come up for air once in a while."

"He did say every night, then amended it to *almost*."

"Aw, hell. Guy's in shock. We gotta take these initial statements with a giant fucking grain of salt." Krause tapped his cigarette with a practiced flick of his finger. Motes of ash floated in a shaft of morning sunlight. He glanced over his shoulder toward the house, fixed Felix with a conspiratorial look.

"Then again, sometimes these initial statements are better. Less time to think of a lie," he added.

Felix didn't reply. He shifted on the thin soles of his dress shoes and looked out across the lawn at the slopes of the town below. A thin stratum of fog clung to the ground. It gave the rows of houses below a hazy, indistinct look like they were floating.

People would be awake by now, pouring cereal into bowls, getting dressed, getting ready to go to work or school. When would they find out a child had been murdered while they slept? Would the trusting citizens of Mariensburg lock their doors tonight when the sun set?

"I'll send a patrol car out to the country club. It's protocol to round up loose family members on cases like this," Krause said.

A stretch of silence, then the captain shot Felix a curious look. "You pissed off I called in the cavalry?" he asked.

Felix *was*, but he wasn't about to admit it and sound like a petulant asshole. "Makes sense. High-profile case," he replied.

"It is." A beat. "You know, Thomas Farney never got much press the way the other rich types did, but he's up there with Carnegie and the Rockefellers. Just as wealthy and just as ruthless."

Felix knew of the wealth and the ruthlessness. Most people in town did. He nodded at the captain, who continued.

"He's pals with Governor Shapp. He's got all sorts of powerful assholes in his pocket. Hell, he had my predecessor in his pocket."

"That sounds like a threat."

"It is." He took a final pull on his cigarette, dropped it. He ground it out on the flagstones with his heel. "Look, the minute Thomas Farney's grandson turned up murdered, the clock started ticking. You understand? We need all the help we can get."

"I understand."

"Good man." Krause reached into his pocket and snagged another burner, then paused in lighting it, his cupped hands cradling the lighter halfway to his face. "Looks like the meat wagon's here." He jerked his chin, and Felix turned to see the coroner's van trundling up the driveway toward them.

"You handle the bagging, okay?" the captain continued. "Make sure everyone's respectful. No gallows humor on this one."

Felix agreed, then walked over to where the van parked. He drew in a lungful of the cool morning air in the brightening day, ready to build his case.

CHAPTER THREE

The phone rang shrill that morning.

It pulled Detective Adam Shaffer from his bed. He lurched in the dark, slapped his hands along the dark hallway until he hit the light switch. He cursed at the yellow flare of the kitchen light, fumbled half-blind at the receiver in its cradle.

"What the hell d'ya want?" he growled, his voice thick with sleep.

He had closed out a case a few days earlier, a real doozy. There'd been a serial rapist in Franklin County who targeted older women—widows, spinster-types who lived alone and were easy prey. Sick shit.

It had dragged out for long months, many of the vics unwilling to cooperate. They were all of a type: prim women who went to church, who kept immaculate homes, whose worst sin involved saying an occasional curse word. They had all been too embarrassed by the nature of the crimes against them, unwilling to sit with a male detective and relive the experience.

Most wanted to put it behind them, forget it, but a lucky break—an offhand comment from one of the few willing vics, something about an unusual car with a two-tone home paint job—landed him at the doorstep of the perp.

Now the rape-o cooled his heels in jail. Adam hoped the accommodations were especially bleak for the bastard. Other criminals looked poorly upon those types: the rape-o's, the pedos, the assholes who hurt children and old people. Adam didn't think it'd be much of a tragedy if some of the other inmates gave the guy a tune-up when the guards weren't looking. It might cheer up some of those women to see his beauty shot in the paper sans teeth.

It had been a job well done, the case coming down to old-fashioned gumshoe work of walking the beat and beating the bushes for leads. After he snapped the steel bracelets on the rape-o, Adam managed the paperwork, wrapped up the loose ends to hand over to the district attorney.

He was owed some rest. Back when he started on the force, he used to get a buzz from solving a case. The moment the handcuffs clinked on the perp's wrists, the moment the judge hammered the gavel with a *crack*, Adam got a jolt—a burst of heat and energy in the center of him that radiated outward until it felt like electricity was about to spark from his fingertips.

Those days were long gone. The thrill of catching bad guys had faded, like the efficacy of most drugs. Now he just wanted a good night's sleep, a few days to rest. A few days to shed the past months like a snakeskin, to slough off the bad juju that came from stalking a rapist piece of shit across county lines. He had planned to sleep in late, drive to the diner. He'd planned on indulging in a greasy breakfast and coffee so strong he could practically chew it.

The phone call ruined his plan.

Late-night, early-morning calls... they always held the same bad news. A bad person did a bad thing, and Adam was called to catch them.

The bad thing this time? A murdered kid in Elk County.

The bad person this time? Adam sent a message out to this bad person, a telepathic communiqué sent over the airwaves, out into the ether: *I'm coming for you, asshole. Enjoy your last days in the free world.*

Mariensburg was situated in the great north-central wasteland of the Commonwealth, a speck of a place nestled between the green swath of the Allegheny National Forest and the Susquehannock State Forest. It was three hours northeast of Pittsburgh, five hours northwest of Philly. For Adam, it was a three hour drive, a hellish trek of twisting two-lanes with the infrequent hairpin turn to keep a man on his toes. It gave Adam time to consider.

It was John Krause who called him. The captain had been a few classes ahead of him at the State Police training school, though those years felt like a century ago. A victim of his Kraut surname,

Krause had found himself railroaded by state brass, even after he had enlisted and spent his wartime career on a tiny island in the Pacific, refueling the planes sinking Hirohito's fleet.

After the war? He might have ended up giving asshole teenagers their driver's license tests if he hadn't had the wherewithal to make a move on his own. He took on the sergeant's role in Mariensburg as the best approximation to a fresh start. He served under the old captain, then took over when the bastard keeled over at a Knights of Columbus dinner.

Krause had a staunch Prussian sensibility. Even on the call that roused Adam from his slumber, Krause had been matter-of-fact. There was a kid murdered in his bed. Grandson to a local business scion. Krause had a handful of detectives, but only the youngest was worth half a damn. He needed help, and quickly.

Politically, it was tricky. Said local scion dined with the governor once or twice a year. He sent expensive Cuban cigars to his congressman to help grease the skids of his business machinations. Krause didn't want control of the case to spiral out of his hands.

Adam understood his concern. He'd worked enough high-profile cases to know how politics could warp even the most straightforward case. Add a very wealthy man with powerful people in his pocket? It was a disaster waiting to happen.

Mariensburg sat perched on the Allegheny Plateau, a geographical anomaly from when glaciers covered the country. Adam piloted his Pontiac Bonneville through the outskirts, scrubby land pocked with run-down houses little better than tar-paper shacks. An old weigh station stood back from the side of the road, tilted and half caved in on itself. It seemed to be the dividing line between rural and city proper.

The shacks ceded to small houses, shabby but neat. There was obvious effort—fresher paint on the trim, bright mums nodding their fat, bright heads in the yards. "The proud poor" his old man used to call folks like that with a sneer, as if the Shaffer family hadn't also toed the line of poverty when Adam was a kid.

Into the city proper. The houses grew bigger, the yards more maintained. Early fall already burnished some of the leaves scarlet and gold. Businesses appeared: A gas station, a burger shack. An auto repair shop with stacks of bald tires against the side of the building. A Catholic church with a banner strung across its entrance that advertised an autumn festival. A massive factory complex with smokestacks scored against the pale-blue September sky.

He'd have to secure a motel room somewhere. His stomach snarled in protest of its missing breakfast.

Both errands had to wait. First, he would go to the barracks, find Krause. He'd meet the green kid who was smart and eager, who could benefit from the expertise of an older, more seasoned detective. Which was how Krause had phrased it on his call, though he had employed more colorful adjectives that were all derivative of the root word *fuck*.

Wunderkind Felix Something-or-other. His new partner for the foreseeable future.

The police barracks sat in the center of town. They were housed in a squat brick pile with high, useless windows set at irregular intervals. Adam slid the Bonneville into an open spot across the street, then tilted the rearview mirror to give himself the once-over. He winced at his reflection. He looked like reheated dog shit.

No, he looked exactly like what he was: a man who had been building up a terrific sleep debt for months on a rape case that made his ulcer flare and burn. He had dark bags under his eyes, and the lines that ran on either side of his mouth seemed to deepen every day. The man staring back at him in the mirror looked an awful lot like his old man.

It wasn't the worst thing, though, looking like dog shit. Adam figured rolling into foreign territory looking a little rough couldn't hurt him. He'd been brought into enough jurisdictions where the local force was less than thrilled by his presence.

The big cities—Philly, Pittsburgh—all had their own detective bureaus. They only brought him in on second opinions, cross-jurisdiction squabbles. Usually, he was called into places with no detectives or no police force at all. The Pennsylvania State Police served as a bulwark against the places without law, the small towns and villages, filling in the gaps as best they could.

The small towns never liked it. Insular, entrenched, they wanted to solve their own problems even if they didn't have the resources. They were suspicious of outsiders. Their hackles were already up, so for Adam to come on the scene looking natty in a three-piece suit like Paul Newman did no one any good.

Better to lean into the ragged, run-down look and put the local yokels at ease. He could almost pretend it was intentional.

"Just keep telling yourself that," Adam muttered to his reflection. He sighed, rubbed his eyes. They felt gritty, like the inside of his eyelids were lined with sandpaper. He twisted the rearview mirror back into place. He rubbed his hand along his jaw and grimaced at the patchy stubble he had missed in his haste to leave that morning.

He climbed out of the car, slid into his suit coat. He put his hat on with the brim angled like how Bogart wore it as Sam Spade. He walked across the street and entered the barracks.

CHAPTER FOUR

Felix supervised the coroner's removal of the body. He crossed himself, muttered the words *"Father-Son-Holy Spirit."* It surprised him how quickly the muscle memory kicked in without conscious thought.

He walked the exterior of the house now that he had daylight to see by. No bloody prints, no footprints in the mud. He walked the entire house, though the team of policemen had already thoroughly documented the mansion. He knelt and examined the lockset of every exterior door, took out his penlight and studied the brass for gouges or nicks that would speak to lock-picking. Also nothing.

With little else to do on the scene, he sealed off the slain boy's bedroom, sealed off the second floor. He returned to the barracks to write out his notes.

And to wait for the cavalry.

Krause calling for help was a letdown. Felix felt like a kid again, sorely disappointed by wanting something desperately—to be picked first for kickball, to get a new bike for Christmas—and not getting it. It was the feeling of a too-tight throat, a sick cramping in his gut. But he held his tongue. He bit back the childish disappointment at having to share his shiny new toy.

Don't be an asshole, he chided himself. *A case about a murdered child isn't a toy.*

He saw Krause's wisdom in calling for help. Felix wasn't stupid. He knew he was green, relegated to small-time crimes because Mariensburg was mostly a small-time crimes sort of place. He also wasn't blind to the bit of good timing that had helped him make detective so young.

The police force dwindled every year as the town's population fell off. The boomtown days were behind them. Mariensburg sloughed off citizens in a steady trickle. Old people died. Young people went away to college or moved to the city for better opportunities and never returned.

There was less to patrol, less to police each year. Fewer tax dollars to fund the entire machine. Felix was one of only three detectives. The other two, Winslow and Haney, were old-timers, the sort of men who found the perfect balance of doing little and still getting paid for it. They were only running out the clock until they earned their pensions. They were already half-retired, often asleep on the job. They grumbled when they had to leave their desks to actually do work.

They weren't asleep now. Both men were in early—miracles never ceased—and both men were bright-eyed, showered and shaved in clean, pressed suits. Their court suits. Winslow with his sad eyes and hangdog face like a basset hound. Weasel-faced Haney, short and skinny, with a too-big skull set on his stalk of a neck.

They think they have a part to play in this, Felix thought. *Even though Krause gave me the case.*

He sat at his desk, crammed in the corner of the bullpen, tucked underneath the industrial clock that ran a reliable ten minutes behind no matter how many times he reset it. He rocked back in his chair and tapped the chewed eraser end of the pencil against his front teeth as he watched the crowd.

The barracks, usually quiet on a Friday morning, vibrated with activity. A murder in Mariensburg was bound to bring out the rubberneckers, even within the police force. Off-duty cops filled the building to the brim, buzzed around, added to the din of ringing phones and slamming doors.

They clumped in groups of three or four and shared their theories with each other. They glanced his way, looked him over. A few tried to ask him questions, but he gave them each the same "no comment" he knew infuriated them.

"Come on, Kosmatka," Winslow said, his voice dolorous. "Bring us up to speed."

"Give us *something*," Haney added. "You caught the big case, buddy. At least throw us some scraps to keep us fed."

Felix tapped the eraser against his teeth, pretended to consider it before he repeated, "No comment," which made Winslow groan. Haney gave a loose jacking-off motion, and they turned away to resume their speculating.

"Hey, Puss!" someone called out, startling him. He groaned at the hated nickname and looked around. Receptionist Rhonda stood by the door, hand on her hip. She gave him a wave, and her red lacquered fingernails glinted and caught the light. "Guy here to see you and the captain. Looks like a used car salesman."

Felix stood up. He took his coat from the back of his chair, pulled it on, smoothed it out. He walked across the bullpen and past Rhonda with her aura of flowery perfume and her shit-eating grin.

"You know, it wouldn't hurt to use my Christian name," he said. "Especially in front of everyone."

"You gonna tattle to the captain about it?" she retorted with that same wide smile.

"I might, Roadhouse," he replied, using her nickname from high school that spoke to her less-than-chaste adventures at the dive bar outside of the city limits. Teenagers with unconvincing fake IDs went to the Roadhouse for bad beer and worse music. Rhonda had allegedly been a regular there during their formative years.

"And I thought you were one of the good ones." She frowned when she said it, a playful moue that ceded to another grin.

Felix shook his head at her with his own mock frown. "No such thing. We're all dogs." He walked through the open door into the reception area.

Rhonda's assessment was apt. The man waiting for him was wide and paunchy, like a star linebacker gone to seed. The suit might have been well-fitted a decade ago, but it strained across the broad shoulders now. The sleeves ended an inch too soon, revealing hairy wrists. He wore a brown felt hat perched at a rakish angle on his big balding dome of a head.

"You Felix?" he asked. He didn't give him a chance to respond before his hand shot out in greeting. "Detective Adam Shaffer, out of Harrisburg."

Felix took his hand, shook it. Pried it out of his vice-grip a beat later. "Detective Kosmatka. We appreciate you coming so quickly."

"It's no problem. I just wrapped up a case, so it was advantageous timing." He looked around, peered past Felix at the hive of activity in the bullpen. He slapped his stomach and turned back to Felix.

"I drove straight through morning," he said. "You know where a guy can scare up some grub? You can fill me in on the preliminaries while I eat."

✱

Felix sent Rhonda off to the local diner for food and better coffee than the precinct's usual burnt swill. Krause wandered out of his office, decades older in the hours since he and Felix spoke at the Farney mansion. He stooped more than usual, his shoulders pulled in and rounded like he expected a blow. He caught sight of where Adam had posted himself beside Felix's desk, and he made his way over to them.

"Adam," he said. The din of the other cops had quieted when Adam arrived, and now that Krause joined the scene, the room got quieter still. Felix could practically hear the creaking strain as they tried to eavesdrop.

Krause shook hands warmly with the state detective, and Felix was surprised to catch a faint smile on the captain's face. It was disconcerting, like seeing a dog walk on two legs.

"John," Adam replied. He glanced around the room at the gossip-mongers milling around for a scrap of fresh news, the sideways glances cast their way. "Looks like you got a hell of a case on your hands."

"A fucking mess is what it is." He glanced around, too, the seam of his mouth etched into a deep frown. "I'm putting the two of you in the conference room for the duration of the case. I don't want these gen-pop assholes distracting you."

"Gen-pop assholes?" Haney called out, hand pressed to his chest in fake dismay. "Us?"

"None other." A beat, and he turned back to Adam. "How was the drive in?"

"Grand. It's nice country up here."

"I'll have our receptionist set you up with a room at the motor court. It's not the Ritz, but I hear they have those coin-fed beds that vibrate."

"I've slept in worse places," Adam said. He jerked his chin toward Felix. "Your guy here already set me up with some grub."

"Ordered in from the diner," Felix cut in. "Rhonda went to get it."

"Good." Krause glanced around the bullpen again, then fixed Felix with a bleary look. "Set yourselves up in the conference room. Walk him through the details while he eats. Then come to my office. We'll lay out a plan."

CHAPTER FIVE

The two detectives made their way to their temporary nerve center. Breakfast arrived in the form of greasy eggs, home fries with unidentified charred bits mixed in for a surprise in each bite. There was a carafe of coffee that smelled like heaven, and Felix helped himself to a cup while Adam dug into his food with the voracity of a starving hound.

Felix sipped his coffee and eyed his new partner. "I don't know how much Captain Krause told you over the phone," he started, "but at approximately—"

The man cut him off with a chuckle. "You get right to it, don't you? No romancing a guy." The words came out muddled as he talked around his mouthful of food.

"I thought you'd want the facts as soon as possible."

Adam swallowed his bite. "I do. But let's take a moment, you know? I like to know a guy if I'm gonna be paired up."

"Alright."

A silence fell over them. Adam resumed shoveling his food into his mouth. Felix watched, fascinated at the speed he forked the eggs, the potatoes into his mouth. The way he rounded his shoulders and hunched, protective-like, over his plate. Felix pressed his thumbnail and left little crescent indents along the rim of his Styrofoam cup while he waited, impatient to start.

Adam reached a moment, two-thirds of the way through his plate, where he slowed down. He took smaller bites, took the time to actually chew instead of inhaling. He looked up at Felix.

"First question. Did that receptionist call you *Puss* or did I hear wrong?" he asked.

Felix huffed. "It's because of my name. First it was *Felix the Cat*, then *Cat*. Given their proclivities toward a certain type of humor, my fellow policemen started calling me *Pussy*, which they eventually shortened to *Puss*."

"Using big words like *proclivities* probably doesn't help your cause with them."

He wasn't wrong. Felix's vocabulary was more hindrance than help around the barracks, but he wasn't about to grunt out monosyllabic words to fit in. He shrugged and replied, "It could be worse."

"Okay, shitty nickname aside," Adam continued, "you ever work a murder before?"

Felix took a sip of coffee. "One. It was open and shut. Husband killed his wife in a drunken rage. He copped to it in the drunk tank after he dried out overnight." He shrugged, continued, "Most of the murders here in Mariensburg are domestics gone bad. Never a kid in my time on the force."

"Those are never easy."

"You've worked a kiddie murder before then?"

"A handful."

Adam took a final bite, then pushed the empty container away with a belch and a pleased sigh. Felix watched him, bounced his leg under the table. He glanced up at the wall clock and saw the second hand sweep around the face over and over again.

The older man blew across the surface of his coffee and took a sip. "Had one case, years back. Divorced mother wanted to remarry but thought her daughter limited her chances." He shook his head. "It never gets easier. I still think about that little girl. I can still see the crime scene if I shut my eyes."

"I think this one will stick with me for a long time," Felix admitted. He knew if he shut his eyes, he'd see the boy—the curled hands on the bedspread, the parted mouth ready to draw a breath—

"Hell, it probably will. Krause gave me the broad strokes. Slashed throat, he said. That's vicious."

"It is."

Adam settled his bulk in his chair, scooted it closer to the table, and sat up straighter. He pulled out his own notebook and pen and said, "Alright, kid. Let's get to it."

Champing at the bit to finally start, Felix let the *kid* wash over him. He could bristle over it after the fact. He stood and walked over to the corkboard that had been cleared of its usual detritus, all the yellowing papers tacked up about union meetings, sign-ups for the summer softball league. He had transferred his thoughts to card stock while he had waited for Adam's arrival, and he tacked them up now as he walked the older detective through the burgeoning case.

Victim: Thomas John Farney, age seven.

Location: The Farney home, located on Briar Lane.

Cause of death: Undetermined. The body sustained a deep cut to the neck, ear to ear. The amount of blood present at the scene inclined one to assume exsanguination.

"The body is with the coroner now," Felix added as he pushed the pin into the board. "We should at least have prelims soon."

"Seems clear he died from a slashed throat."

"Yes," Felix agreed, "but it was such a clean crime scene. The blood was contained to the bed, pooled around the body. You would think there'd be blood everywhere. It should have been messy, but it wasn't."

Felix turned back to the board and resumed laying out his cards.

Time of death: Undetermined, but somewhere between eight o'clock on Thursday night and four o'clock on Friday morning.

"We're basing that on the housekeeper." Felix turned to face Adam, watched as the man took his notes. "She is typically the last to leave and the first to arrive each day. She's the one who found the body."

Adam finished writing, tapped the point of his pen against the paper as he looked up. "The kid was alone?"

Felix shook his head. "His grandmother was in the house, but she is infirm."

"Too infirm to kill?"

"Thomas Farney said she's senile."

"Noted." He bent his head, underlined something. "Keep going. What about the parents?"

"The mother, Abigail, was out of town and is on her way back to Mariensburg. The father, Jack, was supposed to be at the country club playing cards."

Adam arched an eyebrow. "Supposed to be? But not?"

"Undetermined." Felix turned back to the board, started to pin up the names of the family members. He pointed at the one that read *Jack Farney/father* and said, "Krause called for a patrol car to pick him up. We can ask how that went. Thomas Farney also sent his car to retrieve Jack, but we aren't sure where the man is now."

"Interesting."

He pointed at the card, *Thomas Farney/grandfather.* "He said he was at his factory all evening. We have to check on his alibi. He arrived at the scene behind the responding officers. The housekeeper called the police first, then him."

"And this is the rich guy? The one that's politically connected?"

Felix nodded.

"Okay." Adam tilted his head, cracked his neck. "Walk me through the crime scene."

Felix pinned his notes as he went, described the salient points. The lack of weapon, the lack of prints. No obvious sign of forced entry.

"I examined all the locks myself," he said.

"Windows?"

"All locked, too, and the side of the house with the boy's bedroom overlooks a steep drop. It would require a ladder or... I don't know. Rappelling gear, coming in from the roof."

Adam grinned. "What are you thinking, kid?"

Felix noted the nickname again, let it roll over him. He was warmed up now, the case taking its early shape on the board. And now his coup de grâce, his three theories.

"Okay, early thoughts. This is a kid, brutally murdered in his bed with a remarkably clean crime scene. Three theories."

Adam made a flourish with his pen, poised it over his notebook. "Shoot."

Theory one, tacked to the board with an answering flourish, a *ta-da* as he pushed in the pin.

"Jack Farney is a known entity at the Mariensburg county club.

He gambles there nearly every night. There's been spots of dope trouble at the country club too. There's plenty of ditch weed on the streets of Mariensburg, but if you want horse or psychedelics, the country club is the place to go."

"The veneer of respectability peeled back. Tennis lessons at noon, a twist of China white at two."

"Something like that. There's been low-level busts there, but it always seems to come back."

"Gambling has a certain risk factor to it. You thinking debts?" Adam asked, his voice thoughtful.

"Maybe. His father referenced a monthly allowance. He said he spends it all there."

"Theory one is some unsavory blend of gambling debts or drug activity, or both." Adam tapped the end of his pen against the notebook, a staccato beat. "I can get there. What are the other two?"

Another pin, another theory.

"A clean scene like that speaks to a professional. It happened when no one was in the home, and there were few tangible clues. What if it's a serial?"

"A professional could speak to gambling debts too. Or drugs," Adam pointed out. "I can see a mafia hitman or a skag dealer before I can see a serial."

The back of Felix's neck prickled, flushed at the tame critique. He asked, "Why's that?"

Adam chuckled, indulgent. "Every new detective thinks he's caught a serial case. Hell, when I was a rookie, I was convinced I had one myself. People are fascinated by the idea, and everyone knows of Jack the Ripper or H.H. Holmes. But they aren't very common."

"Seem pretty common to me," Felix replied, his voice level despite the flare of irritation at the man's tone. "In the past decade, there's been the Boston Strangler, the Zodiac Killer. Richard Speck. The Tate-La Bianca murders. All that weird, faux-witchy bullshit from the Manson family."

"Did your murder scene have misspelled words written in blood?"

Felix took a breath through his nose, let it out slow through his mouth. "No, but there was the child victim. There was that pair in England. They killed children, and there was the element of cut throats or strangulation."

"Anything ritual in the killing? Missing body parts? Staging?"

"The body did seem staged. A slashed throat with a perfectly tucked-in body seems incongruous."

"Fair enough." Adam looked at him a beat, like he was trying to read whatever thoughts were roiling through his head. He turned back to his notes. "Theory three?"

The last card pinned up.

"Thomas Farney is well-known and wealthy. He's not generally liked. The rich don't get rich by playing nice. He has a reputation as being ruthless, and it's well-earned. He built this town. He *owned* this town for many years."

"Revenge angle?"

Felix shrugged, and with his stack of cards spent, he sat back down at the table. "Wouldn't be out of the realm of possibility. Guy like that, rich and ruthless... It puts a target on him."

"But murder? Usually shit like that is a kidnapping."

"Hence the revenge. A kidnapping would have its motive in greed."

The older man hummed in thought, gazed past Felix to study the partially covered corkboard. He finally nodded, deep and ponderous.

"I'm thinking this was premeditated. Who wants to kill a kid? The kid wasn't the target." He bent his head to write it down. He underlined it twice to drive the point home. "I think theories one and three are the most solid."

"Thanks." It came out dry.

Adam seemed to take something in Felix's expression or tone into consideration. He leaned back in his chair and folded his hands across his stomach. He shot Felix a studious look.

"How are you feeling, having a state detective on your turf? Is that gonna be a problem for you?" he asked.

Felix considered his words, weighed them carefully in his mind before he answered.

"Not a problem," he said, and it was half a lie, half the truth. He stared back at the elder detective, impassive. "I know this case is too important to get tripped on my own ego."

"Fair enough." Adam unfolded his hands and rubbed them together in an eager, let's-get-down-to-business way, then stood up. "Let's go see what the Cap has for us, shall we?"

CHAPTER SIX

The captain sat hunched over his desk as Felix and Adam came in and shut the door behind them. Krause gestured for them to sit, folded his hands in front of him, his face somber.

"Gentlemen," he said. "We have a murdered child and a ticking clock to find who killed him."

Felix nodded. He saw Adam's nod out of the corner of his eye.

"Tell me what you're thinking," Krause said. To Adam's benefit, he turned to look at Felix, gestured with his hand. *Go ahead*, the gesture said. *Take the lead.*

He did. He walked the captain through the case board, his three theories. He glanced at Adam when he touched on the serial theory, caught the man rolling his eyes.

"I told him a serial is about as likely as Bigfoot being the murderer," he cut in when Felix paused.

Felix felt his hackles go up, thought, *Here we go*, thought Krause would agree with Adam since they went back to their academy days. He felt that nebulous golden opportunity slipping out of his fingertips, that vague chance he might solve the case on his own merit and manage to break away from Mariensburg... but Krause only fixed Adam with his usual stony stare and said, "The possibility still exists."

Another eye roll. "Everyone thinks it's a serial now. Serials are sexy, but they aren't *that* common."

Krause rocked back in his chair, steepled his fingers together, and shifted his gaze between the two of them. "Do I think a serial killer singled out a seven-year-old child in the middle of nowhere, Pennsylvania? No. Do I think the likelihood is zero? No."

"But—"

The captain held up a hand, silenced him. "Every serial killer case, there is one moment early on where they had a chance to nail the guy and didn't. The Ypsilanti Ripper strolled into the funeral home where the body of the first victim was laid out. He demanded to take a picture of the body and got turned down. He strolled away and killed more."

His eyes shifted to Felix, and he bent his head in acknowledgment. "If there's even a chance it's a serial, we have to explore it. I'm not letting the course of my career be defined as the asshole who had the chance to catch... I don't know what they'd call him. The Kiddie Slasher? The Slashed-Throat Fucker? I'm not going down as the idiot who let one slip past him."

Adam huffed out, "Fine."

Felix felt a flush of something almost like affection for Krause. Affection-adjacent. If nothing else, at least he seemed to be on the same level as Adam Shaffer. Not the green detective running behind but instead keeping in lockstep with the more seasoned guy.

"Thomas Farney is due at any minute for his formal statement. He's bringing us a list of people with access to the house," Krause said. "Seems like a better place for the two of you to start. I'll poke around on the serial front. Call around to some other jurisdictions and see if they have any unsolved cases with similar MOs."

"Seems reasonable," Adam replied, a tinge of sullenness in his voice.

"I'll have Rhonda call into Bell for phone records for the county club too. I like the gambling and drug angle better than the serial," Krause continued.

"What about Jack?" Felix asked.

"Patrol couldn't find him. Ask Thomas if he knows his son's whereabouts."

"What about the mother?" Adam flipped through his notes, added, "Abigail."

"Driving back from New York."

Krause rocked in his seat a bit, glanced between them again.

"You two are lead on this but remember we have two other detectives in the bullpen if we need them." He saw Felix shake his head and continued, "I know they're about as worthless as a Frigidaire on the North Pole, but they can do the shit-work. They can cross all the t's the district attorney will want crossed before anything goes to trial."

"Might be good for them to build background material," Felix offered. "Winslow and Haney could dig into the Farney family and their dealings."

"They'd have to be quiet about it," Krause warned. "If we send them on a fishing expedition, they'll have to learn discretion right fucking quick."

"We split 'em up. Pair of jokers. Together they're a budget Allen and Rossi. But apart?" Felix shrugged. "They should be fine."

Krause stared a long moment at Felix, and his eyes drifted over to Adam. He finally sighed. Said the plan was fine, he'd talk to the other detectives.

He pushed his chair away from his desk and bent over to open his bottom drawer. With a grunt, he pulled something out, then slammed it on the desktop. It was a thick ledger book, a water-spotted cover with yellowed pages.

"This is strictly hush-hush," he warned, and he turned the ledger around and pushed it toward them. "My predecessor, Captain Fontaine, was in Farney's back pocket. Frenchy bastard got regular payoffs from him."

"For what?" Adam asked.

"Mostly for looking the other way during Farney's less-than-licit dealings."

"Fontaine told you this?" Felix asked. He'd heard stories about the previous captain from Winslow, who liked to wax nostalgic when things were slow. Winslow told him once Fontaine had been accused of skimming from the budget, redirecting funds into his own pocket but the mayor buried it because they were all in the K of C together.

Krause shook his head. "No. He died suddenly while still on the force. Unexpected heart attack, like they tend to be. He didn't have a chance to clean house before he died, and when I took over, I found this in his desk." He tapped a nicotine-stained finger against the ledger.

Felix picked it up, drew it into his lap, and opened it. The cover was cloth-covered cardboard, and the pages crackled against the ancient glue binding. A vinegary smell wafted up as he pinched the pages between his fingertips, turned them. Faded handwriting, spidery and faint, crawled across the pages.

Dates, names, situations. On some of the lines were dollar amounts. Twenty here, fifty there, a couple hundred in others. Big bucks, back then. It went all the way back to the founding of Mariensburg, when it was just a patch town informally called Shale Hollow.

"Is this what I think it is?" Felix asked. His stomach sank with each date, each name.

It was a veritable Ellis Island registry, nothing but Italian, Polish, Slavic names. The huddled masses who came to America looking for streets paved in gold, who instead found themselves deep underground, buried in the stinking dark of the coal shaft. *Barto, Giovonia, DeLuca, Maslovsky.*

He recognized some of those family names. He'd grown up with those family names, went to school with some of them. He saw the surname *Kormos*—Rhonda the Receptionist's family. He didn't recognize the first name, *Helena*, but he saw the amount and wondered what fifty dollars covered up back then.

"Fontaine must not have trusted Farney, so he kept track of every favor," Krause said.

"Insurance," Adam murmured. He craned his neck to read the ledger, too, and Felix turned it to show him.

"Exactly." Krause pointed at the book. "Now, I know this is old news. Fontaine died twenty-odd years ago, so the transgressions noted in there are old. Do I think someone with a decades-old grudge is coming to collect from Thomas Farney? No."

Adam picked up the thread of Krause's thinking. "But it does speak to Farney's bad behavior."

"A tiger doesn't change its fucking stripes, and I don't believe for a moment that Thomas Farney suddenly started playing everything aboveboard. Fontaine kept track until he died. There are disgruntled employees, double-crossed business partners, bad blood between friends and relatives."

Felix closed the book carefully, set it back on the desk. The thing was damned near full, every page overflowing with malfeasance.

"The past may illuminate the present," he offered.

"Precisely."

"Did Farney ever try to bribe you?" Adam asked, and Krause snorted, shook his head.

"The day after I took the captaincy, he stopped in. He gave me a drawn-out fucking speech about the support of law enforcement. A whole nice spiel, smiling at me as he sized me up. He never went beyond that, though."

"You must have an honest face, John."

Krause snorted again. "Or the man didn't have a real need for the police captain in his pocket anymore. The coal mining days were the Wild West, and the mines were shut down before I even got here. He started his carbon factory as the second war geared up. He didn't need off-duty police to rough up miners or put down union drives anymore. His reputation preceded him. No one was stupid enough to test him anymore."

"It is a long shot," Adam said. He jerked his head at Felix. "This one filled me in on the father situation. Jack Farney. It seems a lot more likely there's something going on there. With the nightly gambling at a place known for dealing the harder drugs, maybe Jack piled up some enemies too."

"Agreed." Krause twisted his wrist to peer down at the battered Timex there. "Consider every possibility."

Felix wanted to ask if the coroner had been in touch. The state of the crime scene and the body vexed him, and he opened his mouth to ask the question. A knock at the door stopped him.

Krause called out, "Come in." Rhonda popped her head in, glanced with bright-eyed interest at the three men, and informed them Thomas Farney had arrived to give his statement.

✳

Thomas Farney waited for them in the interrogation room. Outside the closed door, Adam laid a hand on Felix's shoulder and held him back.

"How do you want to play this?" he asked. "You want lead?"

"Yes," Felix replied without a hint of hesitation.

Adam swept his hand in front of him, and Felix opened the door and entered the room.

The wealthiest man in Mariensburg, and its founder, sat at the small table there. He stood when the detectives entered, and he held out a hand to each. His handshake held a vigor that belied his age. He squeezed Felix's hand a touch harder than polite. He stared at him, unblinking, as if he were sizing him up.

A man not used to being the first to blink or let go, Felix noted.

Thomas didn't look like the grief-crazed man Felix had met only hours earlier. He looked like a captain of industry attending a business meeting. He wore an impeccably tailored suit, the slacks sporting a knife-crisp crease. His shirt was blinding white, his tie held in place by a burnished gold clip. His thick white hair was swept to the side, the part perfectly straight and not a strand out of place.

The three men sat down, and before Felix could get a single question out, Thomas asked, "Do you have any leads?" There was a glinting diamond hardness to his voice. He looked at Adam first, then Felix.

Felix bit back the first response that bubbled to the forefront of his head, incredulous. No, they didn't have any leads. Obviously not. They were only a handful of hours from the discovery of the crime. Justice didn't move that quickly, not even for the very rich.

He kept his voice level and said, simply, "Not yet."

Thomas reached into an inner pocket of his suit coat and pulled out a piece of paper folded into thirds.

"Here. This is everyone who has or had access to the house. They all work for me, save the last name on the list. He was a workman hired to fix a handful of windows this spring." He set it on the table and slid it toward Felix.

Felix unfolded it, glanced at the neat columns of typed names, addresses, occupations. He slid it over to Adam who glanced at it, too, before tucking it in his notebook.

"I'd like to take a moment to understand your timeline yesterday evening," Felix continued.

"We went over that already."

"It's procedure. We need specifics. Times and locations. Who you were with, what you were doing. Even the smallest detail could help."

Thomas narrowed his eyes, but after a beat of silence, he did as he was asked.

＊

Felix never had any burning desire to go into business. His second eldest brother, Mark, worked in an office, and job-talk over family meals made Felix want to swallow the business end of his service revolver out of boredom.

Nothing about Thomas Farney's business life led Felix to believe he'd chosen the wrong profession. It sounded so paradoxically stressful and boring. The evening, the night of the murder: a meeting about overhead reduction, a meeting with his lawyer, an overseas call to Japan—late at night because of the time zones—about the possibility of outsourcing the production of certain pressed-carbon components.

I'll never sneer at a boring case again, Felix thought.

The call to Japan cleared Thomas. The coroner's report wasn't back yet, but Thomas had been at his office all night. He had a solid alibi with his lawyer, and if they needed more, they could always learn some rudimentary Japanese and get more from that outfit in Tokyo.

"I appreciate you walking us through your timeline," Felix said when Thomas finished. "And for the list of employees in your home."

Thomas nodded, said nothing.

Felix hesitated, only a split second. Only long enough to get his tone right: not threatening or insinuating anything, but still the no-nonsense quality of a detective.

"Do you know where your son is, Mr. Farney?" he asked.

At that, Thomas narrowed his eyes the barest fraction. It was such a small movement Felix thought he might have imagined it. The barest furrowing of his eyebrows. The barest downturn of the corners of his mouth.

"He's home," he replied. "He returned from the club shortly after you left this morning."

"Your driver found him." A statement, not a question.

Thomas tilted his head. Not a nod, exactly. Open to interpretation. "He drove home in his own car."

Felix wrote in his notebook. *Check timeline on Jack. To/from home Fri morn.*

"Can you think of anyone who would want to harm your grandson or your family?" Adam asked. The elder detective had been quiet, seemingly content to listen. He only took a few notes and mostly watched Thomas as he spoke.

"Sorry?"

"A crime like this, your mind might have gone to one person. Or maybe a few people. It seems unbelievable, but can you think of anyone who might have wanted to hurt your grandson?"

Thomas scoffed at the question, his voice laced with bitterness. "Who would want to hurt a seven-year-old? That's ludicrous."

"Who would want to hurt your family? Or who might want to hurt you?"

The old man stared at Adam for a long moment. He leaned forward, his square hands folded in front of him. "I can't imagine anyone."

"No disgruntled employees? No fellow businessmen where deals fell through?"

Another scoff and a sharp shake of his head. "Of course, but I don't see the connection."

Adam gazed back at him, unperturbed. "You don't have any enemies?"

Thomas scoffed a third time, but quietly, as if the fire was dying down in him. "Perhaps I've stepped on toes, but *enemies* feels a step too far."

Adam made an interested *hmm*, and he wrote something in his notes. The beat of silence drew out, gained heft and weight in the room. Felix caught the faintest twitch on Thomas's face as some thought drifted through his mind.

"This couldn't have happened because of me," he finally said.

His voice, usually a baritone, went up a quarter octave, turned him into a querulous old man in an instant. "If anyone has a problem with me, they would know where to find me."

"Surely you can think of people—employees, partners, whoever—who were angry with you at one point. Stuff like that," Adam said.

Thomas tilted his head back and gazed up at the ceiling tiles. He dropped his head to look at them. He offered them a single nod.

Felix flipped to a blank page in his notebook and tore it out. He laid his pen on top of it and slid both over to the old man.

Thomas sighed. He took the pen in his hand, the nib hovering over the paper. After a moment, he wrote a name, and another. And another.

CHAPTER SEVEN

A thick blue smog of cigarette smoke hung low in the conference room, shot through with the acrid odor of coffee brewed, reheated, and burnt to hell. The top-note of their lunches, ordered in from the same greasy spoon diner as Adam's breakfast, overlaid it all.

He'd unwisely chosen the tuna melt for his lunch. Every time Adam swallowed, he tasted the backwash of the oily fish, the greasy plasticine cheese. He burped queasily and watched Felix tack up all the names they had now.

Like the list of people with access to the Farney house. Eight people in total. One driver, a housekeeper, a cook. Two part-time maids. A gardener to tend the expansive grounds. A nurse for Thomas's wife, a tutor for the little boy.

"What's the difference between a maid and a housekeeper?" Felix asked. He transcribed each name, printed it carefully on a small piece of card stock and tacked it to the corkboard.

"How the hell would I know? We sure as hell didn't have a maid *or* a housekeeper when I was growing up, and the Commonwealth doesn't pay that well."

"Did you have a gardener?" Felix asked. His voice was so deadpan, it took Adam a beat before he realized it was a joke.

"Yeah, asshole. He tended to the dirt patch behind the house where we kept our rubbish bins," he joked back, drawing a chuckle from the younger man.

On to the list of people Thomas Farney considered enemies: His first business partner. A rival mine owner who had laid claim to the same seam of bituminous Farney used to work. An alliance of local farmers who cried foul over groundwater tainted by mine runoff. A secretary he had fired—or more appropriately, the secretary's brother who had made vague threats. Two families whose homes had been seized and demolished via eminent domain back when Farney built his carbon factory.

For someone who couldn't quite think of any enemies at first, the man had built up an impressive roster of aggrieved fellow businessmen, employees, and regular ol' citizens who felt they had suffered because of him. "Stepped on toes" was how Thomas framed it, but the people in the ranks of the wronged might disagree. From where Adam sat, it looked less like stepped-on toes and more like being steamrolled, ridden roughshod over. Lost jobs, lost homes. Those weren't minor infractions.

"Man has more enemies than I have friends," Felix grumbled. He wrote those names, too, pinned them in a neat grid on the board.

Adam grinned at the back of his new partner's head. Krause had described Felix as green and hungry. Greenness was a given. The kid was barely thirty, young for a detective even by backwater standards. The hunger was obvious too. When Adam asked if he wanted to run lead on Farney, the kid jumped at the opportunity.

"That's because you've never founded a town, you lazy bastard," Adam replied.

Felix paused in his task, held his middle finger aloft for Adam to see.

Adam responded with a scoff of mock outrage. "Rude shit like that is how it starts, the acquisition of said enemies," he said. Felix chuckled, flipped him the bird again, then continued pinning names of possible suspects.

✱

Of the eight employees' names Farney provided, they eliminated three as suspects within hours.

Felix and Adam began with the simplest tasks. Adam always thought of a case as a spiral with the crime in the dead center. It made more sense to start right in the middle with the crime, then work outward. Most of the time, that's where the solve lay anyway—people close to the tragedy, the family or friends or acquaintances. Adam had only ever worked a few cases where the perp had been a true stranger to the victim.

They took statements from each person as they came in, one

at a time, nervous or outraged or bewildered to find themselves in an interrogation room, answering questions about a child slaughtered in his bed.

The driver was an easy name to cross off. He'd been in the break room of the factory, listening to the Pirates lose to the Cubs the night before. Nelson Briles on the mound, he said, the asshole with the hard slider who sneered at the hometown fans.

Adam cocked an eyebrow at Felix, who took a sidebar to murmur, "Briles said Pittsburgh fans have mill-town mentality. People are still upset about it."

"Damn straight," the driver declared. "Attitude like that, go pitch for the Yankees."

More to the point, the driver wasn't some kiddie murderer, according to him. Some of the second shifters saw him. Some of the third shifters too. He was clear on that, jabbing his index finger against the top of the table to drive home his point. He did not kill any kid, he said. How dare they even think he could do such a thing. He had kids of his own. Hell, he had *grandkids.*

Felix made a note to send Winslow or Haney out to the factory to check. They were digging into the Farney family anyway, so it gave them another thing to do, a crumb of the case tossed to them. And it shored up any future case that may go to trial, like Krause said. It proved they had followed every exhaustive lead to the bitter end.

The cook, Susan. A jittery woman with small, darting eyes. Another easy one to eliminate. She worked a second job at a nearby bakery, worked late into the night kneading dough and shaping pastries for the next morning.

"My husband is out of work," she explained, her voice tinged with shame. "We have debts."

A phone call later to the bakery, and they crossed off her name.

Last came the tutor. Hired by Thomas Farney to help his grandson with the trickier bits of math and grammar. A student out of the community college two towns over, the kid nearly pissed himself from fear when Adam and Felix sat him down and questioned him.

Jitters in the interrogation room could be a sign of guilt, Adam knew. The tutor seemed too soft, though, like he'd burst into tears if he accidentally ran over a squirrel with his car. He was lucky to be in college. A guy like him wouldn't survive basic training, let alone fighting half a world away in Vietnam.

He had an alibi anyway. He'd pulled an all-nighter at the campus library with his study group, and at least three people, including a security guard, could place him there.

Before the college kid left, though, he turned to Felix and Adam.

"Did he suffer?" he asked.

Not a second of hesitation. Adam shook his head. Said no, Junior hadn't suffered a single moment.

The tutor nodded. He swiped his runny nose with the back of his hand. Once he left, Adam turned to Felix with a rueful shrug.

"I know I wasn't at the scene, but no sense in making the kid feel worse than he already did."

"I get it," Felix replied. "When I was a patrolman, I used to say the same thing. When someone's family got killed in a crack-up, we always lied and said death was instantaneous. Bad enough they've lost a loved one. Why make it worse by admitting yes, they suffered before they died?"

"You think the boy suffered?"

Felix shifted his eyes from Adam's, turned his head away.

"I have to hope he didn't," he said.

They eliminated more names that afternoon.

The two part-time maids had both been home with their families. The gardener showed up, his arm wrapped in a dingy plaster cast. He fumbled his way through signing his statement, his signature an illegible scrawl. Adam figured with his dominant hand out of commission ("Tripped over a root and broke my wrist," the man had said), he wasn't likely to be slashing the throats of children.

The nurse who looked after Clara Farney came in. She was a

well-preserved woman, as Adam's mother used to say—too old to be pretty but too young to be handsome, in some indeterminate middle age. She sat down and introduced herself as Laura.

"I work for Mr. Farney on a part-time basis, caring for his wife," she said, and she looked at them expectantly. She seemed poised, calm, except for the faint tremor in her hands that only stilled when she folded them in her lap. She caught Adam noticing them and gave him a tight smile that trembled at the corners of her mouth.

"Sorry," she said, halting. "This is all... it's a lot to process."

"I understand it's upsetting."

"He was such a sweet boy. And just a child..." She took a couple of deep breaths. She smiled at Adam again, and it looked steadier.

"Can you walk us through your evening, ma'am?" Felix asked.

She did, the thankless catalogue of a home nurse's duties. Adam's mother had worked at a nursing home when his father left them, so he was sympathetic. He remembered how his mother ached at the end of each day. How she traded away her own strength to turn and heave the slack weight of the elderly, gave them sponge baths, changed their sheets. He remembered the smell of that work—baby powder and encroaching death— that clung to his mother. Adam nodded as Laura listed through her job duties. It was all familiar.

Her evening had been uneventful, she said. She had helped Clara Farney bathe. She coaxed some food into the old woman, coaxed pills down her throat. They helped the old woman sleep.

"She wanders at night otherwise," she said. "Before Mr. Farney hired me, they tried locking her in, but she'd get frantic. She is easily disoriented."

Adam raised an eyebrow, glanced over at Felix and caught his eye. Laura tracked the motion and shook her head.

"It's not like that."

"What's that?" Adam asked.

"You're thinking there's a possibility she did this."

"She was in the house at the time," Felix pointed out, his tone gentle.

Another shake of the head. "Yes, but she weighs all of eighty pounds. Ninety, if I can keep her fed up. She barely has the strength to shuffle from place to place, let alone do much else."

"You said she used to wander," said Felix.

"She still does, but she always tries to wander *outside*. She heads for the front door, always. She's only a danger to herself, getting lost in her condition."

"We'd like to talk to her all the same," said Adam. "Maybe she heard something that woke her."

"It's always possible, I suppose."

She laid out the rest of her evening. She gave Clara Farney her pills, sat with her until she fell asleep. She bade the housekeeper farewell and went home.

"What time was that?" asked Felix.

"Around eight."

"And the housekeeper..." He flipped back a page in his notebook, consulted earlier notes. "... Martha. She was still there?"

"She usually leaves not long after I do, but yes. She's usually the first there in the morning and the last to leave."

"Is it common for there to be no one there at night other than a young boy and an infirm old woman?"

The woman took a moment, her face thoughtful as she considered the question. "Mr. Farney often works late, but he usually comes home at some point in the night. And Abigail—that's the boy's mother—is often there, too, unless she has an event or is visiting family or friends in New York."

"And the boy's father? Jack?"

Laura's gaze settled first on Felix, then Adam. For the briefest second, Adam swore he saw something in her expression, hard to place because it came and went so fast. A second later, it disappeared, replaced by a placid expression.

"I don't usually see Jack," she said.

Felix didn't bother to write the note down, but Adam guessed his partner registered the change in attitude too.

Jack Farney, he thought. *Could a father do this to his own child?*

He knew the answer already. Of course a father was capable

of filicide. History was littered with fathers killing their children, from Russian czars to Joseph Goebbels. Hell, there was even a story about it in the Old Testament, how Abraham stood over Isaac with a knife, poised and ready to slaughter his own blood.

"He's a nice man," Laura continued, and she put a slight emphasis on the *nice*. She sounded more magnanimous, as if she'd caught herself and was correcting for her initial tone. "I only see him occasionally. I'm usually in the same few rooms with Mrs. Farney."

"And where did you go after you left the Farney residence?"

"I went home."

"Can anyone vouch for you?"

She shook her head. "I live alone. I made myself a snack and watched some television, then went to bed." A beat. "I suppose you could talk to the neighbor. He sits near his living room window. He always seems to know everyone's comings and goings."

Laura glanced from one detective to the next, watched as Felix made his notes. She glanced at the watch on her slender wrist.

"I apologize, but I have to leave to attend to Mrs. Farney. I'm already late, I'm afraid."

Adam nodded and stood, and he made his way over to the door. "I think we're good, ma'am," he said, and he opened the door and stood aside so she could walk past him.

"We'll reach out if we think of anything else," Felix added.

Laura stood, took her purse from where it sat on the table and hooked it over her shoulder. "I'm happy to help however I can." She paused, gripped the strap of her purse tighter. "I'll be praying for the boy. Poor little mite."

CHAPTER EIGHT

After the nurse left, Felix and Adam returned to the conference room. Felix shut the door behind them and watched as Adam dropped into a chair and leaned back. Someone—Krause, probably—had left the developed photos from the crime scene. Adam reached for them, paused. He reached into his coat pocket instead and pulled out a cigarillo and a lighter.

"You mind?" he asked. Felix shook his head. When Adam lit it, the room filled with the familiar scent of his childhood. Swisher Sweets. His dad had smoked those on Sunday afternoons as a treat, a break from his usual Winstons.

Felix sank into a chair, too, and propped his elbows on the table. Dropped his head into his hands and shut his eyes. His head buzzed like electrical lines. The too-clean crime scene. The names crossed off—alibis secured—but so many names to go. People to question. A ledger book full of Thomas Farney's past malfeasance. An absent mother. A missing father known to frequent the one place in town where serious card games and serious dope could be procured.

There was the victim, Junior. *"Poor little mite,"* the nurse had called him him. *"Lonely,"* claimed one of the maids, the one who turned chatty once she realized she wasn't in trouble. *"A child needs brothers and sister as his first friends, but... well. The less said there, the better,"* she had said. A child left alone with only a sick old woman locked in her own room.

Felix rubbed his hands together, brisk. He built some heat in his palms from the friction, pressed them over his closed eyes. His thoughts roiled. The dead child kept surfacing in his mind's eye, and he kept pushing it back down.

"You okay there, kid?" Adam asked. Felix could hear the man paging through the crime scene photos, heard Adam's punched-out exhale a moment later at whatever picture he examined. Felix didn't bother to open his eyes to see what had elicited a reaction from his partner. He'd seen it in person.

"Trying to get my thoughts squared away," he muttered in reply.

"First day's always an onslaught." Felix heard him take a puff. He smelled the fresh plume of smoke a beat later.

"Before you square your thinking too much, tell me what's sticking out to you," Adam continued.

Felix sighed and removed his hands, opened his eyes. Sparks lit in his peripherals, a sure sign one of his killer headaches was on its way. They flared up on occasion, usually due to changes in the weather or poor sleep or stress. Which was the trifecta he lived at the moment. He turned to face Adam, who smoked serenely, his inscrutable gaze shifting from the stack of photos to look at him.

"What's sticking out to *you?*" he replied, trading one question for another.

"Jack Farney is an interesting one. His old man seemed cagey when you asked after him."

"You think he's covering for him?"

"You tell me."

Felix thought about it. He considered the old man's grief from early that morning.

"Maybe Thomas was wrong about where Jack spends his time. Country club isn't far away. It doesn't account for all the time Jack was missing."

"Anywhere else around town a guy can play cards?" Adam asked. "Maybe there's another place with hot tables."

"There are rumors about high-stakes games at the Polish club. We could ask around." He paused, smiled despite the pressure building in his left temple. "One of my cousins got into trouble there once. It's supposed to be a family secret, but I can ask my mom when I finally get home."

"You still live with your mom?" Adam asked. Felix could hear the lilt of surprise in the man's voice. He supposed it *was* surprising. Not many thirty-year-old men still slept in their childhood bedrooms, especially men with decent jobs who were reasonably well-adjusted and not complete dipshits.

"Yes," Felix said. He tried not to sound defensive even though he knew his voice took on a petulant tone. "She's been sick, so I moved back home to help her out."

He didn't add how he'd been guilted into moving back after his father died. That he had an apartment downtown, a swell little bachelor pad over a shoe shop. That, when the five Kosmatka boys had circled around their widowed mother's request for someone to move back in, for someone to keep her company, Felix was the one too slow on the draw, the last one to say "not it."

"Shit, kid, no judgment here. Family stuff is hard."

He nodded at the understatement. Family stuff was hard. Family stuff felt uncomfortably like shackles. Every night he fell asleep in the same narrow bed he had occupied as a child, and every morning he woke up thinking, *Maybe today is the day I slip the trap.*

Felix cleared his throat, opened his eyes again. He saw Adam watching him, that same inscrutable expression on his face, so he changed the subject back and said, "The country club."

"Yeah, right. You think Jack might be in hock to some bad people? Or swept up in drugs somehow?"

"It's always possible. The drug bust from a while back included some of the wealthy patrons. It wasn't all dishwashers and golf caddies."

Adam nodded, thoughtful. "You know the guy personally?"

"No. He's about four, five years older than me. He only went to school here for a few years before he got shipped off to boarding school out East."

Felix never had much awareness about Jack Farney growing up, but his older brothers had known him. Felix had the haziest memory of Albie, his eldest brother, talking at the dinner table about the rich kid on his Little League team.

Felix reached back into his memory, deep into those nebulous ones that faded a little more each year. The rich kid could only have been Jack Farney. Mariensburg had a middle class, plenty of people with nice cars and houses, but there were no other truly rich people in town.

He remembered Albie talking about how Jack didn't ride his bike to the ball field like the other boys did. A sleek black car picked him up and dropped him off for each game. The boys had made fun of him because he didn't have a bike at all, didn't even know how to ride one. They had made fun of Jack's fielder's glove, stiff on his hand. He hadn't known how to soften the leather, to shape it around a baseball at night so it was ready for game play.

The memory became clearer as Felix turned it over in his mind. He could see his brother in his red-and-white jersey, CHLUDZINKSI TOWING emblazoned across the chest, number 30 because Rip Sewell was Albie's hero. His brother at the kitchen table as he talked about the teammate no one liked, and their father gently admonishing him to be nice, that people can't help which family they're born into.

"Richie Rich" they used to call him, Felix remembered. *Another lonely boy, just like Junior.*

A knock at the door pulled him out of his reverie. Krause stuck his head in first, then folded the rest of his stooped body into the room and shut the door.

"Jack Farney. He's on his way in now."

"Speak of the devil, and he shall appear," Adam said.

"Remember what I said. Work him, but *carefully*. Not kid gloves, but... I dunno. Fucking kid gloves—adjacent."

Adam tapped the ash off his half-smoked cigarillo, snuffed out the cherry, and carefully tucked it back in its pack. "We'll be courteous about it. The man did just find out he lost his son, after all."

The captain nodded his craggy head. "Another thing. Coroner called. He's got his preliminary report ready."

Adam shot Felix a look. "When it rains, it pours, kid. Interview first, then we can head over to the morgue."

The sparks shimmered at the edge of Felix's vision again, and his temple throbbed in time with his heartbeat. It was going to be a hell of a headache later. Maybe he could stop off for a coffee and some aspirin before they hit the morgue. He looked past Adam to the board behind him; all the names listed out in neat columns, some already crossed off with heavy black lines.

They scraped their chairs back on the linoleum floor, stood, reassembled themselves. They grabbed their notebooks, ready to talk to the father of the murdered boy.

*

Growing up, Felix had always heard family resemblance could sometimes skip a generation or two. His entire family—parents, brothers, grandparents—were all cut from the same template. Himself, he was some rarer strain of Kosmatka, apparently a spitting image of a great-uncle he'd never met.

It was a recurring joke when he was a child, how Felix belonged to the mailman, though his father always chucked him on the shoulder, said he guessed he'd keep him anyway.

The Farney family seemed to be the same. Where Thomas was tall and broad through the shoulders even in his older age, Jack Farney was shorter, more compact. He wore thick-lensed, wire-rimmed glasses that made his washed-out blue eyes seem slightly agog. It gave the unfortunate effect of looking surprised. Despite the wan face, Jack Farney looked more startled than sad to find himself sitting in front of the detectives investigating his son's murder.

His hand, though, trembled when he shook with Felix and Adam. What drove the tremor? Was it sorrow? Guilt? Was it the consequence of some addiction left unaddressed so that he could come to the precinct to give his statement?

Felix and Adam extended their condolences. They bade Jack to sit, offered him water or coffee, which Jack turned down.

"We understand how difficult this is for you," Adam said.

Jack tilted his head in acknowledgment. He said nothing.

"Can you walk us through the last twenty-four hours?" Adam asked. "Where you were, who you were with?"

He did. In a reedy, slightly breathless voice, Jack gave his whereabouts from yesterday morning until now. Adam broke in here and there, clarified or dug deeper as Felix took notes.

Thursday morning began at the factory. "I worked all day, then went home to change my clothes. Then I left for the club," he said.

"What time was that?"

Jack shifted his eyes to the clock hanging behind Felix and pursed his lips. "Around six, I guess. Maybe closer to seven."

"When you stopped home," Adam said. "Did you see anyone? Talk to anyone?"

Jack folded his hands in his lap. "I saw Tommy," he replied, his voice low.

"Your son?" Felix asked.

Jack nodded. "I stopped by his bedroom to look in on him, and he was playing. Just sitting on the floor and playing. He'd found some matchbox cars somewhere. Maybe Martha gave them to him, or one of the maids. And he sat there, rolling them around the carpet, and when he saw me in the doorway..." He shook his head at the memory, only a day old.

"What happened when he saw you?"

"He looked up at me like he got caught. Like he was in trouble." Jack lifted his gaze and fixed them with a watery look, his eyes swimming behind the lenses of his glasses.

"And was he?" Felix asked. His pencil was poised over his notebook. "In trouble, I mean?"

"Not from *me*. My father. His grandfather."

"For playing with toy cars?" Felix glanced over at the other detective, caught the thoughtful look on his face.

Jack shook his head. "My father has very definitive ideas about how one should spend their time. Those ideas extend to children."

"He runs a tight ship, your father?"

Jack's mouth twisted into a sardonic smile that held no humor. "There's no room for play in his world. Not when there's work."

"Even for a child?"

"A child's work is to study, according to my father."

Felix wrote it down verbatim, sketched a little question mark beside it. He asked, "And then?" and Jack continued.

"Tommy looked at me with this guilty expression, so I shushed him. Held up my finger." He demonstrated, lifted a hand and pressed a trembling forefinger to his lips, dropped the hand back into his lap. "Told him I wouldn't tell if he didn't tell, and he... he *laughed*."

He took a deep breath, tremulous, like he was on the verge of crying. But he pulled himself together and added, "That was the last time I saw him."

Felix and Adam both gave the statement a moment of silence to settle in the room. They both bent their heads, studied the whorls on the faux-wood tabletop to acknowledge the man's grief.

Adam broke the silence, asked, "What happened after that?"

The rest of Jack's evening and night: Cards at the club, though the game broke up early. It had ended up with a few of them watching the Olympics. Sailing, Jack said. He used to sail in college. It had been a nice evening, good food and drink, good company.

"We'll need the names of the people with you last night."

A beat before Jack nodded, and Felix wondered if it was hesitation or just a grief-addled mind trying to keep up.

"We heard you spend a lot of time playing cards. You don't owe anyone money?" he asked.

Jack sat back in his chair. He blinked at them in surprise. It gave him the look of a cartoon owl. "No. Not at all."

"Have you owed people money in the past?" Adam asked.

Jack lifted a hand and tapped the top of the table to drive each point home. "I don't have debts. I play with the same guys, in the same places. If someone has a problem, anyone knows where to find me."

Felix glanced at his new partner, arched an eyebrow at him and caught his answering nod. *Go ahead*, it seemed to say. *Lead him into deeper waters.*

"No one knew where to find you this morning," Felix pointed out.

"I was there. At the club." His expression turned stony. He pressed his lips together until they were a bloodless line.

Felix said nothing. He let the implication hang heavy in the air. He waited for Jack to fill in the silence, and the man did after a long beat.

"Sometimes I indulge too much," he said, his voice waspish. "I sleep it off there. Last night... early morning, I guess... I started to drive home but pulled off on the side of the road. I was tired and still drunk, so I parked and stretched out in the backseat."

It was flimsy as hell, but playing devil's advocate, Felix guessed it wasn't outside of the realm of possibility. The country club stood outside of town, set apart in a sprawl of acres that butted against the low, forested hills. There were two roads in and out of the place—a main one and a service one—but members used both equally. It was possible patrol and Thomas's driver alike only checked the main one.

"And?" Adam, encouraging the man to continue.

Jack sighed and pushed his hand through his hair, then dropped it into his lap again. "When I woke up, I felt awful. I went home and found out m-my son... had—"

He broke, a sudden bark of a sob cutting off his words. Felix startled at the force of it, such a loud noise from such a spare man. He turned, looked away as whatever dam holding back Jack's roiling grief finally broke. The man slumped in his chair, pressed his forehead against the edge of the table, and tried to rein in his weeping.

Felix knew in his gut that no matter where else the truth settled out, Jack's anguish over the loss of his son was real.

✱

They cut Jack loose with the promise to be in touch soon. Preliminary statements done for the moment, they went to see the coroner.

"As far as alibis go, 'I was asleep in my car' is pretty damned thin," Adam said. He piloted his Bonneville as Felix pointed out the turns from the passenger seat.

"I've slept in my car before."

"Seems mighty coincidental."

"He seemed genuinely torn up about it. That didn't strike me as acting." He pointed, added, "Turn right here."

Adam took the corner too sharp and hit the sidewall of his tire on the curb. The man cursed, then asked, "But is that grief or guilt?"

One question out of a mountain of questions. Felix pointed out the next turn, then shut his eyes and pressed his fingertips against the throbbing headache that had settled and taken root in his temple.

Someone had killed Junior Farney. Someone had a motive. Someone had planned it all out: access to the house, the mode of murder, the tableau of the slaughtered child in his bed. Someone had done this terrible thing, and now they moved through the world like him or anyone else, eating and drinking and drawing breath while a child lay dead.

Felix's mother whiled away her daytime hours by doing jigsaw puzzles in front of the television. They were always infuriatingly complex, usually nature scenes where every piece looked the same. Her strategy was to isolate the corners and straight-edged pieces first, to get the framework set before filling in the middle.

That's how Felix thought of the case now as his headache thundered through his skull: the list of names, the early elimination of suspects was framing out the puzzle. The coroner's report would be another piece of the edging, a corner to anchor the rest of the investigation.

Piece by piece, he'd fill it in. Piece by piece, he'd reveal the someone who killed Junior Farney.

CHAPTER NINE

The house was quiet.

The house was always quiet, but that quiet was nothing special. That quiet, the everyday kind, was a lack of noise, an emptiness that carried no weight and held no emotion.

This quiet was something else. It had heft. It was a tangible thing that took up space in each room, filled it to every corner where the walls met the high ceilings. It pressed against the floors and windowpanes until anyone standing in its presence felt as though they were suffocating.

The hired help tiptoed around. They kept their steps light. They communicated by pointing, by shaking their heads. The only sound was the occasional wet sniffle. No one dared to weep outright. They retreated to the bathroom reserved for the servants if they needed to have a cry.

They held their breaths, unwilling to disturb the silence with even an audible exhale. It felt like that—like the silence was a living thing lying in wait, a slumbering dragon waiting to be awoken. It was something that, once roused, would drag them away like a flood or a fire that swept through a place and left a ruined landscape in its wake. They were only on the periphery, but tragedy had a way of spreading like any other infectious disease.

She moved quietly too. It was second nature. Her training as a nurse taught her how to move through tragic scenes without a sound, but even before, she'd been a quiet child. A watchful one. "Little Gattina" her father used to call her, padding around on light feet and seeing everything while rarely being seen herself.

It had been a game when she was very small, before tragedy swept through her life and left ruin in its wake. A game between Gattina and her papa, how she crept in the shadows at the corners of a room. How he called for her as if she was far away, how she dodged his gaze until the last second when she pounced and scared him. It made him laugh as he swept her up into his arms and laid smacking kisses on her cheeks until she shrieked and demanded to be put down.

She realized years later he had only been playing along. He had acted slower and stupider, pretended to be blind so his daughter could win the game.

Still, maybe those early games had been a primer to stalking from the shadows. To sticking to the corners, out of sight until the right moment to pounce and win the game.

*

She arrived late, but she knew it didn't matter. Normally it'd be grounds for dismissal, but the old man's stringent rules seemed toothless now.

The household was in flux. Much of the house remained off-limits, and the second floor remained cordoned off by the police. The bottom of the stairs was sealed off with bright-yellow police tape. The oppressive silence seemed strongest when she peered up the steps toward the crime scene, though of course there was nothing to see. The door to the boy's bedroom was shut tight.

Most of the help had been sent home and told to stay there until further notice. The house, the grounds could wait. Only Martha and Susan, the cook, remained—to feed the family, to care for them.

And Laura remained, to care for Clara with her soup-for-brains, her fractured memories and hands gnarled with arthritis.

Laura went straight to the mansion after the police precinct. She had given her statement, answered their questions. She had tried not to openly gawp as the floozy receptionist led her through the building. Laura had never been inside a police station before, and it disappointed her to see it looked like an ordinary office building, staffed by ordinary-looking men. Television had lied to her.

She knew she had to be a suspect. She was in the house every day. She knew the family, knew their schedules, knew when they would and would not be home. She doubted she was the first or even the second suspect, though.

No one ever believed a woman could do such a thing.

It was easy to let the mask slip when she spoke to the detectives. To give a glimpse of dislike and distrust of Jack, then to pull it back. Poor Jack. *"A nice man"* she'd called him. Emphasis on *nice*, the way people used the word as a placeholder for the real adjective they wanted to use but couldn't because it was impolite. She played the role of the loyal servant trying to see the best in her employer's feckless son.

Bette Davis, eat your damned heart out.

She'd seen both detectives notice it. The young skinny one and the older fat one. They looked like Laurel and Hardy, but they seemed perceptive. She couldn't underestimate them. She knew the police force would put everything they had into solving this case.

Maybe they'd solve it, after all. Maybe her story ended in handcuffs, in a jail cell, in a courtroom with a placid expression on her face as jurors glared at her. As some district attorney called her a monster. She wouldn't say a word if they did. If they failed to see how she acted on God's will, it would be their failing, not hers.

She could easily shift from God's vengeance to God's martyr. Heaven held all variety of saints.

Or maybe her story would keep rambling along as it always had. Little Gattina, seeing everything while rarely being seen herself. Our Lady of the Shadows, Patroness of the Hidden.

Laura went to Clara's suite of rooms and put her purse on the dresser, shed her jacket and hung it up. It was early afternoon, and the old woman lazed in the sunroom, stretched out and soaking up the weak autumn sunlight while she still could. There was no rush to attend to her yet. She was probably still lucid, only starting to get fuzzy around the edges.

Laura would check on her later. She made her way to the kitchen instead.

The kitchen in the Farney mansion was sinfully large, big enough to cook for a battalion, though the cook rarely had the opportunity to put it to full use. Thomas Farney preferred meals that lay light in his stomach and didn't challenge his palate. Clara ate as much as a bird, ate the diet of the classic invalid—toast with a scrape of butter, clear broths. The occasional pudding to help her put on weight. Jack usually ate at the club. Abigail was a ghost: a whiff of expensive perfume, the soft sound of her expensive clothing whisking against itself as she came and went, never settling to eat with the family.

And the boy? Laura remembered the boy sitting alone at the kitchen table, his small legs swinging as he ate a grilled cheese sandwich, drank a glass of milk. She pushed him out of her mind before he could settle there and take up residence. What was done couldn't be undone. No sense in dwelling.

The cook and housekeeper were both in the kitchen. Both sat at the long, broad island in the middle of the room, their heads bent, whispering furiously.

Susan's head shot up as Laura walked in. Martha glanced up a second later. They both looked terrible, but Martha looked far worse. She seemed to have aged in the past few hours, and she seemed to have lost weight, too, though Laura knew that was impossible. The woman looked drawn, the plump cheeks sagging, the bird-bright eyes now set like dull stones above the heavy bags under her eyes.

If Laura had one regret, it was that Martha found the body.

It hadn't been her intention, but it couldn't be helped, she supposed. The housekeeper had the habit of walking the house when she arrived early each morning, some holdover from when she raised her own brood and took a headcount to make sure none of them had snuck out in the night to stir up mischief.

The sweet, stupid old bird. They'd sent her home to recover from her hysterics, but she was loyal to Farney and had worked for him forever. No one was surprised when she wandered back to the mansion to drift around uselessly until she could help in some way.

Martha fixed her bleary gaze on Laura and asked, "How are you holding up, dearie?"

Principle one: Why lie when you don't have to? In Laura's

experience, people asked questions but didn't care to really hear the answer. People just waited for their chance to speak.

She pressed her lips together in a grim line, shook her head. It was answer enough. Martha shook her head, too, mirrored Laura, and a fresh film of tears glazed her eyes. Susan clucked her tongue sympathetically, and she rushed to put the kettle on, to pour them some tea. She urged them to drink, gripped Laura's forearm and squeezed it in a gesture of comfort before she passed the lemon slices and sugar.

When Laura lifted the cup to her lips, she let it rattle a little against the saucer, the delicate chink of bone china chiming against itself. She'd done the same thing at the precinct, let her hands tremble just enough to be seen. From the corner of her eye, she caught Susan noticing it, and she knew the gossipy old broad would tell everyone she knew about how torn up they all were.

Poor Martha, can you imagine discovering a child like that, dead like that? Can you imagine? And I had just made him dinner that night, the last thing the boy ate.

Laura knew the phone lines would buzz. Susan and Martha would both take calls over the weekend. Both women would suddenly be the stars of their circles of friends and acquaintances. They'd tell it over and over, and she—Laura Lucas, the nurse for the poor invalid Clara Farney—would have a periphery role in the retelling. She'd not be a suspect but a fellow victim, an upstanding woman thrust into a violent crime investigation, steady nerves fraying at the horror of it all.

I could have had a fine career on the stage or screen, she thought, and she lifted the rim of the cup to her mouth to still the smile that wanted to form.

CHAPTER TEN

Felix hated hospitals.

The morgue lurked in the basement of the city's hospital. Though Felix had been there plenty as a cop, he always felt like a little boy again: his cold, clammy hand clasped in his mother's, him being dragged to visit any one of his grandparents. They all got sick around the same time, one right after the other, all four of them.

The memories of those days bubbled to the surface of thoughts, summoned by that unique hospital odor of bleach and sickness. His headache throbbed against the inside of his skull and made his stomach twist with nausea. He must have looked peaked because Adam glanced at him in the elevator and remarked that he looked like shit.

"Headache," Felix replied. "And I hate hospitals."

"Well, hell... everyone hates hospitals."

Felix rolled his eyes. The elevator stopped and chimed, and the metal doors slid open to deposit them in the morgue. It was cooler in the basement, and quiet. At least upstairs, in the hospital proper, there were the constant sounds of life—the beeping of machines, the clicking of heels on the tile floor. It made the silence of the morgue stand out in stark relief.

"Fine, but I hate them more than the average person, okay?" He dropped his voice to a near-whisper.

"Touchy." Adam didn't soften his voice, and it boomed off the tiled walls. "Lead the way."

Felix jerked his thumb to the right and turned on his heel toward the morgue. Adam kept stride with him, and Felix could feel the weight of the older man's stare as they walked.

"If you want to sit this out, I can handle the coroner," he finally said as they approached the door at the end of the hallway.

"I don't want to sit it out."

"No shame in it. It's never easy to see 'em on the slab."

"I've seen plenty of dead bodies."

"You look a little green around the gills, is all I'm saying. Don't want you tossing your lunch, you know?"

Felix clenched his jaw, gritted out, "I'm fine. I'm not going to throw up. Let's go."

*

Almost as soon as he got inside the morgue, Felix puked.

Two steps in, and everything hit at once: the sterile scent of industrial disinfectant over the fainter scent of decay, of the dead leaking noxious fluids; the chill in the air to help preserve the bodies.

And the boy, tucked under a white sheet. His was the only body laid out, a macabre centerpiece to the clean, tiled room. Impossibly small, and Felix already knew what he'd see when the coroner peeled back the sheet. It was the same thing he saw when he shut his eyes—the deep-slashed throat, the small hands curled alongside, the bluish lips parted—

He turned and dashed to the waste bin near the door, his mouth suddenly flooded with saliva. He barely made it in time. A few seconds later and his stomach cramped and heaved, deposited the half-digested remains of his lunch. Felix cursed himself for choosing the roast beef sandwich earlier. It looked and tasted worse the second time around.

Adam, blessedly, didn't say a word. Neither did Doctor Miller. The older detective and the coroner exchanged introductions. They pointedly ignored Felix as he swept his sour mouth with his tongue, spit into the trash can until the rancid taste subsided. He stood, swiped the back of his hand along his mouth. He heard the soft tread of footsteps, heard rustling behind him and the quiet *thunk* of the small refrigerator being opened, then closed.

"Detective Kosmatka," Doctor Miller said. Felix turned to face the man, who pressed a bottle of ginger ale into his hand. The Doc kept a supply of it on hand. He had enough people with weak stomachs pass through his domain.

"Migraines acting up again?" the doctor asked.

Coroners, Krause told Felix once, were fucked-up individuals. It took a certain sick sort, the captain had said, to learn medicine and *not* heal the living. Who spent all that time and effort in medical school just to cut open dead bodies and root around like a kid grubbing around a cereal box for a toy?

Felix liked Miller, though. He always found the man respectful and efficient, and the two always fell into more mundane topics of conversation once the work-talk finished. They had the same taste in books, both read Larry McMurtry and had definite opinions on which stories were better.

And fucked-up individual or not, Doctor Miller had been the one to crack the code of Felix's infrequent but powerful headaches.

"Those are just migraines," he had said once when Felix was in the morgue for a case, a hunter who had been shot during doe season.

"I was worried it was a brain tumor," Felix had replied, grateful for the free diagnosis. The headaches had plagued him since high school but, like everyone else in his family, he treated most of his ailments by ignoring them and hoping they would go away on their own.

"Oh, don't worry," Miller had said cheerfully, clapping him on the shoulder after he signed off on the paperwork to rule the shooting accidental. "You could still get one of those someday."

Now, Felix only nodded at the man. He sipped at the ginger ale and felt his stomach accept it without complaint. He jerked his chin in the direction of the body and Miller caught the motion.

"I've never performed an autopsy on a murdered child before, and I'm sad to have reached that milestone in my career."

Felix took another mouthful of the soda, swished it around to get the acid taste of vomit out of his mouth. He stood up straighter.

"Tell us what you found, Doc," he said.

*

The doctor didn't remove the sheet at first. He gestured for the men to join him near the slab, but he kept the body covered while he went over his notes.

"Let's review the obvious first. The deceased suffered from a single, deep incision to the front of the neck. The right end starts approximately an inch below the ear and terminates at an inch below the left ear with a slight trail abrasion. Both the jugular vein and the left carotid artery are severed."

Miller paused, sat his notes down, and held his hand over the covered body. "Given the facts of the injury, I'd say you're looking for a right-handed person. They stood to the left side of the victim. They started on the right, or far side, and pulled the weapon toward themselves." He mimed the motion as he described it, slashed his empty hand over the boy's body.

"The person is right-handed," Felix said. "What about the weapon?"

"Nothing was recovered at the scene, but there's nothing unique about the wound. There's no tearing, which would suggest a serrated blade like a hunting knife. Given the cleanliness of the cut and the depth, and the entry point, I'd say it's a single-edged blade. Something like a standard kitchen knife."

"Doesn't narrow it down much," Adam grumbled.

"No." Miller picked up his notes and glanced at them. "Detective Kosmatka, you were at the scene. Did anything strike you?"

"The cleanliness of it," Felix replied immediately. "It should have left a terrific mess, but it was all pooled on the bed."

"The blood loss was contained. There was no spraying, no vertical distribution."

Adam shifted beside Felix, put his hands on his hips. "Most slit throats happen from behind, with the vic standing or sitting up. Wasn't the boy lying down?"

Miller and Felix both nodded, but the doctor sat his notes back down and grasped the edge of the white sheet between his fingers. He glanced between the two, read their expressions. He peeled the sheet back, tucked it over on itself at the boy's chest.

He folded his hands in front of him and bowed his head, solemn.

Let Krause think what he would about coroners, Felix liked this about Doctor Miller, too, his respect for the bodies in his care. Felix had been a policeman long enough, attended enough scenes with the dead, to know the old-timers could become numb to it. The gallows humor crept in, and they stopped seeing the body as a person.

Not Miller. Every body, every victim—from the homeless man who died of exposure to the middle-class mother who died in a car crash—received the same solemn care and respect.

"Yes, the victim was lying down," he finally said. His voice was quiet, and he gazed at the boy's slack face. "But still, given the violence of the injury, there would have been arterial spray. Even if he'd been asleep, even if he wasn't entirely aware of what was happening, the body would struggle to survive. The perpetrator would have been covered in blood."

Felix kept his eyes level on the doctor's face. Out of his peripheral, he could see the body. Pale, even smaller on the slab than he'd been in his bed. Under the edge of the sheet, he could see the thick black stitches where the Y incision began. He could see the lurid gash to the neck, even worse now that the drying blood had been cleaned away—the severed muscles, the bit of white bone gleaming through the gore—

He cleared his throat, rough. "There was no spray. No blood spatter."

"Blood moves through the body due to the contraction of ventricles, usually. Simply put, a beating heart pumps blood around the body. At death, the only thing left to move the blood is gravity. That's why we use lividity. The pooling of blood in a dead body is a reliable way to determine the ballpark time of death."

Adam caught on a beat faster than Felix, his gears turning faster. "Are you saying the cause of death wasn't the cut throat?" He gestured at the body, his tone one of blatant incredulity.

"Yes."

Miller stepped away from the body and strode over to where

his desk was tucked away in the corner of the room. He pulled out a second file folder and returned to where Felix and Adam stood. He handed the file to Felix.

"Everything is in there, Detective," he said. "The boy was already dead when his throat was cut. The blood at the crime scene was only pushed out by gravity. Or maybe by pressure in the arterial system if the arterial wall musculature hadn't relaxed yet in death. It's consistent with the lack of mess at the scene. The blood only oozed out of the wound, since the heart had already stopped."

Felix opened the file in his hands. He scanned the technical medical terms he was only half-familiar with. "It doesn't make sense," he murmured as he read. "Why... How..." He was unsure of what the right question even was.

"I can't answer all of those questions yet," Miller replied, and he reached out to cover the body again, the white sheet obscuring the boy. "But the body doesn't lie. One would expect to see some aspiration of blood. If he had been breathing, there would have been frothy blood in the lungs. Add to that the lack of defensive wounds..." He held his hands out, palms up, entreating them to understand the facts of his investigation.

"So how did he die?" Adam asked.

"I'm testing samples, and I sent some off to another county coroner. Given the scrutiny this case will get, I thought it prudent to verify any findings."

"Any theory in lieu of test results?" Adam again.

"Strangulation would have left a bruise, so I'd guess poison or suffocation. There are no other obvious injuries to the body beyond a scraped knee that was already half-healed." The doctor laid a gentle hand on the slab, not touching the body but pressing his palm near him. He gazed at the covered boy and shook his head. "He had a scraped knee. An everyday injury for a little boy."

The doctor exhaled heavily through his mouth. He patted the enamel of the slab as if he were trying to offer comfort.

"This has been ghastly, gentlemen," he continued, and there was a roughness to his voice, his words taut like he'd forced them out. "Once I know what the cause of death is, you'll know too."

✳

"Damned bizarre," Adam muttered on the drive back to the barracks. His words were quiet, but Felix caught them anyway. When he turned to face his new partner, Adam turned, too, caught his gaze and shrugged.

"Sorry. Still not used to having a buddy riding along," he said.

Felix snorted at his word choice, *buddy*, then turned to look out the passenger-side window. Traffic grew thicker as the workday ended and people went home. When they passed the factory, the usual line of cars crept into the complex as the first shift went home and the second shift arrived for their turn at the blast furnace and assembly lines.

The sun sunk steadily, and it cast the streets in a ruddy golden light. Times like this, Felix thought his hometown close to beautiful. Draped in the rosy light of sunset, Mariensburg looked like a painting: the hard edges and worn-down dinginess softened to Norman Rockwell Americana.

He and Adam had burned most of their daylight hours taking statements and gathering names of potential suspects. They steadily approached the twenty-four-hour mark. Now, at least, they had this other crucial piece of the coroner's report, but even that made little sense. The slashed throat and the neat crime scene. It baffled him.

Adam braked at a red light. Felix studied the faces of the people who crossed in front of them. They all looked shifty. They all looked guilty. The old woman with her pocketbook clutched in her hands. The slouching teenaged boy with the beady eyes. The young mother, a baby slung precariously on one hip and a bag of groceries balanced on the other, her mouth etched into a deep frown.

He knew, logically, it wasn't any of them.

He also knew it could be anyone, including any one of them.

His headache had eased a bit, but his thoughts swarmed and buzzed like a hive of wasps. Flashbulb memories, only recently formed within the last day, sparked: The boy's small hands curled on the green coverlet of his bed. The boy's small hands curled under the white sheet in the morgue. Thomas Farney pacing behind his desk. Jack Farney staring at his hands in his lap as he stuttered out *"my boy,"* his sole moment of emotion during his statement.

The traffic light snapped to green. Adam eased into the intersection, then turned toward the precinct.

CHAPTER ELEVEN

The job took little effort.

Clara Farney was a model invalid. Laura had worked with dementia patients before. She was familiar with the slow skid of the disease. It always began with simple forgetfulness and ended with being bedridden, incontinent, and lost in their own slushy brain matter. Clara was somewhere in the middle of that skid. She was prone to wandering, and more often unmoored in time, but she was pliant, easy to handle.

Laura had handled far more difficult cases in her career.

Hospital work, for example. She'd worked at plenty of them. Small ones with a single story, a single wing. Large ones that took up an entire city block. She had hopscotched her way across the East, cut a haphazard path from Boston to Concord to Rochester and smaller towns in between. Every sort of ward, from the chaos of the emergency room to a veteran's hospital to the tucked-away terminal cases.

She had staffed maternity wards but found them unpleasant, all the bleating and wailing of labor, the milky odor of babies covered in waxy vernix. She had drifted toward the care of the elderly and those with catastrophic brain injuries. She'd worked with brain cancer survivors missing chunks of their frontal lobes, car crash victims, people with bullet fragments buried in their skulls.

It fascinated her endlessly, how a single moment could change an entire person's personality, the sweep of their life. How a sweet-natured young girl could turn into a creature of pure, snarling rage after driving headfirst into a tree. How a family man could kill his wife and kids because of a lesion or a tumor.

How the essence of a person was never fixed and settled. How a single moment could shift the entirety of what made a person them.

Laura had honed her skills at the hospitals. But before that?

Before that, in the war, the great sea change that swept up so many men of her generation and, like her, some of the women too.

She tried not to dwell too much on the *before*. She kept it locked away in a separate part of herself and only visited it on rare occasions. The single moment that had shifted her. Laura wondered sometimes if her elderly patients, her brain injury patients were aware of their own sea changes. Did they recognize who they had been and what they had become, like she did?

It was hard to say. Laura had tried to ask the formerly sweet-natured girl once if she remembered her life from before. Did she remember the candy-striping job, or babysitting her younger sister, or playing double Dutch at recess? Did those memories still exist in her scrambled brain, and did it hurt more to know what she had been? To realize what she had lost and would never be again?

The question had gone unanswered. Instead, the formerly sweet-natured girl had grinned at her—leered, actually—and gestured for Laura to lean closer, as if she was about to impart some deep-held wisdom. When Laura obliged, the girl had only whispered a string of invectives, called Laura a *"dirty bitch,"* then laughed wildly at the look of disappointment on the nurse's face.

Most people who experienced a sea change only ever got one: a single moment that changed the trajectory of their fate. Laura got two.

The first happened early, when she was just a child, that nebulous *before* she kept locked away in the farthest chamber of her heart. The second came later as she settled into womanhood.

Nursing hadn't been a passion for her. She had no deep love of healing the ill and infirm. Neither, it had to be said, did many of the girls in her nursing class. Half were only there for the proximity to doctors, the ultimate catch for a husband. The other half were homely girls, unlovely things with too-small eyes or too-large noses or lumpy bodies, who had no hope of finding someone to marry them and therefore had to rely on themselves.

Laura had enrolled in nursing school half-heartedly. It was a stab at carving out some stability, of being able to take care of herself. She could have gone to secretarial school instead and learned shorthand and typing.

The war barely crossed her mind most days back then. Hitler and his gang of goose-stepping thugs conquering countries she couldn't even place on a map—who cared? What did it matter to her what happened over there? She had problems enough over here.

Then Hirohito bombed Pearl Harbor. The war hit home, but only comparatively. Pearl Harbor, Hawaii... it had still seemed as distant as Poland or Paris.

Providence, then, the second great sea change. It wasn't any patriotic stirring that put her on her path. It was a newspaper article about the men who bombed the harbor. Sent up in planes without landing gear, a mission with no return ticket. They accepted their own doom in pursuit of their greater mission. Laura had sat at the dining room table at the boarding house, bent over the days-old newspaper, and marveled at the dedication of those Japanese aviators.

Another girl at the boarding house found Laura like that—lost in thought, staring at the tiny black type marching like ants across the newsprint. The girl had misread the situation, patted Laura on her shoulder, told her everything would work out alright.

Laura, only half hearing her, had nodded along and agreed. Everything would work out alright. Yes, it would.

Providence. The still, small voice inside her, whispering at what purpose could do.

See what a person can achieve, the voice whispered. *See what a single person can do when they take the rage that fills them and whets it into a fine, sharp weapon?*

Laura had nodded again at the voice. *Yes, I see.*

Providence. The voice of God speaking to Laura in a boarding house in Philadelphia, commanding her to put her feet to the path He would lay out for her. If she listened to Him and obeyed His will, He would lead her back to Thomas Farney.

He would reward her with vengeance against the man who took everything from her.

✻

After her tea with Martha and Susan, Laura went to the sunroom to check on her patient. It was as she expected. The old woman was stretched out on the chaise, drowsing in the late afternoon sun.

"How are you doing, lovey?" she asked Clara, and it took the woman a few moments of blinking at Laura before the gears in her head caught and turned.

"It's getting cold outside," Clara replied. "The roses will need to be collared."

Laura reached past her for the blanket draped over the chaise. She shook it out, covered Clara with it.

"We can let the gardener know."

Clara's face went slack the way it always did when she began to sundown. Laura could practically see her sifting through names and faces, all a muddle in her head. After a long moment, her face lit up with joyful triumph.

"The gardener," Clara said. "Jacobs."

"That's exactly right."

"He'll need to know about the roses. They'll need to be collared."

Laura laid a soft hand on the woman's shoulder, pushed her to lie back on the chaise again.

"We'll tell him," she repeated, and she put on her official nurse's voice—low, soothing, with a thread of unswerving authority. "Why don't you rest a bit more and I'll see what the cook has planned for our dinner?"

✻

She left Clara and made her way to the old woman's first-floor quarters. Most of the house remained off-limits, but the police had given Clara's suite a cursory once-over and cleared it.

It had been a parlor at one point. When Clara Farney began wandering at night, Thomas spared no expense in converting the space into a bathroom and a pair of bedrooms (a small, but lavish, one for Clara, and a smaller, sparser one for hired help). The hired help was Laura, and she didn't spend the night yet. Clara remained manageable.

The medicine helped. The nightly white tablet eased down Clara's throat with tapioca pudding or broth. It kept her docile and quiet through the night. No more wanderings, no more anxiety edging against full-blown panic.

Laura heard the nightly tablet could cause euphoria. She wondered what that felt like.

She crossed to the far side of Clara's bedroom and went into the smaller bedroom reserved for the help. It held a narrow bed, a single chest of drawers that were empty save for the lavender sachets Martha put in every nook and cranny in the house. There was a nightstand beside the bed.

That's where Laura kept Clara's medication tucked away, where she couldn't find it. She used to keep it in the bathroom medicine cabinet, but she'd caught Clara on more than one occasion rummaging through it, mindlessly searching for something she couldn't remember, even when asked.

The innocuous brown bottle, the label with SOPORAL writ in large red letters. It was habit-forming, Clara's doctor had told Laura, but senility only worsened, never improved. Who really cared if an old woman became an addict, so long as the old woman stayed obedient and easy to handle? Everything was palliative now.

Still, what sort of nurse would Laura be if she didn't count pills?

✳

Martha was still in the kitchen with Susan when Laura walked in. The old bird didn't seem to know what to do with herself, so she leaned against the counter as the cook prepared dinner. Laura offered them each a smile that wasn't quite a smile, one of those tight-lipped near-grimaces that served more to acknowledge the sad situation.

"I'm about to go to the police station to give my statement," Martha said. "Mrs. Farney alright?"

"She doesn't understand what's happened."

"No sense in telling her, I say. Poor dearie won't remember even if we did."

The cook glanced up from where she sliced the bread that would become Clara's toast points for her bland dinner of scrambled eggs.

"A blessing," she added.

There was nothing else to say, so the silence stretched out. Laura watched the cook as she cracked the eggs against the edge of the bowl, whisked them with a bit of milk. She waited until the eggs were poured into the pan—the burst of sizzle against the melted butter—before she cleared her throat.

"I wanted to ask," Laura started, then hesitated. She furrowed her brow and pulled on an expression of uncertainty until she had both Martha's and Susan's attention. Once she felt their expectant eyes on her, she reached into the pocket of her cardigan and pulled out the bottle of Soporal. She gave it a little shake, let the few remaining pills rattle loose in the bottle before she set it on the counter.

"I don't want to bother Mr. Farney with this, given the tragedy." She paused. "But I noticed the other day Mrs. Farney's pill bottle seemed light, so I did an inventory. I counted back to when I was at the pharmacy last, and the math doesn't add up."

"Has Mrs. Farney been sneaking 'em, you think?" Susan asked. She turned back to her dinner preparation, pushed the spatula around the edge of the eggs.

"I don't see how she could," Laura replied. "I keep her medicine tucked away in the spare room. I doubt she even knows I store her medication there, and she couldn't open the bottle with her arthritis anyway."

It always took a deft hand with the housekeeper. Martha Donoghue might look harmless and even a bit stupid: the plump body that scurried around, the crooked incisor, and the slightly bulging eyes. She may seem a simpleton, but she was far from it.

Naïve? Yes. A bit too trusting? Yes.

Both of those traits served Laura well. It had been so easy to single Martha out as Farney's little lieutenant who kept his life running smoothly. Easy to join the congregation at Saint Boniface, to attend the same Mass, to bump into her and make her acquaintance.

God had helped by delivering Clara's diagnosis. Laura only had to obliquely mention to Martha that she was a nurse, how she was taking private clients after a career in hospitals, and if she knew of anyone hiring...

Naïve, trusting Martha. But not stupid.

Laura never said anything outright to Martha. No declarative statements and only the mildest of opinions. Instead, she insinuated, she alluded, and she let the housekeeper believe she drew her own conclusions instead of being carefully led.

Laura reached out and tapped the top of the bottle. "These are addictive. I'd hate if they fell into the wrong hands because I didn't lock them up better." Nudging against the conclusion she wanted the housekeeper to draw, Laura widened her eyes as if she just had a realization, asking Martha in a hushed whisper, "You don't think one of the maids took them, do you?"

Laura expected the firm shake of the head. She expected Martha's spirited defense of her girls, and the housekeeper did as she expected.

No, they were good girls, her maids, Martha told her. No, they didn't truck with dope. No, they'd never steal from their employer, let alone the sick old woman who relied on those pills.

Laura held up her hands, palms up in surrender. "I hate to assume the worst," she said, her tone apologetic. "I remember how the police busted those dope dealers out at the country club..." She shook her head sadly. "That sort of thing happens in the big cities, but not places like here."

When she ducked her head, she chanced a sideways look at Martha. She could see the woman thinking, her goggled eyes narrowed as she worked through the mystery on her own. Laura had laid out the possibility. Missing pills plus a mention of the country club... it could equal Jack.

It was only one possibility among hundreds of possibilities. Laura tried to cover every single one. Martha might mention the missing pills at some point. Martha Donoghue with her big heart and her bigger conscience. She'd spill every mundane detail and maybe a few of the ones Laura had planted. She'd treat the police barracks like a confessional.

She was Thomas Farney's most loyal soldier, after all. She'd be keen to help in any way she could.

CHAPTER TWELVE

C aptain Krause waited for them at the precinct. As soon as they hit the door, the man was there, a half-smoked cigarette clamped between the fingers he used to point at Felix and Adam.

"You two," he said without preamble. "Conference room. Now."

Adam swept his arm in front of him, gestured for Felix to lead the way. In the conference room, Krause shut the door behind them, turned to face them.

"How'd it go with the coroner?" he asked.

They summed it up, gave him the broad strokes before they arrived at the punch line: the body with the slashed throat was dead before the throat was slashed.

"Doc is running tests. He sent samples out to double-check any findings too," Felix explained. "But he was certain the boy was dead before his throat was cut."

The captain leaned against the edge of the table and eyed the corkboard with its neat line of names. The stub of cigarette smoldered in his hand as he processed the new information, and he absent-mindedly tossed it in an abandoned cup of coffee where it hissed and sputtered.

"Haney spent the afternoon at the carbon factory," he mused, still staring at the list of names. "He confirmed the driver's alibi and confirmed the first half of Jack Farney's day yesterday. Jack was in his office all day, as he said."

"Doesn't confirm his flimsy 'I slept in my car' bullshit story for the time of the murder, though," Adam said.

"True." Krause turned to face them. "I watched during his statement. What are your impressions?"

Adam held a poor opinion of the man. He pointed out the dodgy alibi, asked what sort of father left his young son alone at night to gamble and do God-knows-what else. He'd been pale,

Adam said, shaky hands that had been clammy. Proof of a dope habit? He pointed out Jack's lack of emotion until the very end of his interview.

Felix bristled at the other detective and his use of the word "acting." Jack's outburst had felt genuine to Felix.

"I disagree," Felix said. "A man grieves too hard and he's acting. He does the stiff upper lip thing, he's acting. You can't judge a suspect on the range of human emotions. Grief makes people act strange."

He didn't add his own experience with it, how he and his brothers had each reacted differently to the sudden death of their father. Albie with his down-to-business pragmatism. Mark and his flippant disbelief. Mike and his histrionics, how Stevie focused his anger on Mike, scrapped with him at the funeral luncheon to the horror of all.

He didn't add his own reaction to death, which wasn't that different from Jack's. When he found out about his dad's death, Felix had clicked right along, never missed a beat. He'd been convinced that a mistake had been made, so he never let the sorrow sink in until long after the funeral.

Krause's gaze bounced between Felix and Adam. "Okay, so we confirm Jack's evening yesterday. Reach out to the names he gave as alibis," he said.

"Got it," Felix said.

"We keep working the people with access to the house," the captain continued. "I'll do a quiet inquiry into homicides with postmortem injuries. Hell, who knows? Maybe it is a serial fucker after all."

"There is a certain element of competence to this," Adam added. "This seems too sophisticated for a first-time killer." He sighed, rolled his head around until something in his neck popped. "I'm coming around to the possibility of it."

Felix crossed the room and plopped into a chair. He propped his elbows on his knees, cradled his head in his hands. Behind the darkness of his eyelids, white sparks crackled and sputtered in time to the throbbing in his head.

"While you were gone, the mother came in," Krause said, and Felix kept his head down and his eyes shut. He heard the rustle of paper and the captain's rumbling voice.

"There was nothing much there. She seems to have taken a... let's call it *inactive* role in her son's life. It sounds like Thomas ran things when it came to his grandson."

"That jives with what Jack told us," Felix mumbled, head still in his hands.

"No ideas on who could have murdered her son?" Adam asked.

"She was oddly distant."

Felix opened his eyes and lifted his head. "*Distant*? After her son was *murdered*?"

Krause shrugged. "People deal with it differently. You just said so."

"Could be shock," Adam added.

"She gets a pass, but Jack doesn't?" Felix asked, and he caught Adam's rolled eyes.

Krause ignored the comment. "She doesn't know of anyone who'd hurt the boy. Then again, it doesn't sound like she's around enough to know. She comes from old New York Dutch money. She's there more often than here."

"And we don't think it could be her, right? No angle where the mother is upset about her only son being commandeered by Old Man Farney?" Adam asked.

"Doubtful, but I have a call in to the police up there. They're gonna check in on her whereabouts last night, on the QT."

Adam stood. He walked over to the corkboard and clasped his hands behind his back like a professor about to deliver a lecture. Before he could get out whatever deep thought he had, a knock sounded at the door.

Without waiting for anyone to call out, Rhonda poked her head in.

"Woman here to talk to you," she announced. "About the Farney case."

✳

Martha Donoghue sat at the interrogation room table, her handbag clasped in her lap. She started to rise when Felix and Adam entered the room, but Adam waved her off the formalities, and she settled her bulk back into her seat.

Felix studied her as she gave them the preliminaries of that evening, how she left the mansion a bit after nine that night and went home to her husband—"My Paul" she called him—and then straight to bed.

This was the woman who found the body. It showed in little ways. Her froggy eyes were threaded in fine red lines, the burst capillaries spoke to hard crying. Her restless hands snapped the clasp on her purse as she talked, her words punctuated by the quiet *click* of metal on metal.

"I always do one final sweep of the house before I leave for the day," she said.

"What does that entail, ma'am?" Felix asked.

Click, click, click went the metal clasp on her purse as she explained. She walked through the Farney mansion every night before she left and every morning when she arrived. It was a habit, a way of taking stock of her workday, of inventorying what needed done and what could wait. It was also a way of inventorying who was in the house and who was out.

"Mr. Farney is a busy man," she explained.

"What about Jack?" Adam asked. He leaned forward in his seat, hooked an elbow on the laminated tabletop. "And Abigail?"

"Oh, *them*." She sniffed, curled her nose in obvious dislike. "*She* is almost never here. Too good for us here. She spends most of her time in New York with her Barnard friends."

"Are she and Jack separated?" Felix asked. It wouldn't surprise him if they were. They certainly didn't seem to hold any of the hallmarks of a loving couple. They had arrived at the barracks separately. They weren't a united front in any obvious sense of the term.

Another derisive sniff. "They were barely together even in the beginning. A poor match, if you ask me."

"Do they fight a lot?" Adam asked.

Martha shook her head. "No fighting. She goes to her fancy Park Avenue apartment, and he goes to wherever he goes."

"They both left their son behind?" Felix looked up from his notebook. He glanced at Adam to see if the other detective's expression gave anything away, but his face was neutral, slightly nodding his head to encourage Martha to keep talking.

At the question, the woman's face lit up. "Oh no, it's not like that," she said, and she sat forward, her eyes lighting up as she described the life of Junior Farney. How Thomas, God bless him, took a special interest in the boy, his namesake.

How he hired a tutor to prepare the boy for his future in prep school and college—all a foregone conclusion for the grandson of a scion. How he took the boy to the factory sometimes, plunked a white hard hat on him and walked him across the factory floor, said it would belong to him one day. How he groomed the boy, started to mold him to be his heir.

Interesting, Felix thought. *Thomas talking about succession with his young grandson instead of his son.*

The conversation meandered, circled back. Martha relaxed and stopped the maddening clicking of her purse. She offered gossip and opinions. She scattered in important facts, like the time she left the house and the time she returned, which helped firm up the timeline of the murder.

Intel on the other people in the house, the hired help and the family alike. She had opinions on all of them, but she spoke of Thomas Farney as though he were responsible for setting the sun in the cosmos. It was obvious the woman was fiercely loyal to her employer.

"I've worked for him since I was fourteen," she said, the pride apparent in her voice. "I started on as a maid in the mansion. It was brand new. I was there when Mr. Farney brought his new bride home, and when they had Jack and when Jack married, when Junior was born... A lot of life, and now *this*."

"Surely you have a theory," Adam said. His voice was soft, charming when paired with his winning smile. "Surely you've thought over who could do such a thing—"

"I *cannot* imagine it," she replied, a fierce shake of her head driving the vehemence of her answer. "I cannot imagine who could slaughter a child in his bed."

She sat back in her seat. Twin spots of color burned high on her cheeks, and her neck was splotchy red as well. Her hands returned to the purse and resumed toying with the clasp, the steady *click-click* like a metronome in Felix's head.

Adam paged through his own notes as they waited for her to add something, and he saw something on an earlier page that made him cluck his tongue thoughtfully.

"On your walkthroughs of the house," he said, tapping the point of his pen against the notebook. "Can you describe how you lock up each night?"

If she had been planning on saying something, she forgot it at Adam's question. Felix could see the way her face crumpled, could already guess at the guilt behind her expression. Her eyes shifted from Adam's face to his, her mouth working soundlessly until she could get the words out.

"I've thought about it," she replied. "Do you think I forgot to lock up? Did I forget? Is this my fault?"

Fault had always been an interesting concept to Felix. He was fascinated by culpability, by the fine line between responsibility and atonement, how they overlapped. There was no way he could explain to Martha Donoghue, though, that Junior Farney had been murdered by someone with know-how. Felix guessed that locked door, unlocked door—the killer was always going to find a way inside.

"It's not your fault," Adam said, preempting any comfort Felix might have given. "It's not your fault at all."

＊

In the conference room afterward, Adam stood at the board while Felix sat and went through his notes.

"Everyone hired by Farney with access to the house, so not counting family here." Adam turned to the names, tapped each as he went.

"The driver, the maids, the gardener and cook, and the tutor. All cleared. All have solid alibis that have been confirmed."

"We can check on the housekeeper tomorrow, but her alibi will likely clear too."

Adam grinned at him. "She was a chatty one, huh?"

Felix held up his notebook, flipped through the pages filled with his writing. "Half of these are hers."

"That leaves the nurse." Adam turned back to the board. "She lives alone, so no alibi."

"She said her neighbor might serve."

"Wouldn't hurt to try."

Felix pushed away from the table, the chair legs scraping against the floor. He stood and stretched, twisted until his lower back did its satisfying pop. He took the few steps around the table to stand beside Adam.

"Krause made some headway with Farney's list of enemies while we were at the morgue," he said, and he gestured at the second line of names. "Looks like he identified all of the ones who are dead."

Adam snorted. "Yeah, that's a solid alibi there." He squinted and read the captain's note on the card labeled as *Steph. Aiken/ Partner-coal mine*. "'I couldn't have murdered that boy, officer,'" he mimicked. "'I've been dead since 1947.'"

"The partner from the coal mine, the rival mine owner, and the city councilman are all dead," Felix added, tallying the crossed-off cards. "Anyone left jumping out at you?"

"Maybe the brother of the fired secretary? Man made a threat, so we can't ignore it."

Felix pointed at another card, the one with more than one name—the local farmers with the mine runoff tainting their groundwater supply. "Might be worthwhile to check on these ones too. Their complaint is recent, and there's several of them."

"You think this is a two-man job?"

Felix shook his head. "No, but I'd hate to not check on it."

"Fair enough. Add it to the to-do list."

Felix glanced at the clock on the wall. It was getting late. The dull roar of the bullpen had steadily quieted in the last few hours. Adam caught the motion and waved at him, shooing him away.

"You should go home," he said. "Sleep off that headache. We can hit it fresh in the morning."

At the mention of sleep, Felix felt a massive yawn creep up the back of his throat. He stifled it against the back of his hand at the last minute. He shook his head and protested, "There's too much to do. Gotta call the names Jack gave us as his alibis."

"I know that, but if I've learned one thing, it's that a tired detective is a sloppy one. Hell, I need at least a few hours of shut-eye myself. I can make those calls before I leave. Get those names lined up to come in first thing tomorrow."

Felix knew he was right. He'd pulled plenty of double shifts, plenty of days with the one-two punch of the day shift, then night school. He knew he got dopey when he was tired. Maybe it didn't matter much for the usual misdemeanors, but this was high-stakes. One misstep could cause the case to unravel.

"Yeah, okay," he groused. "You situated with a place to stay?"

"Yeah. Your receptionist set it up. Room at the motor court, color television, vibrating beds. I'll break a dollar for change and have a swell night." Adam repeated the shooing motion. "Go on. We meet back here early."

Felix stifled a second yawn, then gathered his coat and his notebook. He turned to leave. A single backward glance over his shoulder revealed Adam, turned back to the board, already deep in thought.

Felix's glance fell onto the scatter of folders and paperwork on the table, and he saw the ledger book. Krause's predecessor, the man who held the accounting of Thomas Farney's sins. With Adam's back turned, Felix reached out and snagged the book, tucked it under his arm with his notebook, and draped his coat over both.

"Have a good night," he called out, but Adam only grunted his farewell, waved at him again without turning to look at him.

CHAPTER THIRTEEN

He didn't stay much longer once Felix left. He got the phone numbers of the three possible alibis for Jack, but two said they couldn't help—they'd been part of the contingent who'd drifted away that night when the cards petered out. The third and most promising was nowhere to be found. The phone rang and rang when Adam tried to call his house.

They'd have to try again in the morning. Adam made a note on the board.

The exhaustion hit him somewhere between his stroll out of the precinct and his drive out to the edge of town. He usually felt pretty good, but right now every single one of his years weighed on him. He could have pulled off any given side street, ratcheted his seat as far back as it would go, and slept.

He pulled into the burger shack he'd passed on his way into town. He ordered two cheeseburgers with extra fried onions, a massive scoop of french fries, and a six-pack out of the cooler. He slid a tenner across the greasy counter and gathered his change and his food, then returned to his car.

The motor court was shabby but clean. A bored-looking young man staffed the front office. He sat reading, feet on the counter, but he snapped to attention when Adam strolled in.

"Help you?" he asked.

He sat his book down, and the cracked spine drew Adam's gaze. *The Exorcist* by William Blatty, and the young man looked like he was about two-thirds through it. Adam had tried to read it when it first came out, but his nerves failed him early on. Besides, he saw enough sick shit in the human world. No need to invite in the demonic.

"I have a reservation," he said. "Under *Shaffer*."

"Got it." The boy laid the register in front of Adam and added, "You're the only reservation."

"Not much business this time of year?" He printed his name

and address back in Harrisburg, then signed.

"Not much business any time of year." The kid turned to face the line of hooks with keys dangling from them. He pulled one and set it on the counter. "Sometimes we get hunters."

"I bet the hunting's good up here. Lots of wildlife."

"I guess." The boy turned the register book back toward himself. "You a hunter?"

Adam pocketed the room key. He thought of the case he had just closed, the serial rape-o that seemed a million years ago. He thought of the perp as prey, of the long days turned into months as he stalked crime scenes, gathered clues like a tracker following its quarry.

He thought of the case now. He barely had the lay of the land. Would this case stretch out into long months? He knew it wouldn't. Adam knew he and Felix had only a scant amount of time to make an arrest.

"I guess I am a hunter," he told the kid. "In a manner of speaking."

*

He tossed his suitcase down and settled into his room. He inspected the bed and found that Johnny Krause had been sorely misinformed. It did not vibrate. It only sagged in the middle, a faintly wet scent of mildew wafting from the burnt-orange polyester bedspread.

He clicked on the television, listened to the pop as the tubes warmed up. He knew he was in the dregs of summer programming, but he liked the noise of it. Life on the road was lonely, and when Adam was younger and much spryer, he would find the local watering hole, maybe chat up a local lady.

Now he felt old and exhausted. The CBS Friday Night Movie was fine enough company.

He cracked one of the beers, drained it halfway before he came up for air. He unwrapped the first cheeseburger, wolfed it down without tasting it. It sated the gnawing hunger in his gut enough that he ate the second one at a more leisurely pace. Bloody grease ran down his wrist, and he daubed at it absentmindedly as he stared at the television.

The movie was some goofy spy film with Vince Edwards playing the lead somewhere between Bogart and Bond. Adam rolled his eyes as he snagged a handful of fries and chewed them. Maybe he should have gone Fed, joined up with the FBI or the CIA. The movies made it look more fun. Busting crooked assholes with a bevy of lovely ladies waiting in the wings?

"Sure would beat sitting in the middle of nowhere by myself," he groused. He opened a second beer, tipped it in a mock toast toward the television screen where Vince threw schlocky fake punches at bad guys.

He could review his notes, but there was nothing there yet. A preliminary coroner's report and a handful of statements that elucidated little. He sat, let his mind drift. He finished his second beer and moved on to the third. He took some deep swallows, felt the beer settle in his gut and warm him.

He knew once he got halfway through the six-pack, he'd be able to conjure his younger sister, Amelia. She'd take form in the room, a hazy shadow that'd grow firmer, more distinct as the hours passed. His constant companion.

He aged every day. She stayed forever sixteen.

She had wanted to see the world. She'd kept a battered atlas in her room, Adam remembered. She'd marked every place she planned on visiting, from Paris to the length of the Amazon.

This was the best he could do: summon her shade in shabby motel rooms across the Commonwealth. A sad, too-short life and now an afterlife keeping her lonely brother company as he hunted monsters.

Adam made it four deep into his six-pack before sleep claimed him. He dozed sitting up, his chin tucked to his chest, until he woke with a jolt early in the morning with a cottony mouth and a crick in his neck.

The clock radio by the bed read 2:23 in the morning, so he stumbled to the bathroom, relieved himself of his earlier beers, stumbled back to bed for a few more hours of rest.

His dreams, as always, were a muddle. They spooled backward, grew grainier the further they cast back. He dreamt of little boys with thick, black-stitched Y incisions on their chests. He dreamt of Felix writing out the names of serial killers and pinning them to the board, Felix clicking his pen over and over, the same metallic *click-click-click* of the housekeeper fiddling with her purse.

He dreamt of a parade of older women, all victims of the same rapist, their prim mouths set and their eyes pleading with him to leave it, to let them forget it happened.

He dreamt of the other victims, the ones from early in his career when he was young, green, still hopeful. Further back to Dog Red, Omaha Beach. The noise and stink of death, his boots sucked into the squelching sand as Kraut bullets whizzed past his head. The wash of the shoreline slick with viscera, injured men reduced to boys crying for their mamas in their final minutes of life.

He dreamt of his sister in her casket, his mother's ceaseless weeping at the wake until his aunt led her away and plied her with enough sherry to keep her docile.

When he woke again, this time for good, his dreams melted away. As always, he was left with the same unsettled feeling, the same sense of dragging ghosts behind him like rattling chains, even if he couldn't make out their faces.

CHAPTER FOURTEEN

While Adam paid for his greasy sack of cheeseburgers, Felix pulled into the driveway of his house.

He rested his forehead on the steering wheel, but only for a moment. He'd already seen the curtain in the front window move when he pulled up, the dark silhouette watching. His mother had been waiting for him.

She always sat up and waited. For his entire teenaged and adult life, save for the period he had escaped, Irina Kosmatka always waited in her ratty robe with her face shiny from cold cream.

He sighed, picked his heavy head off the steering wheel. He took a deep breath, but the influx of oxygen coaxed his headache to flare brighter. No sense in delaying it. If he waited too long, she'd toddle over to the side door and yell out at him, destroy the quietude of the night.

He climbed out of the car and arranged his face so he looked merely tired, not dragged down by one of his headaches. The only thing worse than a migraine was Irina smothering him with her maternal care. She blamed his migraines on his absence from church, told him how she and her altar committee friends prayed for his return to the flock every single day.

Felix could tell his mother was waiting for him because the television was turned down to a murmur. She usually let it blare all hours of the day until the speakers crackled from the effort. He entered through the side door into the kitchen and toed off his shoes, shrugged out of his coat.

"You're late," she called from the living room.

"Work," he called back.

"Your father was never late."

He said nothing in reply, didn't bother to point out his father had worked at the county garage, servicing the county's fleet, a job with set hours. Detective work was much more erratic.

"I made you a plate." He heard her climb off the couch, the squeal of protest from some rusted spring deep inside it. He heard the familiar *slap-slap* of her house slippers, the faint wheeze of her breathing as she made her way into the kitchen. "I can heat it up for you."

"It's fine, Ma." He beat her by a step, reached the icebox first. He pulled the wrapped plate out and peeled back the foil. Cabbage rolls. The gassy smell hit him first, made his stomach roil. They looked sad, pale and limp in their congealed pool of greasy tomato sauce.

He replaced the foil and put the plate back in the icebox. "I had a late lunch," he said, not adding that he'd puked his lunch up at the morgue. "I'll eat 'em later."

"That's why you're so skinny." She pulled out a chair from under the kitchen table and sank down into it. "That's why people think I'm not feeding you."

Felix rolled his eyes. He reached into the cabinet and pulled out a carton of saltines. He shook a handful loose onto the counter and ate one. He replied as he chewed, "No one thinks that. I can feed myself."

"Ha!" Irina gestured at him, a broad sweep of the hand that took in all of Felix—from the top of his head down to his socked feet—and his measly dinner of crackers. She turned to the tabletop and reached for her pack of cigarettes. She shook one loose, tore a match from the matchbook tucked in the pack. She lit up and drew a deep lungful that she exhaled slowly with a phlegmy cough.

"You on the murdered kid case?"

"You know I can't talk about it."

"You can say if you are or you aren't."

"I can." He plucked another cracker and popped it into his mouth. "But I won't."

Irina grumbled, took another lingering drag on her cigarette. "Helen said she saw you at the hospital."

Helen: one of many in the Saint Callistus's gossiping club. They were legion. They joined every committee at the church, used every moment to hash out the lives of everyone in the neighborhood. The phone lines ran hot between their homes on an average day. Felix had to imagine that today, with news of a murdered child, the lines probably sizzled.

CIA spooks have nothing on bored church ladies, Felix thought.

"Helen said you were there with a man she didn't recognize," she added.

"Did Helen say if she saw you smoking?" he asked, dodging the bait. "Because I'm pretty sure the doctor told you to stop."

Irina inhaled deep. The cherry on the cigarette flared bright red. She blew out a plume of smoke. "It's not hurting me."

"It makes your breathing worse."

"Getting old makes my breathing worse."

He knew which way the conversation would go if he pushed it. The Kosmatka family, like many in their neighborhood, had a healthy distrust of doctors. They put those in the medical profession around the same level as door-to-door salesmen, shifty types who used slick language and an aura of confidence to foist medicine and hospital bills on them.

Most ailments, Irina believed, could be cured with folk remedies. What couldn't be cured could only be endured, offered up to the Lord.

If Felix pushed it, the conversation would turn to Irina's overblown sense of martyrdom. How much she suffered, a widow for years now. How she prayed for the Good Lord to take her, how she had no pleasure in life but little things like cigarettes, and who could begrudge her that, after all she had suffered through?

He let the thread drop. He ate a last cracker and brushed the crumbs into a neat pile he rinsed down the kitchen sink.

Maybe his mother sensed his headache, because she didn't push for any gossip. He knew having a son on the police force gave her a certain amount of cachet amongst her friends. Irina would milk it the next few days. She'd plaster on her knowing smile, as if she held all the details and simply couldn't share them yet.

"If you're not gonna eat those cabbage rolls, I'm gonna take them next door tomorrow. Mr. Dobos has been feeling poorly," she finally said.

He nodded. Turned to make sure the door was locked and hit the switch to turn off the outside light. He remembered the gambling thread he and Adam had been tossing around and turned to his mother.

"Hey, remember when Richie got in trouble?"

"Richie, who? Cousin Richie?"

"Yeah. Down at the Polish club, remember?"

Irina threw her hands up, made a disgusted *bah.* "Oh, *him.* Always trouble, even when he was a baby. You never saw a worse-tempered baby. You? You were sweet. Never cried. Never fussed at all. Him? He—"

"Ma." He put his hands on her shoulders, squeezed her gently to stop the litany of the Numerous Sins of Richie. The gravest sin was being born to Irina's younger sister, the two extending their childhood rivalry into adulthood by pitting their children against each other. Felix and Richie were only a month apart. They'd always circled each other as children, like two prized gamecocks set in the ring by their mothers.

"I was curious what the trouble was. I heard it was gambling."

She lifted her shoulders in a shrug. Underneath his hands, he could feel how skinny she'd gotten. The bird wings of her shoulder blades would cut him if he squeezed her too hard.

"He ran a lottery scheme. He had people buy into a pot, then he'd buy a bunch of numbers." She shrugged again. "One of the guys complained because the numbers never hit. They thought he was pocketing the cash, so they kicked him out."

"That's it?" It had been a long shot anyway.

"As far as I know." She tilted her head and peered at him. "Why are you asking?"

"Just curious," he said. "I'm heading up. It's been a day."

He leaned down to brush a kiss against her cheek, felt his lips slide across the greasy cold cream she slathered on. She reached with her free hand to pat his face.

"You work too hard, *duci*," she said, and he murmured good night to her.

*

In the bathroom, Felix brushed his teeth. He swallowed three aspirin and hoped they'd put a dent in his headache before he had to wake up and tackle day two of the case.

He changed into his pajamas and set the ledger book of Farney's sins on the nightstand. He thought about leafing through it, but his head already swam with names. He could peruse it later.

He lay on top of the covers, listened to his mother downstairs as she turned off the TV and made her way up the creaking stairs. Past his room and into her own, then the snap and low static of the radio. She liked the classical station out of Buffalo. It came in grainy and fuzzy if the weather was bad, but she played it low for the background noise. It helped her sleep.

Sure enough, not long after, Felix heard her snoring.

He waited another long moment and studied the ceiling of his bedroom in the dim light from the streetlamp. A long crack in the plaster ran from one corner to the center. As a kid, Felix had gone through a spell where he was afraid to sleep in case the crack suddenly widened and tried to swallow him.

He'd outgrown it when he tried to explain it to his older brothers. Albie had scoffed at him, but Mark—always the meaner of the two—had twisted the skin on Felix's arm until it was rubbed raw, then called him a baby.

At the thought of Albie, Felix swung his legs out of bed and crept out into the hallway. He knew the creaky boards and by-passed them on socked feet until he was downstairs and perched on a chair in the kitchen. He dialed his brother's number and glanced at the oven clock. It was late, but Albie was a night owl too.

Sure enough, his brother picked up. "Hello?"

"It's me."

It was a late-night call, and Albie's mind went to the obvious. "What's wrong? Is it mom?"

"No, nothing's wrong. Sorry to call so late."

Felix heard the sigh of relief over the wire. "Jesus, you scared me." A beat, then, "How's the old girl doing?"

He glanced in the direction of the stairs and replied, "Same as always."

"Heard about the Farney kid. You on the case?"

"Yeah."

"Got any inside information?"

He started to protest, but Albie cut in, his voice sly, "Because you know the girls down at the altar committee are dying to hear—"

Felix let loose a weak laugh. "Fuck off."

His brother laughed, too, said, "You kiss your mother with that mouth?"

"*Your* mother, you mean? Sure do."

Albie's chuckles died down, and he asked, "What's up?"

Felix leaned his head against the wall and closed his eyes. "You knew Jack Farney from back when you were kids, right?"

"Shit, yeah, but barely. It was his kid that was murdered, huh?"

"Yeah." Felix let silence stretch out over the line, and Albie filled it in a moment later.

"He was a year behind me in school. I think he fell between me and Marky, but we all played on the same ball team one summer."

"What was he like?"

Albie hummed in thought, and Felix could see him in his mind's eye rubbing at his jaw, the same absent-minded gesture their dad used to do when considering a thoughtful question.

"Hard to say. We weren't friends at all. Weren't enemies either. He was barely there, I guess you could say. Most of the time, we forgot he was even on the team until he flubbed a pop-up or struck out."

"He wasn't very good?"

"Hell, none of us were."

"His father ever go to any games?"

Albie chuckled. "I hate it when you interrogate me."

"What interrogation?" he replied, grinning. "This is a friendly, brotherly call."

"Bullshit." Albie chuckled again. "I don't remember much. I remember making fun of him. He used to get chauffeured to the games, and we gave him flak for that."

Felix replied with a thoughtful hum, and Albie added, "Why all the questions?"

He gave his brother a non-answer sort of answer. "Just curious is all."

CHAPTER FIFTEEN

While Adam paid for his dinner, and Felix slumped against his steering wheel, Laura tied off loose ends.

She spent the evening with Mrs. Farney. She helped spoon scrambled eggs into her mouth, held the toast points for her to take a delicate bite. She daubed at her mouth with the cloth napkin, as gentle as a mother feeding her baby.

She gave her the nightly allotment of her pills. She helped her into her nightgown, brushed her hair, tucked her into bed. She watched the old woman's taut, confused face go slack, her eyes turn dreamy as the pills took hold. Once Laura knew the old woman was truly asleep, she stood and secured the blanket more firmly around her. She left, shut the bedroom door behind her with a firm click.

She took the route past Thomas's study. The door stood ajar, and she slowed her steps and glanced in as she walked by. It was only a glimpse. The larger-than-life man laid low, slumped over his desk. Head in hands. Heavy, chuffing breaths that could only mean he was crying and attempting to hide it. Mourning in solitude despite having the rest of his family—his son, his daughter-in-law—together for once.

Laura bit back a smile at the sight.

*

She drove home, parked in her driveway. She made a show of it, slammed her car door, walked into the house slowly. She gathered the mail jammed in the slot of her front door. She stood in the open doorway a beat, pretended to sort through the envelopes and flyers. She clicked on the lights once she was inside so the message was clear. Laura Lucas was home for the night.

Just like the night before.

Then dinner, a thick-sliced piece of buttered bread, some soft cheese. She sat in front of the television with the newspaper open in front of her. There was nothing about the murder, but the *Mariensburg Gazette* pulled most of its news from the wire service and went to print early. They didn't put out a Saturday edition, so the Sunday one would almost certainly be dedicated to the murder.

She was keen to see what they might write. The *Gazette* only employed a handful of reporters. She imagined them drawing straws. It'd be an exciting change of pace from covering high school sports and Kiwanis meetings.

After dinner, she went upstairs. She shed her home nursing uniform—slacks and crisp button-down, softened by a cardigan—and slipped into dark pants and a dark shirt. She brushed out her hair and braided it in a tight plait she pinned to the top of her head. She covered it with a black cap. She pulled on her boots, a size and a half too big but still manageable when she stuffed the toes with newspaper. She'd seen that once on *Perry Mason*, how to mask one's shoe size.

She went back downstairs. She left the lights and the television on, and she removed her phone from its hook. If anyone tried to call her, the line would be busy.

A busy phone line was coverage. If anyone tried to reach her, she already had a story ready to go. An old nursing friend from back East called, a long-winded catch-up about the good old days.

She went out the back door in the dark. She crept through her backyard in the darkness, past her tumbledown potting shed, and into the alley that ran behind her house and parallel to her street.

Laura often thought of herself as two distinct people. It helped to compartmentalize things. There was Laura, the mild-natured nurse. Never married, no children. Devoted member of Saint Boniface Catholic Church. Lived alone in the trim little house she bought when she moved to Mariensburg once she got tired of living in big cities.

Then there was Gattina. Quiet, watchful. Stalking from the shadows, waiting to pounce.

Laura drove a Buick Riviera, deep blue. It was one of her few nods to luxury amongst a life of austerity. She loved the leather-and-wood interior and took obvious pride in her car. She washed it every Sunday and buffed it dry with a chamois until it gleamed like a gem. Her father would have loved to have such a car.

Gattina? She drove a black Impala. One of the most popular cars on the road, no one took any notice of it. Just an everyday car, covered in road dust and rusted along the wheel wells. She'd bought it used, cash, from a lot in Youngstown. She'd given the seller an entire made-up spiel about it being for a son, how she and her husband thought a boy should have his own wheels. Just an everyday reason to buy a used car. Nothing to raise flags, though the seller had certainly forgotten her and her made-up story by now.

She kept it parked at the end of the alleyway. No one took notice of the Impala. Still, she looked around. Did a quick scan of the nearby houses with lights still on. She always got that feeling of eyes on her, of being watched. The hair on the back of her neck bristled, stood up.

There was no one there. No one watched her.

Even if they were, what would they see? There were no streetlights in the alley. The moon, and a handful of back porch lights, threw the barest bit of light. At best, anyone looking would see a dark figure walking toward a nondescript car.

As far as anyone might notice, Laura Lucas was home. Her Buick was in the driveway. Her lights were on, and if one pressed their ear to the front door, they'd hear the television murmuring inside. If one were to call, the line would be busy.

It was Gattina who crept through the night, who turned the ignition to the dusty Impala, who piloted it in the direction of the country club. It stood on the edge of town, edged against the wild spread of second-generation forest. Most people knew about the two roads into the club—the main road and the service entry—but few knew about the old logging trails that crisscrossed the area. Some were in better shape than others. Some were little more than deer paths with two ruts cutting through the undergrowth.

Not everyone knew about them, but Gattina did.

Jack Farney did too. That's where he stashed his own second, secret car.

She could always thank him, if it came to it. She'd gotten the idea to buy the Impala from him.

*

She'd found it by accident.

It was one of the first mysteries she had faced when she returned to Mariensburg. *Where does Jack Farney spend his time?*

Everyone always said the same thing. Jack was at the club. Jack was always at the club. Jack played cards, spent his allowance as fast as Thomas gave it to him. Jack was hanging out with his good-for-nothing buddies, drinking, gambling, doing God-knows-what.

Where others took it at face value, Laura had doubted it. He didn't have the hallmarks of a longtime drinker—no burst capillaries in his face, no shaky hands. He didn't seem to have a dope habit—no nodding off, no clammy skin. If cards were his vice, he didn't seem to get irritable or restless on the rare occasion he wasn't able to go to the club for a few days.

He had to go somewhere else, at least sometimes. She wanted to be certain. She wanted to know if her chief fall guy had an airtight alibi or not. She wanted to know his schedule better than anyone else.

Failing to prepare was preparing to fail, and Laura had never failed. She trusted God to guide her, but she also knew she couldn't ask too much of Him. It was best for her to handle what she could and leave the true miracles up to Him.

She had staked out the country club. She parked where the hired help parked and watched from there. She trawled both of the roads in and out. She followed Jack's grey Kraut car, the only BMW in town, from a distance.

She discovered the second car after weeks of watching. She followed Jack, watched him park his BMW by the tennis courts... then watched him walk *away* from the country club. It had been an early summer evening, the sky still light enough to see. The man's head ducked low. Furtive. He gave a quick glance behind him before he disappeared into the brilliant-green undergrowth.

It took her a few more weeks to find it. She limited her trips to the club so no one took notice of her. No one ever did; the summer was busy. People churned in and out for tennis tournaments, pool parties, special dinners, and dances at the clubhouse. No one noticed a middle-aged woman with a forgettable face sitting in her car.

She found the older-model Cutlass Supreme on one of the old logging roads, tucked back in a turnout carved from the underbrush. It was backed in and roughly camouflaged by hacked-up saplings pulled over the hood and the windshield. She nearly missed it as she drove past. She only found it because a glint of sunlight caught the corner of her eye.

She had been looking for something, and she found it.

She staked out the Cutlass. She figured out the pattern of his movements. She was in good shape, so hiking in and waiting in the shadows beyond the turnout was easy. She saw Jack do his quick-paced walk in from the direction of the country club. She watched him move the brush, unearth the car, and drive off.

She waited for hours after that. She dozed, woke up to pressure on her bladder. She crouched behind a tree in the darkness, relieved herself, hunkered back down. Nodded off again and woke to the sound of a motor.

Near dawn, and Jack had returned. He backed the car into its usual place, covered it again. He walked back toward the country club, now with a noticeable spring to his step.

She cracked the code on his comings and goings. Tuesdays and Thursdays were when he slunk into the woods, climbed into his nondescript car, and drove somewhere. Two days a week, Jack Farney escaped somewhere the people in his life couldn't find him.

Laura tried to follow him once or twice, tried to wait at the different access points to the logging roads. She caught him once out on the highway but lost him behind a slow-moving tractor trailer. She never cracked that part of the code.

She guessed it might be a woman, a mistress tucked away somewhere. Maybe even a man. Maybe Jack had a male lover, and maybe it was the great secret of his life he worked so hard to keep hidden.

It was all speculation. It worried her, but it didn't consume her. Jack Farney had his secrets. He could have an airtight alibi for that night. Maybe he didn't have one. Maybe he did, but he wouldn't share it. Maybe he couldn't account for every hour either way.

It was a worry, but just a small one. She didn't lose sleep over it. Even if she got caught, hadn't she already won?

Now, she piloted the Impala down the logging road. The roads here weren't maintained, so they were pocked with deep hillocks and holes from the upheaval of freeze and thaw every year.

She took it slow. The last thing she needed was a busted axle.

She parked a quarter mile from the hidden-away Cutlass. She pulled on a pair of leather gloves, checked her pocket, and climbed out to hike the rest of the way.

The quarter mile was an easy walk, even in the ill-fitting shoes. At the Cutlass, she tested the driver's side door. Locked. The passenger door was locked too. She reached a gloved hand into her pocket and pulled out the key.

She had gotten the idea from the cop shows she watched at night. She had waited until Jack was away at the factory, playing at being a businessman like his father. She crept into his bedroom. On the dresser sat a cut-glass bowl, the type men used to dump the contents of their pockets at the end of each day. She rifled through it: the loose change, the lint, the half-used matchbook. And on a plain plastic fob, a single car key.

It only took a minute to press the key carefully into the soft bar of soap, to get the imprint of the jagged cuts of the metal. She wiped the key clean from the bits of white soap, placed it back where she found it, then pocketed the soap to cut her own key once she got home.

That evening, hours later and with a cramped wrist and a small pile of metal dust on her kitchen table, she'd tossed the mangled blank aside and thrown the soap impression away.

"Damned television," she had muttered to her empty kitchen.

The next day, she did the next best thing. She pocketed the key, made up an excuse of needing to refill a prescription for Mrs. Farney. She went to the locksmith and had a copy made. Her hands had sweated so much she nearly fumbled it when she handed it over to the man. She had a story ready (teenaged son keeps losing his key), but the locksmith hadn't asked, and she didn't offer. He barely even looked at her as she paid him.

She had the original home in time to slip it back into Jack's room, no one the wiser.

Laura unlocked the driver's side door with her pilfered copy now. The inside of the car smelled like the ghost of the astringent cologne Jack wore.

She reached into her pocket. She pulled out the empty brown bottle with SOPORAL written on the label. She gave it one last swipe against her jacket, even though she'd wiped the face of the bottle earlier.

She tucked the bottle under the driver's seat, far enough back it was hidden from view and out of reach for a casual pass of a searching hand. She didn't need to plant the Soporal bottle. The police may never even find the car.

She took these steps because she enjoyed it. She felt a trill of pleasure spark along her spine when she tied off these loose ends. It was the clever Gattina outsmarting everyone, and she never felt pleasure quite like when she was outmaneuvering everyone else.

CHAPTER SIXTEEN

A dam returned to the precinct before dawn. He thought he'd beat his partner there, and he wanted a moment to regroup for the coming day after the thin sleep he'd gotten the night before.

No such luck. The bastard was already there, waiting. The pale, puking man from the day before was gone and replaced by a plucky asshole with good color back in his face.

"Get your beauty sleep, princess?" Adam asked as he strode into the room.

Felix greeted him with a Styrofoam cup of coffee. He pointed at the box of doughnuts on the table and told Adam to help himself.

"A little on the nose for cops, ain't it?" he grumbled, good-natured. He flipped open the lid to the box and helped himself to a cruller.

"Bakery is the only place open this early."

"Fair." He took a bite and joined Felix where he stood in front of the board. "Any thoughts on the plan for today?"

Felix pointed at the lists of names with his own half-eaten doughnut in hand. "We should split up this morning. I want to firm up the alibis of both Jack and the nurse. I saw your note. No luck on getting ahold of them last night, I guess."

"Two claimed ignorance, said they'd wandered off after the card game ended. The third one never answered the phone."

Felix hummed thoughtfully. "Interesting." He took another bite, chewed it as he gazed at the board. "And Farney's enemy list. It'd be worthwhile to talk to that group of farmers, like I said. And the brother of that fired secretary."

"Good so far."

"And I thought you could reach out to any contacts you have in the Commonwealth. Krause is checking on similar cases to cover the serial theory, and we have a call into Bell for phone records from the country club. But in the meantime, you could reach out and see if there's anyone running paper in the area. Or pushing dope. The LaRocca family territory extends to here, I think. They seem to mostly truck in football pool sheets and illegal lotteries, but I've heard of high-stakes poker games too."

"That's a long shot, kid."

Felix lifted a shoulder in a shrug, seemed to acknowledge it. "Yes, but when you pair the idea of gambling and drugs against such a clean crime scene..." He let Adam fill in the rest.

Adam polished off the rest of the cruller. He licked the glaze off his fingers and brushed away the crumbs dusting his front. "I can put in a few calls. So, you want to split up?"

"For the morning. Reconvene around noon."

"Tired of me already?" He picked up his cup of coffee and took a careful sip. It was lukewarm. The kid must have gotten into the precinct *much* earlier than he thought.

"We can cover more ground," Felix said.

"A man with a plan," Adam said. "Tell me where I'm going and I'm on my way, kid."

Adam drove beyond the city limits, out to where the old mines honeycombed the countryside.

It was like stepping back in time. The scrubby family farms looked like they'd been recently hacked out of the wilderness. The low hills were cleared of trees, but the forest stood sentinel at the edges, ready to take it all back.

Rolled and wrapped bales of hay marked the landscape in regular intervals. Dried stalks of corn lined the muddy furrows. The farmhouses were all the same narrow-windowed, plain-faced buildings with uniform sagging porches and peeling paint.

Adam eventually found the place. The farm belonged to Charles Bernhalter, the unofficial leader of the consortium of local farmers. They'd been a problem for Thomas Farney in recent years.

Adam had called ahead from the precinct, had been worried

he'd disturb the slumber of Bernhalter and his family so early, but the wife had answered on the second ring and sounded like she'd been up for hours already. Farmers, Adam remembered a beat too late, rose and retired with the sun.

When Adam climbed out of his car, the farmer was already striding across the front yard with his meaty hand extended in greeting.

"Call me Chuck," he said, pumping Adam's hand before he released it. "Everyone does."

Adam judged the situation on the fly. He didn't bother to sugarcoat the reason for his visit. He went for plain-speak, which in his experience went over better with the rural folk.

"A boy was murdered Thursday night," he said. "Thomas Farney's grandson."

Chuck crossed his arms, and his expression softened. "I heard. Sorry to hear it." A beat, and he lifted his head and gazed at Adam down the length of his nose. "You here to ask where I was the other night?"

Adam crossed his arms, too, mirrored the farmer's stance. "Heard you had some problems with Mr. Farney."

The man said *yeah*, but it came out in a grunted *yuh*.

"Can you account for your whereabouts on Thursday night into Friday morning?"

"Sure can. I was at the Grange for a spaghetti dinner. One of the members has a sick kid in the hospital in Pittsburgh. Leukemia. We were raising funds to help 'em."

Adam clucked his tongue. "That's tough. I'm sorry to hear it."

Another grunted *yuh*. "We take care of our own."

"You were there all night?"

"Until about eleven. Me and the wife, we helped tear down. Cleaned up, did the dishes, all that. We came straight home and went to bed." He jerked his chin in the direction of the house. "You can talk to her if you want."

"Can you tell me about these problems you have with Mr. Farney?" Adam asked.

"We been pursuing legal action."

"Who's *we?*"

Chuck uncrossed his arms and swept one hand in front of him, taking in the scenery around them.

"Four family farms. Farmers can handle about anything, but we can't fight against polluted groundwater. It poisons everything." He paused, took his cap off, and ran his fingers through his greying hair before he resettled his hat on his head. "You know, our lawyer was at the spaghetti dinner that night. You can always contact him if you need to check on us."

Adam made his notes, murmured he'd take the name of the lawyer down, but he'd need names of everyone included in that *we.*

Chuck did him one better, though. He strode over to the passenger door of the Bonneville, said, "How about I introduce you to everyone instead? And I'll show you what I'm talking about while I'm at it."

*

Adam found himself bouncing along back roads with the ponderous Chuck beside him. The farmer had one beefy forearm slung out of the rolled-down window despite the chilly morning air. He pointed out each turnoff to each farm. They paid a visit to each one.

Adam got the same story each time. They all were at the Grange spaghetti dinner the night of the murder. They all hated Thomas Farney but would never kill a child. They all said it so matter-of-factly, stung at the accusation, that even Adam was practically affronted by his own questions around alibis.

After they did their rounds to the other farms, Chuck didn't let Adam off. He climbed back into the car but pointed in the opposite direction of his own farm.

"Head up that way," he said. "Got something to show you."

This would be a good way to get myself murdered, Adam thought. He rarely—no, scratch that—he *never* went off with a possible suspect (though he guessed Chuck and his gang of farmers could be safely ruled out) to an unknown location.

It was a day of firsts, he guessed.

Chuck pointed out a patch of flattened grass where the woods edged against someone's far field. Adam killed the ignition, climbed out, and followed the man into the thicket. His shoes slipped and scrabbled on the soft ground, and he grasped at low-hanging branches to keep his balance.

"Here," the other man said. He pointed at a middle distance a few hundred yards away where a creek burbled.

"This is called Sinking Creek, officially," Chuck continued. "Because it starts underground and breaks aboveground about a quarter mile back."

"Officially?"

"On maps, like. Unofficially, we call it Stinking Creek." He pointed off to the distance. "Over that way are the mines. Farney's mines. Started out as his and a few other outfits, but he ended up owning all of them in the end."

"I'm following so far."

"The mines played out. There's still coal there, mind you, but it's too deep and too expensive to get to. So Farney quit."

Adam put his hand on a nearby tree and leaned against it. He nodded at Chuck to continue.

"When you decommission a coal mine, there's protocols. You don't just walk away, but that's what they do anyway, these owners. They just roll up the carpet and leave without sealing off the mines, so you get leaching. All the shit they dug up with the coal, and they left it lying around. It rains. It gets into the groundwater."

He pointed at the creek. "Look at it. You wanna drink a glass of that?"

Adam heaved himself from his leaning, and he walked to the water's edge. A deep burnt-umber color stained the rocks in the creek bed. Pale-orange foam swirled where the water broke along the shoreline, and when he crouched lower to peer at it, he could smell it better—a gassy, eggy smell. *Stinking Creek.*

"Sulphur," Chuck said. "And other things. Over there"—he pointed to the far shore, and Adam saw a boxy contraption sunk halfway in the mud—"is monitoring equipment. One of the farmers has a nephew at Penn State. He got them to come out and do a study. Water's full of all sorts of heavy metals Farney left us to deal with."

"It's affecting your crops?"

"It affects everything. The last shaft working the seam finally closed down in '52, but they dug around here for nearly half a century. Fifty-plus years of all that bad shit stirred up. Fact is, every ton of coal dug up brings up a certain amount of waste material. He took the valuable stuff and left the bad stuff."

Adam stood from his crouching position. He looked closer.

He'd grown up in the city. His only sojourns with nature were within the parks of Philadelphia, anemic green patches amongst the concrete and din. His mother had kept African violets that died every winter along the windowsills. Adam knew jack-shit about nature.

Looking closer, he saw what Chuck meant. The trees were spindly here, twisted and bent. Their leaves were limp, looked worm-eaten and ragged. The longer he stood there, the more the creek seemed to smell. He could guess what it smelled like at the height of summer.

"It affects everything," Chuck repeated after a moment of quiet. "Those graduate students out of Penn State did more research and thought it mighty suspicious such a small city had such a high rate of cancer."

Adam turned and made his way back up the slight slope. "What are you saying?" he asked.

"I'm saying the study concluded Mariensburg is a cancer cluster, and I'm saying it's because of the mines and their tailings poisoning the water. Turns out the state is full of these clusters, I guess. At least that's what the university people told us."

"If the state's full of them, why doesn't the state do something about them?"

The farmer shrugged. "Who knows? Laziness. Corruption. Half the mines in these coalfields went bankrupt, so who would even pay for it? Taxpayers in Philly and Pittsburgh don't care much about us out here." He clenched his jaw, the muscles of his face rippling in anger as he spat out the rest. "But Thomas Farney never went bankrupt. He took what he could to make his fortune, then left the ugly business of cleaning it all up to us."

CHAPTER SEVENTEEN

Felix always got a post-headache bounce of unsubstantiated optimism.

After he slept off the pain and nausea in that blessed handful of hours, Felix woke feeling chipper and ready to face the day. He picked up coffee and doughnuts. He went to the precinct to lay out a plan and wait for Adam.

Splitting up for the morning helped. It allowed them to cover more ground, and it assuaged the bit of guilt he had from knocking off the night before. He could finish up the corner pieces and edges of the puzzle and could work his way inward until a picture started to form.

Most important were the Farney family and the people with access to the house. They were the edge pieces, the ones who framed the whole case. He was surprised Adam agreed to split up. He was doubly surprised when he agreed to take on the farmers, though they seemed a long shot.

The nurse didn't live too far from Felix's house. For a brief, mad second, he considered dropping in and seeing Irina before heading back to work, but the insanity passed almost as soon as he thought it. His mother was the best detective he'd ever known. She sussed out lies and half-truths as only a mother could.

She'd be able to work out that he was in the area for official business, which could spark a firestorm of gossip over the phone lines. The altar committee at St. Callistus, once unleashed, could whip themselves into a mob before dinnertime. Their frenzies were legendary. Only last year, they had protested outside of the movie theater during a showing of *Billy Jack* so vehemently it made the news outside of town, a little blurb in one of the Pittsburgh papers.

Best to leave them be. Best to leave Irina be.

When Mariensburg was still just a patch town owned by the coal company, the neighborhood had been divided into factions based on nationality. Felix and his mother lived on Larch Street where the Eastern Europeans—the Hungarians, the Poles, and the Czechs—lived. Laura Lucas lived only a couple of blocks away on McKinley Street, where the Italians and Irish had settled.

He found the address and pulled along the curb. At a glance, Laura lived in the same company housing he did: The same wood-frame construction. The same front porch. The same side stoop and narrow walkway leading from the sidewalk.

Laura's house looked neater. The flower beds had already been cut back and twined together for the coming snow. The paint along the trim looked fresh. It made Felix grimace at his own home's shabby appearance.

Laura had mentioned a neighbor who might vouch for her whereabouts. She had framed it more delicately, but Felix read the subtext. Her neighbor was one of those old, lonely bastards who sat by the window to monitor the street all day.

Speak of the devil and he will appear. Felix climbed out of his car and took stock of the street when he saw movement out of the corner of his eye. He turned, looked, and sure enough... there, across the street. A wizened hand like a claw holding the curtains back, and a pale, drawn face peering out of the window at him.

He's noting my license plate in case he has to call the police, he thought. He shook his head, then made his way over to where the old, lonely bastard waited for him.

The neighbor, Mr. Castaldo, proved true to Laura's assumption. He could vouch for her whereabouts that night. His hands trembled with a palsy—or excitement, Felix couldn't be sure which—as he tottered over to his easy chair and retrieved a yellow legal pad covered with dates and times. He showed it to Felix, a look of triumph on his face.

All of the comings and goings on McKinley Street. Laura Lucas, Mr. Castaldo said after a moment of consulting, had arrived home at exactly 8:23 in the evening. She did not leave again until the next morning, a little after nine.

Sensing the man's loneliness, Felix frowned, played along. "But it's possible she left after you went to sleep, isn't it?"

"*Ach*," he replied, waving his hand in dismissal. "The doctor has me on this damned medication. Makes it so I can't sleep. I stay up with the television until the national anthem plays, then I switch to the radio."

"You're up all night?"

"Most of it," Mr. Castaldo conceded. "I catch a few hours here and there in the afternoon, like a cat." He paused, peered at Felix from his hunched-over position. "This about that murdered boy? Miz Lucas works for them, huh?"

Felix hummed, made a non-committal sort of noise in the back of his throat, and then he started the long process of extricating himself. He politely declined all offers for coffee, for tea, for the bit of Danish Mr. Castaldo's niece brought over the other day.

He only got out by promising to visit again, to really sit and listen to the man's concerns about the neighborhood—the speeding cars, the loud music the kids played. He had called the police plenty of times, after all, and Felix was the first one to finally turn up to speak with him.

*

The drive out to the suburbs only took fifteen minutes, but it took another ten to find the address. The sprawling red-brick ranch sat back on a dead-end street, and the house number was obscured by an overgrown rhododendron.

Jack Farney had given his friend, Henry Murray, as one of his alibis. The two of them had met at the club years ago. From card-playing buddies to fast friends, Henry was the closest thing to a contemporary for Jack. His father owned the Chevrolet dealership in town, and the Murray family was likely the second richest family in Mariensburg, albeit a distant second to the Farneys.

"You can call Henry," Jack had told them yesterday. "The other guys... well, I don't know who noticed if I was there or not. But Henry will vouch for me."

It took a long while for Henry to appear. His wife answered

the door, a twitchy woman with two young children close at her heels. She ushered Felix inside, had him sit in the living room. The children stared at him from around the doorway until she herded them away, casting a baleful backward glance at Felix.

Ten, fifteen minutes later, Henry Murray appeared. If Jack Farney was compact and unassuming, Henry was the opposite. He was taller but already rounding out into soft middle age. His stomach strained at his golf shirt, and his carefully combed hair valiantly tried to hide the shiny scalp peeking out underneath.

"Detective," he said, clasping his hand in a firm shake. It was pure car salesman, likely honed at his dad's dealership, but his hand was moist with sweat.

Felix offered his own introduction, gave him the broad strokes of his visit. "I'm only here to cross some t's. Can you walk me through your Thursday evening?" He smiled to try and put the man at ease.

"Well, let's see. I was at the club. We got a few hands of cards in but then one of the guys had to leave, so we sort of lazed around."

"Who else was there?"

"Me, Womack, Schmitty. Jack."

Womack and Schmidt. The two other names Jack had offered. The two men who had told Adam they couldn't be much help, that they'd drifted away after the card game folded.

"What did you do?" Felix asked.

"We had the baseball game on the radio, but then we put on the Olympics."

It all jibed with what Jack told them. Every question Felix asked, Henry answered a near match to Jack's story. The comings and goings of the other men, the drinking, Olympic sailing on the television.

Hell, Henry even verified that sometimes the men slept in their cars, that they all kept a change of clothes in the locker room for the morning after a night of sleeping rough. They'd lost a friend a few years back, cracked up along a sharp turn after one of their boozy card games. They'd decided to be smarter after that. Not enough to give up their drinking and gambling, but at least sensible enough to not leave their wives widows and their kids partial orphans.

Henry answered every question perfectly, but his eyes never quite met Felix's. And Felix thought the man might be a shit card player because he had a tell: after answering each question, the tip of Henry's tongue darted out, quick like a lizard, and licked his lips. An unconscious sort of motion.

As Felix shook the man's hand again and saw himself out, he couldn't shake the gut feeling he was being lied to.

CHAPTER EIGHTEEN

A fruitful morning. Felix snagged the last alibi for the hired help with access to the mansion, got the preliminary alibi—albeit shaky, in his opinion—on Jack... *and* he finished early enough to procure lunch for him and Adam. The post-migraine bounce of pep surged in his veins. He took a bite of pizza.

"Got the border in place," he muttered around his mouthful of greasy pepperoni and cheese.

"You cracking up on me, kid?" Adam said from the doorway, startling Felix. He took the few steps to the nearest chair, then dropped into it. "Next time, we draw straws for who takes a damned nature walk with a pissed-off farmer."

Felix eyed him as Adam reached for a slice of pizza. His thick-soled brogues were caked in mud. The cuffs of his pants were damp, as if he'd been walking through early-morning grass covered in dew. Which, apparently, he had.

Between his wolfish bites, Adam filled him in. Farmers were a no-go. They could hand the alibi verification off for Winslow or Haney to work on, but Adam doubted it was them.

"How do I put it?" Adam said, swiping at his mouth with a napkin. "They're stoned on their own virtue. Really playing the downtrodden little guy versus the big, bad robber baron."

"Which isn't an exaggeration," Felix pointed out.

"Very true. Farmer Bernhalter gave me a tour of a nearby creek polluted by the mines. He was angry. He was also offended by the thought of murdering a child. And the man's no actor."

"What about the other ones?"

"Nah. They just want to be heard."

Felix stood and walked over the board. He popped the cap on the black marker and hovered it over the piece of card stock labeled *Bernhalter et al./farmers.*

"Cross it off, then?" he asked.

Adam nodded. He reached across the table and helped himself to another slice of pizza, then sat back in his chair and eyed the board. "Notice you crossed off the nurse."

"She was right. Her neighbor is one of those old guys perched at the window all day and night."

"Sentry-type."

"Yes. He has a yellow legal pad and notes dates, times, and make and model of cars." He paused. "What about the other guy you were looking into?"

Adam shook his head. "Handed it off to..." He snapped his fingers, thinking. "Which one is the squirrelly-looking guy?"

"Haney."

"Him. I did a quick check of the city directory before I left for my nature walk but couldn't find him. So I passed it off."

"We can check on his progress after we eat."

Adam pointed at the board with the crust of his pizza. "Sum up where we're at. There are eight employees with access to the house, and they've all been cleared. We've cleared a handful from the list of possible suspects from Thomas Farney."

"Of the family, we've cleared Thomas and Abigail as well."

"Which leaves Jack and Clara," Adam replied. "How'd Jack's alibi shake out?"

Felix hesitated before he answered, and he covered it by taking a wide bite of pizza and chewing slowly. His gut told him Henry had been lying about Jack, but a quieter part of his gut also said Jack wasn't the perp. He couldn't reconcile the mild-looking man with someone capable of slashing his own child's throat.

"It seemed legit," he answered, splitting the difference. "But the guy also seemed jittery."

"*Jittery* because he had a detective in his house on a Saturday morning, or *jittery* because he's lying?"

"Hard to say." He hesitated again, then added, "I don't think we can cross off Jack."

"We also can't arrest him without anything concrete."

Felix swabbed at his mouth with his napkin. "Agreed. That leaves Clara. I don't see a senile old woman having the wherewithal to murder her grandchild, then stage a scene with the cut throat."

He sat down, twisted in his seat to look at the board. There were a fair number of names, many crossed off, but there were so many missing pieces. No weapon, no prints.

"If it were Jack, what would be the motive?" he mused.

"Housekeeper said the old man was setting the grandson up to be the heir. Could come down to greed, envy, anger. All the classics in the deadly sins."

"We could ask Winslow and Haney to gently probe that line of questioning. Maybe Thomas changed his will. Or maybe there were rumors he wanted to," Felix replied. He grabbed a blank piece of card stock and wrote *Poss. MO - money/inheritance.* He stood, leaned over and pinned it to the board under Jack's name.

"What're your thoughts, kid?" Adam asked after a beat. Felix turned back to face him, and he saw the tilt to the older man's head, like he was trying to read him.

He sat back down, turned to the board. He laced his hands behind his head. "It's both personal and professional."

"Go on."

"It feels like there's a message in the killing, yet there's no passion to it. If it was a message, it should have been messy. Something horrific for them to discover. On the other hand, it's too precise to be random. If it were a serial who got his kicks killing children, there's better targets. Let's be honest. It'd be easy to kidnap a child and take them to a second location."

He didn't turn around, but he heard Adam rustling for his smokes. He heard the gentle tap against his palm as he shook one out, then the *snick* of the flint as he lit it. A moment later, the smoke curled around him in tendrils.

"How'd I do?" he asked Adam, his tone aiming for sardonic but landing on something closer to a teacher's pet scrounging for praise.

"You're asking the right questions," Adam offered.

"I'll put you down as a reference, then," he joked, but he felt the tiny thrill of approval anyway.

"A sure way to get yourself blackballed," Adam joked back,

but then he added in a more serious tone, "my radar is twinging pretty hard on the father."

Felix turned around to face his partner. Adam sat forward, too, ticked off his points one by one on his fingers.

"Thomas Farney seems barely tolerant of Jack and seemed to put his future hopes on the boy. Jack spends his spare time out of the house, gambling at a location that's been busted for drugs in recent history. His 'sleeping in the car' feels flimsy, and you said the alibi didn't feel solid."

Felix could concede all of that. He could get to what Adam implied, except for the scant evidence—or total lack thereof. Police had swept the Farney mansion, shot a hundred rolls of film. Jack's bedroom was down the hallway from Junior's. It had been thoroughly combed through, catalogued. They'd found no knife, no blood-spattered clothing, no notebooks filled with mad rantings against his son.

It was all circumstantial, all lack. He told Adam so.

"People have been convicted on less," he pointed out.

"There's something pathetic about Jack, but I don't get a ruthless air from him."

"Pathetic men snap all the time. The meek man with the job and family who cracks one day and takes to the clock tower with his rifle. Like *that*." He snapped his fingers to emphasize the last word.

"My gut says it's not him."

Adam snorted, shook his head. "Gut instinct is like anything else in this work. You might have a talent for it, but you hone it with years on the job. Experience, kid."

Felix bristled. He opened his mouth to protest, which Adam silenced by holding up a conciliatory hand.

"Experience comes with time is all I'm saying. Don't take it personal."

It was hard *not* to take it personal. That original sick-stomach acid-churn of jealousy roared back. The disappointment of being too green, of not being ready. Of a once-in-a-career case falling into his lap, a case that could launch him out of this damned town, and not being *ready* for it.

Still... maybe he was compromised on Jack Farney. Felix didn't add anything about his late-night call to Albie. The secondhand memory of young Jack, lonely and friendless. Was Felix swinging too far in the other direction, so concerned about running every lead that the answer was right in front of him?

Felix grumbled but didn't add anything else. He stood and straightened up. He crushed the pizza box, gathered the balled-up greasy napkins, jammed it all into the trash bin near the door. He heard footsteps outside and stepped back as the door swung toward him to admit Captain Krause into the room. The old man shut the door behind him, looked from Felix to Adam and back.

"Where do we stand?" he asked. He scrubbed a hand over his face.

They brought him up to speed quickly, picked up the threads of each other's statements, listed it all out. The captain perched against the edge of the table and listened.

When they finished, the captain gave one final, pensive nod. Then he reached into his jacket, pulled out a piece of paper.

"Doc Miller called while you two were out on your road show," he said. "He has a cause of death. The coroner over in McKean County he's working with came to the same conclusion." He held the paper out, and Felix snatched it out of his hands.

"Cause of death was an overdose," he read from Krause's blocky print. "In testing the stomach contents of the victim, they found evidence of a sedative." He glanced over at Adam, then back at the captain. "Any idea what kind?"

Krause shook his head.

Sedative could mean anything. Felix reached back into his memory, tried to list out the ones he knew. He'd taken a workshop on drugs in Pittsburgh a few years back. There were barbiturates, benzos. Opiates like codeine and horse. Haldol and quaaludes. Muscle relaxants.

Sedatives were one of the drug classes caught up in the country club busts, mostly yellow jackets and China white. Barbiturates and heroin. Was *that* the link?

Krause broke his musing and continued, "In closer examination of the body, Miller also found a hidden injection mark between the boy's toes."

"My god," Adam breathed out.

"He's sending over an updated report, but he has the sequence of events. The perp drugged the victim, likely by slipping a sedative into a glass of chocolate milk, hence the stomach contents. That was enough to subdue the boy but not enough to make him sick. No vomit on the scene. Then a hot shot between the toes, which killed him. Then the slashed throat, which conclusively happened after death."

In the only other murder Felix had investigated, it had been a murder of seconds. A drunk husband, a querulous wife, a loaded gun. A second to pick up the gun and pull the trigger. Seconds for the bullet to tear through the body and cause irreparable damage. It was one drunken decision. But this?

This was drawn out. It was an entire series of steps. It was...

"Overkill," he muttered.

"Doc said the boy went without any pain," Krause said. "If that helps."

"Like putting a fucking dog down," Adam spat. "Then slicing its throat for fun afterwards." He rapped his balled-up fist against the table in a sudden fit of anger. "My *god*."

Felix thought of how his mother always reacted to that particular phrase of cursing, which usually made him roll his eyes in mild exasperation. In this case, it seemed bitterly apt: God had nothing to do with this. God, in His infinite wisdom and benevolence, had been far from sight when the boy was murdered.

A dam was typically slow to anger. It was part of what made him a good detective. Keeping a cool head, keeping a certain amount of distance from the victims allowed him to review facts without any passion clouding his judgment.

This damned case. The kiddie murders in his past had been grim, had left him sleepless long after they were solved. This would probably be the same: the image of the little boy drinking a glass of chocolate milk juxtaposed against the slit throat, the posed body. Just another ghost for him to drag around.

Felix must have sensed the anger coursing through him. He sat quietly, paged through the original coroner's report, read through Krause's update. Adam felt eyes on him, glanced up to see his young partner eyeing him from beneath his drawn-together eyebrows.

"What?" he barked.

Felix shook his head. "Nothing."

"Say whatever you're thinking, dammit."

Another shake of his head, but he cast his eyes back to the folder in front of him and said, "You should call your connection to cover the mob angle—"

"Wasn't a damned mobster did this," he cut in. "The kid drank drugged chocolate milk. It was obviously someone he knew."

"Of course it was someone he probably knew, but we have to eliminate every possibility."

Adam grunted, said nothing.

"We can go back to the scene of the crime. We can try to question Clara Farney."

It was as good a plan as any, and Adam offered a curt nod, a jerk of chin to show he agreed. He grunted again, then sat up. He reached across the table and dragged the heavy black phone toward him, lifted the receiver. He punched in the number to a guy in the Commonwealth who liaised with the feds on RICO cases.

No one answered, so Adam hung up, told the kid he'd try again later. He could leave a message with the switchboard if he had to.

It wasn't a damned mafia hit, and it wasn't a damned serial either, but he didn't want Felix's quiet judgment. He fixed his gaze to the board of names. He stared at *Jack Farney/father* so long and so hard the letters blurred and swam together.

*

The ride out to the mansion was tense. Felix drove, and Adam stewed in the passenger seat. It took them three traffic lights' worth of mileage before Felix finally asked, "You alright over there?"

When he thought it safe to speak, he turned to Felix and said, "You were right earlier."

"With what?"

"When you said there was no passion in this. You were right." He paused and looked out the window at the scenery rolling by. It was only early afternoon, but the day was cloudy and grey. It made it seem later than it really was.

"I've never worked a case like this," Adam continued. "Most murder cases I've worked, it was a fit of passion. A moment where the perp isn't themself, you know? They talk about it sometimes, once they get caught. How they don't even remember doing it, or how they felt like they were watching themselves do it."

"Like they were out of body. I've heard of that."

"Exactly." He took a breath, pushed it out through his nostrils so he sounded like a bull, snorting and pawing at the dirt. "I would bet my last nickel our perp was fully in the moment. There's not an ounce of passion in this. It was clinical."

"Except for the slashed throat."

"Exactly." Adam turned in his seat to face Felix again. "It's psychopathic, and I don't use that word lightly."

To be so green in such a small jurisdiction, Felix had probably only investigated crimes borne from the more common human conditions: boredom, envy, lust. He likely had never come across the sort of madness so calculating it made the investigating detective's blood run cold.

But did that mean that Jack Farney was a psychopath? Was the meek little man with the thick eyeglasses truly a cold-blooded killer? Was his lone display of emotion during his statement a calculated bit of theater? Was he capable of slaughtering his child, a step progression of poisoning, drugging, then staging the body? Did he have what it took to slash open the throat of his own son?

Adam had only faced a psychopath once. He never wanted to cross that class of murderer again, but it looked as though he might already be in the middle of it.

✱

The Farney mansion rivaled anything Adam had seen in the wealthier enclaves of his travels around the state.

It also sent an icy finger of dread down his spine. He suppressed the urge to shudder at the dark stone, the heavy paned glass of the windows. It took him a beat to realize what the mansion reminded him of, and it occurred to him just as he and Felix came to the front door.

"It's like a smaller version of Eastern State Penitentiary," he murmured. The old Gothic prison had finally closed about a year ago, its remaining inmates bundled off to the slightly more modern SCI Graterford.

Felix didn't reply. He pressed the bell, and Adam leaned out of the doorway, craned his neck to study the place. If he were rich, he would have built the opposite, an airy Spanish villa with stucco and clay tiles, high ceilings, lots of light.

Imagine being a kid in a place like this, he thought, his mind casting to Junior Farney. *Imagine growing up in a house like this.*

His thoughts didn't extend a generation further. He didn't offer the same sympathy for Jack, though he would in the future, after the case was closed and after almost everyone else had moved on.

✱

If the exterior of the mansion put Adam in mind of a hulking old prison, then the inside reminded him of a mausoleum. It was cool, and quiet like a held breath. Somewhere nearby a clock chimed bright and chipper, a jarring moment before the home fell silent again.

The housekeeper, Martha, led them into a parlor that reeked of the artificial lemons of furniture polish. She offered them tea, coffee, but both Adam and Felix declined.

"I'll fetch Mrs. Farney and Laura, then," she said, but she lingered a beat too long, cast a backward glance over her shoulder. It was like she waited for them to invite her to stay, to offer her own opinions on the investigation.

"Nosy," Adam grumbled once Martha was out of earshot. He'd seen those types his whole life, both when his sister died and later when he became a detective. People with boring little lives and boring little jobs, suddenly a few degrees removed from a tragic moment. When he first started in the state's detective bureau, he had worked under an older, grizzled guy who used to call those types "grief tourists."

But if Martha was a grief tourist, the nurse seemed the opposite. She entered the room with Clara Farney, slow and careful. She hovered at the elbow of the old woman, who was so thin and brittle a sneeze from the other side of the room might knock her over. Once Clara settled into a nearby chaise with a thick blanket tucked over her lap, Laura turned to leave.

"Oh, no," Felix responded. "You can stay, Miss Lucas."

"Laura, please." Then, "Are you sure?"

Felix nodded at her. He nodded again, a smaller gesture, toward Clara. "You can help if she... uh, needs you."

"Of course." She sat in a nearby chair, apart from the trio of detectives and old woman, but close enough to intervene if Clara needed anything.

Felix, God love him, played it gentle. Probably had to do with his own sick mother, but the younger detective finessed it, kept it light.

"How are you doing, Mrs. Farney?" he asked, and the smile on his face was open. Genuine.

The old woman returned his expression with her own version

of it, the corners of her thin mouth trembling from the effort. She tilted her head as if to say, *I'm doing as best as I can,* but she didn't say anything.

"I'm Felix and this is Adam," he continued. He didn't reach for his pencil and notebook. He kept his posture open and friendly. "We want to ask you a few questions, if that's alright."

Another tilt of her head upon the stalk of her neck, but she replied, "We rarely have visitors these days."

"You have a lovely home," Adam offered, and he was rewarded with another tremulous smile from Clara.

"The other night," Felix said. "Do you remember where you were?"

Clara gazed back at him, her eyes narrowed in concentration. It hurt Adam to see the earnest way she looked as she tried to cast back into her addled memory.

"Well, I suppose I was here," she finally answered. "We rarely have visitors, and I rarely go out anymore. I've been ill."

"Of course." A beat, and Felix continued, "You were here the other night. Do you remember anything strange about that evening or night?"

"Strange?"

"Perhaps you saw someone you didn't expect. You have such a lovely home. Maybe there was someone in it who didn't belong."

Another narrowing of her eyes as she tried to focus. Her eyes turned filmy with tears as she stared, unblinking, at Felix. After a moment, her eyes widened at some memory.

"Jack was here. My son."

Adam chanced a look at his partner, who caught his glance and tipped his head the barest fraction to acknowledge him.

"Your son Jack was here?"

Clara nodded, eager. "Oh, yes. He was just back from Cheshire, visiting."

Adam caught movement out of the corner of his eye and saw Laura, shaking her head faintly. When she saw him watching her, she mouthed something he couldn't make out, but he could guess.

"Your son, Jack," he cut in. "How old is he?"

"Fourteen," she answered. "Though he'll be fifteen in a month's time. I've been missing him since he went away."

"To Cheshire?" Adam asked. He glanced at Felix again and noted how the younger man sagged in his chair, deflated or defeated or both.

Another eager bob of her head. "It's one of the best schools. J.P. Morgan attended Cheshire and look at what he accomplished in his lifetime."

"You must be very proud, ma'am," Adam said gently. There was no point in continuing the line of questioning, he supposed. The old woman was gone, lost to her scrambled memories. Worst-case scenario, she could lead them down a wrong path, make them waste precious time.

"My father knew J.P., you know. They were both members of the Church Club—"

Laura rose from her seat, laid a calming hand on Clara's shoulder, interrupting the old woman as she reminisced about the glory days. "The gentlemen need to leave soon, Mrs. Farney," she said softly. "And perhaps you'd like a rest as well?"

Clara's sparse eyebrows drew down as she considered the nurse's words. She turned her head to face the wide windows.

"We'll have to talk to the gardener," she said. "The roses will need to be collared soon before winter."

*

Laura led them out of the parlor after she tucked Clara more firmly into her blanket against the chaise. Adam spared a single glance backward as they left the room, and the old woman was already dozing.

"I apologize," Laura said. "She's been scattered these last few days."

Adam and Felix followed her through the mansion, and Adam was again struck by how quiet it was. The faintest scent of flowers threaded under everything, that half-sweet, half-decaying scent that reminded him of funerary arrangements, tight clusters of carnations and roses.

"Where is everyone?" He kept his own tone hushed.

"Half of the staff is gone," she replied over her shoulder. "It's just me and Martha. And Susan. The cook," she amended.

"The family?"

"I assume Mr. Farney is at the factory. Jack and Abigail... I'm not quite sure. Martha mentioned a meeting with the funeral director, but I believe there was a question around..." She paused in her steps, turned to face them. She glanced around, furtive, then dropped her voice to a whisper. "I believe there's a question around when the body would be released."

"Soon, I think," Felix replied, his voice quiet too.

"It'll help, putting the poor mite to rest." Laura's eyes sought both of them, seemed to be peering into them to find something. "The sooner we can find a semblance of peace, the better I think Mrs. Farney will be."

Adam clucked his tongue in sympathy. "She doesn't realize, does she?"

She offered a sad smile. "But isn't that a blessing? She thinks her son is visiting from boarding school and all is right with the world."

Both Adam and Felix agreed it was a blessing. Felix said he'd like to walk the house again, that Adam should get the layout, and she said she guessed it was okay, but she could get Martha, if they wanted.

"Before you go," she said, and her voice was still low, almost conspiratorial. "I have a bit of a problem and I'm not sure who to talk to about it."

"What is it?" Felix asked, and she gestured for them to step into another room with her, away from prying eyes.

She told them. Halting at first, clearly uncomfortable with the position she'd been put in. Then all at once, in a rush of words: How a bottle of Clara Farney's medication had turned up missing. How she didn't want to burden Mr. Farney, but how she also didn't want to get in trouble. Should she file a report with the police?

She twisted her hands in front of her, her cool composure

shattered at the thought of getting someone else—or herself—into trouble with the law.

Felix took out his notebook and made a note. He asked her to spell the medication for him.

"S-O-P-O-R-A-L," she said, her hands wringing in anxiety.

"What kind of medicine is it?" Adam asked.

"Well, it's a quaalude that helps Mrs. Farney sleep," she replied, her face guileless as she looked between him and Felix. "It's a type of sedative."

CHAPTER TWENTY

A dam sat silent on the drive back to the precinct. The radio played softly, and Felix considered the nurse's bombshell.

She hadn't even realized she'd given them a possible murder weapon.

There were a million questions, a handful of answers, and a growing sense of unreality. Nothing quite lined up. The puzzle pieces didn't fit into place neatly.

The Farney mansion—a monstrous stone fortress, but easily infiltrated.

The Farney family—hardly a family. Thomas always at his factory, Clara lost in her own degrading memories. Jack at the club with his friends, little more than a passing stranger in his own son's life. Abigail even more absent with her pied-à-terre in New York.

The victim—contradictory. Heir apparent to a vast fortune, a legacy of a name, yet left alone the night of the murder.

Felix thought to mention his musings to Adam. When he glanced over at him, he had the same stormy expression from earlier, the same flexing of his jaw as he ground his teeth together. Maybe he should give him a little breathing room as he worked through whatever he was dealing with.

Felix left him alone.

On the radio, The Jackson 5 sang about stopping, slowing down, that the love he saves might be his own. Felix sighed and reached out to snap the music off, but then remembered the oppressive silence of the Farney home and thought better of it.

✱

Back in the precinct and settled in their nerve center, Felix excused himself and went into the bullpen. Haney was there, waiting. He stood up from his desk when he saw Felix, and he offered his usual smarmy smile, shifting across his face like a slick of oil on top of water.

"How's the case coming?" he asked. He fell into step as Felix strode across the room. "I looked into that one guy. It's no bueno, hoss. Guy's been locked up in county for a few weeks on check-kiting charges. Can't make bail—"

"Thanks," Felix replied. "We'll add it to the list."

Haney persisted. "You thinking it was a former employee? You think you're close to—"

"Excuse me." Felix cut him off, yanked open the door to the reception area. He didn't turn around, didn't hold the door open for Haney. He barely heard the man's startled cry as it slammed in his face.

Rhonda sat at her post, a P.D. James hardback in her hands. She glanced up at Felix, then tucked in a scrap of paper to mark her place before she closed the book.

"What's up, Puss?" She smiled at him, a near smirk that lacked the oiliness of Haney's similar expression.

"Want to try that again, Roadhouse?" he asked, but he smiled back. He could remember when she was a hellion with scabbed knees, and he a boy with an untamable cowlick. Felix felt an ease with her that made the teasing more companionable, possibly toed the line of flirting when the light hit it just right.

"Any update on the phone records?" he continued.

She laughed, incredulous. "That was a big order. It's going to take a while."

"You couldn't get them any sooner?"

"Even I have limits to my considerable powers," she said. She jerked her chin toward the door to the bullpen. "How's it going with your new buddy?"

"Why do you think I came out here? I needed to see a friendly face."

Rhonda laughed again. "It's a bad day if I'm the friendliest face you've got."

"Still better than Haney."

"Anyone's better than that rat-fink." She gazed at him, and her smile faded as she turned serious. "How are you doing with the case?"

Felix shrugged. "We're working through it—"

"No." She cut him off with a shake of her head. "I asked how *you're* doing. This is dark stuff, Felix. A murdered kid? How are you holding up?"

He considered the question. "I'm okay," he answered honestly. "As okay as I can be."

*

Haney was exiting the conference room just as Felix returned. Felix shut the door behind him and turned to Adam who sat and paged through paperwork.

"What did he want?" he asked.

"Dropped off his notes on the fired secretary," Adam murmured, not looking up. "That's a dead end." A beat and he added, "There's other stuff there to sort through." He pointed at the center of the table where an untidy stack of papers sat. "And a message from John. He was off to see the district attorney to update him. Apparently, Thomas Farney is rallying his troops. Krause wanted us here when he got back."

The stack of papers was all the intel gathered in their absence, as if they'd set baited lines in the water and returned to a creel full of trout. Felix had a million questions and few answers, but maybe one or two lay in the sheaf of paperwork.

The easiest piece of intel to lay to rest: Captain Krause's call on the QT to other jurisdictions, the hush-hush inquiry into similar murders. Did anyone in Pittsburgh, Buffalo, Youngstown have any kiddie murders with slashed throats? No signs of forced entry, remarkably clean crime scenes? Any slashed throats with no arterial spray?

Apparently not. Krause had expanded his grid to reach farther onto all four sides of the compass. Even northward into Canada, where baffled detectives in Hamilton and Toronto said no, no cases like that in their territory.

"So not a serial then," Felix said.

"A one-of-a-kind case," Adam agreed. "Aren't we lucky ducks?"

Felix turned the paper face down on the table and reached for the next report. It was the coroner's updated findings, printed in duplicate for him and Adam. He pushed one folder over to his partner, then pulled the second one to him and started reading.

It was the same information they already had, with the updates on the stomach contents, the hidden needle mark. Adam, the quicker reader, found the salient update.

"Says here the drug in question was methaqualone." He tapped his report with the blunt tip of his forefinger. "Both injected and ingested."

"Quaaludes." The hair on Felix's arms stood up, and he looked at his partner who stared back at him, his expression grim.

"Quaaludes." He jerked his chin in the direction of the corkboard. "Go ahead and add it."

Felix felt the queasy churn in his stomach as he reached for a blank card and marker, wrote *overdose/quaalude/C. Farney meds?* on it and pinned it onto the board.

"We can call the area drug stores in the morning," Adam said.

"There's two in town. Three if you count the one at the hospital."

"Might as well check all three. See how many prescriptions for quaaludes they've given out over the past few months."

"I'd say we could give it to Winslow or Haney, but maybe we should handle that ourselves. Speaking of..." He snapped the folder with the coroner's report shut and reached for more from the stack. "Here's Winslow's fishing trip on the Farney family."

"What'd he come up with?"

Winslow's research was biographical. Much of it was common knowledge, now with the added depth of facts and figures. Farney came from an old banking family in Philadelphia and had moved west across the state to strike out on his own. Winslow had researched all of Farney's holdings past and present, his net worth.

His net worth was a boggling number. It didn't look real on

the paper. It looked like a pretend number a child just learning their numbers would scrawl out.

Then on to Jack, a similar biographical slant. Jack Farney, born 1937, only son, etcetera. Sent off to Cheshire to prepare him for college. A degree in business from Vanderbilt—

"Shit," Adam broke in. "Daddy gets into Princeton and Sonny Boy has to settle for Vanderbilt. That's gotta sting."

"I guess money can't buy everything." Felix bent his head and kept reading. After college, Jack returned to Mariensburg to work at his father's factory. Then his marriage to Abigail, the birth of Junior.

"Winslow found a gap," he said. He ran his forefinger over the neat handwriting. "Looks like for most of 1966, Jack Farney wasn't here."

Adam leaned back in his seat and crossed his arms. "Where was he?"

"Somewhere in New York. A place called the Haverhill Center." He flipped the page, continued reading.

"Sounds like a place you'd send a rich druggie to get clean. Did Winslow say what Jack was in for?"

Felix scanned the page. "He tried, but patient files are strictly confidential. He did manage to confirm that yes, Haverhill is a sort of catch-all for various problems. Nervous breakdowns, drying out alkies. Druggies getting clean."

Adam nodded, a knowing tilt of his head that grated on Felix's nerves. The action had the same smug aura of superiority from before when he dismissed Felix's initial thoughts on a serial killer, when he'd dismissed Felix's gut feeling on Jack.

Which was exactly where Adam's thoughts were carrying him.

"You know we're narrowing in on Jack," he said. His arms were still crossed over his chest as he stared at Felix. There was a hint of challenge in his voice. He obviously remembered their earlier conversation too. "You gotta ignore your gut and look at the facts right in front of you."

Felix refused to rise to the challenge. He knew Adam was right. He knew the scant evidence trickling in pointed to Jack. He also knew that his gut had never misled him before, even if he'd never worked a murder case—and his gut told him that Jack was hiding something, but the man was no killer.

CHAPTER TWENTY-ONE

Adam and Felix circled each other, wary as alley cats with their hackles up. Adam couldn't understand why the supposedly bright young detective couldn't see the bare facts of the case blaring Jack Farney's name like an air raid siren.

He started to formulate a speech in his head to offer Felix some of his wisdom when the captain strode into the room. Krause hadn't been gone long. The meeting with the district attorney must have been quick.

"That was miserable," he said. He yanked a chair out from where it was tucked under the table and sank into it. He hooked his elbows on the table and looked between them. "Asshole thinks he's the next Arlen fucking Specter instead of a county DA."

"That bad?" Adam asked.

Krause reached into his jacket for a cigarette. Once he took a few calming puffs, he looked at them again and said, "I needn't remind you of the pressure we're under here. Show your cards."

Adam had let the kid take the lead for most of their time together, but he always felt like a father teaching his boy how to drive—the illusion of control while he kept one hand on the wheel. Now he moved fast to talk over Felix, lest Krause side with the first one to talk.

"My money's on Jack Farney," he replied, and he ignored the sharp inhale from his partner, the scowl of frustration. Adam stood and pointed at the board, quick to get his point across before the kid started blathering about his gut instinct.

"Jack Farney had access to the house and access to the type of drug that killed the boy," he said. "The nurse said Clara Farney takes quaaludes to help her sleep. She also said a bottle of pills turned up missing recently."

"When was this?" Krause leaned forward, his cigarette smoldering where it was tucked in the corner of his mouth.

"We just found out when we went to talk with Clara Farney.

We got the coroner's report too."

"That's all circumstantial," Felix cut in, seeing his chance. "It doesn't put the syringe in his hand, and there's still no knife."

Adam turned to face Felix. He fixed his hands on his hips and glared at the younger man. "It's pretty obvious Jack was being passed over in favor of his own son."

Felix scoffed. "Something being pretty obvious doesn't mean it's fact."

"I don't buy his alibi for one second. How about that?"

The younger detective pushed his chair back and stood too. He crossed his arms over his chest. "Henry Murray vouched for him."

"You said yourself he seemed hinky."

"I said *jittery*." Felix shook his head. "That's a low bar for making a case. We should arrest the damned housekeeper and the tutor, too, if we're going with people who get twitchy around cops."

Adam threw his hands up in frustration. He dragged his ghosts behind him every damned day, heavy as lead chains. Felix had none yet. He still had the gleam in his eyes, the bounce in his step as he did this work. The ember hadn't been snuffed out of him yet. He could afford to see the best in a man like Jack Farney, but no longer. Adam refused to coddle him.

He wanted to be a man, be the lead detective? Let him haul Junior Farney's ghost around then, that tiny body on the slab with the thick black stitches from the autopsy. Let that silent shade trail behind him with his accusing eyes and his soundless mouth gaping like a chasm.

Adam turned to John, braced himself against the table, and jabbed each point with his finger.

"It's Jack Farney. It's either him or someone he knows, but if I were a spoiled rich asshole with a gambling problem and my gravy train was about to end, I'd do anything I could to keep it rolling."

He heard Felix's scoff of outrage. "You really think he killed his own son because he was getting cut from the business? Or getting cut out of the will? That's completely unsubstantiated!"

Krause glanced from his detective to Adam. "That true?"

Adam paused, uncertain for a beat. "It's a theory I've been kicking around."

Another scoff from his partner, and a "that's convenient" muttered under his breath.

"Look, John." Adam pulled his chair back out, sat, and leaned across the table toward his old academy buddy. "The simplest explanation is usually the correct one. Remember what they taught us at the academy? Occam's Razor. This isn't a serial killer or some revenge fairy tale. It's plain ol' jealousy and greed. Jack Farney's hiding something. It's either him or someone he knows."

Krause's flinty grey eyes drifted from Felix to Adam, then back to Felix. Finally, he turned to Adam with a sigh.

"It is all circumstantial. I gotta agree with Kosmatka," he said, almost apologetic to not be agreeing with him wholesale. "We can't build a case on circumstantial. Go question the alibi again. Both of you. If he was jittery with one cop, maybe a second will break him. If there's anything there to break."

"Thank you," Adam said.

"Fine," Felix said, speaking over him.

Krause stubbed out his cigarette and sighed. "Play nice, boys. Call me when you're done."

A call to the Murray home found Henry unavailable.

"He's at the country club," his wife said. The bitter resignation in her voice made it clear this was the usual state of affairs.

The drive there was dead quiet.

The country club was a blink-and-you'd-miss-it turnoff along the highway, marked by a tastefully understated sign that read LAUREL RIDGE COUNTRY CLUB. The drive cut through the woods, the trees and brush cleared back to give it a wide berth. Late-afternoon autumn sunlight filtered through the turning leaves, casting their fiery scarlets and yellows into brighter hues.

"Nice place," Adam said, and he meant it sincerely. "Why Laurel Ridge?"

"Name of the mountains here," Felix replied. The words were tight, like he forced them out through clenched teeth.

Some part of him wanted to apologize for not talking through his thoughts first. He rarely worked with a partner anymore, usually caught solo cases with the state bureau. He was out of practice, lost his company manners. He liked the kid, really. He thought him earnest with a good head on him, a decent sense of humor that hadn't turned grim from the job yet.

The other part of him wanted to reach over and smack the kid. Who cared if he was green? Who cared if he was the wunderkind of some shit-hole backwater town's police force? *Grow up*, he wanted to tell Felix. *We're here to do a job*.

Instead, Adam said nothing. He watched the golden autumn landscape slide past and let the silence sitting between them settle in.

Adam and Felix discreetly flashed their badges to the attendant in the main building, who discreetly called around to see where Henry Murray was holed up.

They found him in a small lounge. The room was paneled in dark wood and held a small bar stocked to the brim with liquor. A massive television set in an expensive-looking wood console was the centerpiece of one end of the room. A fireplace stood at the other end.

Henry Murray, alibi to Jack Farney on the night of the murder, sat smack in the middle.

The man must have started early. Adam could smell the booze fumes from ten paces away, and he wondered if the man would catch fire if he lit a cigarette.

Bullshit on jittery, he thought as Felix explained they were just checking a few things. *The guy's practically vibrating from fear.*

Henry was bleary-eyed and borderline slurring, but his story stayed the same as when he'd talked with Felix. The same names of people who drifted in and out that night. The same card game that petered out, the Olympics on the television, the drinking.

Adam watched him as he spoke. He kept his hands in his lap, his right hand tight around the rocks glass and his left wrapped around it. Like he was physically holding himself back from trembling.

Bullshit on jittery around cops, Adam amended. *This asshole is lying.* He knew it in the core of his being, honed from long years of sitting across from liars and cheats, from people terrified of being found out.

"You know it's a crime to lie to the police," he said. He watched Henry as his words hit him. He saw the slight flinch, the glimmer of fear in his eyes.

Henry reared his head back. "I... no. *No.* I'm not lying."

Adam said nothing. He scowled at the man, an expression that said he didn't believe him a bit.

Henry swallowed hard, the column of his throat rippling at the effort. "I'm n-not. Maybe I had too much to drink and aren't remembering it right—"

"You're not lying or you're not remembering it right?" Adam cut in, and the question earned him a cleared throat from Felix, a warning to ease off. Adam ignored him and plowed ahead.

"Jack wasn't here at all that night, was he?" A guess, but he wasn't looking for an answer so much as he was calibrating the man—laying out guesses to see how they landed. A man with a secret was like a radio: it was all static until Adam could twist the dial enough to make him sing.

"He was." His watery eyes implored him. "I swear he was! He played cards with us—"

"But he left after that, didn't he?"

"I don't... I mean, his car was in the lot. He didn't—"

"But you didn't see him when it got late. You can't vouch for Jack Farney after a certain time."

Henry swallowed hard again, an audible gulp. His eyes darted between Adam and Felix and finally settled on the younger man's face, which likely seemed friendlier by comparison.

"Look, okay. Fine. I didn't see him after cards, but he was probably in the other lounge." He held a hand up in supplication.

"People always drift in and out, even when we have a good game going. Jack always drifts off..." He ran a shaky hand through his thinning hair.

"When did you last see Jack Farney on Thursday night?" Felix asked. His voice had the same teeth-clenched, too-tight quality from the car ride. Adam chanced a look at him and saw anger bubbling beneath the surface of his stony expression.

"Around eight, I guess." Henry sat back, deflated.

"You lie for him often?"

The man nodded, the misery plain on his face. "Yes."

"What sort of lies?" Adam cut in.

"Same as this." He lifted his hand again, pointed between the two detectives. "If people come asking about him, I'm supposed to say he was here all night."

"People like who?" Felix leaned forward. "Bookies? Loan sharks? Drug dealers?"

Henry blinked, and his bafflement was genuine as far as Adam could tell. "What? No. Nothing like that."

"Who then?"

"His old man."

"Why?"

The man shrugged, still baffled. "Who knows? Keeping tabs on him, like he always does."

"What do you get out of it?" Adam asked.

Here, Henry laughed, humorless and laced with rancor. "He kicks me cash when I'm tight on funds. It wasn't a big deal until now. Christ almighty, a dead kid?" He shook his head. "I can't see Jack doing that. I just always thought he had a side piece tucked away somewhere."

They left Henry twisting in the wind, a toothless comment about the obstruction of justice and aiding and abetting. Maybe it was mean, but Adam couldn't muster much sympathy for the man.

Adam was on the scent now.

He ducked into a tucked-away manager's office and used the phone. He called Krause and updated him. He could hear his own heartbeat in his ears, the steady thrumming amped up by the adrenaline rush he always got when he closed in on a perp. Felix stood in the doorway, and the hectic flush along his neckline spoke to perhaps a similar rush for the younger detective.

"What do you think, boss?" Adam asked Krause, and he heard the sigh, could picture the man rubbing his hand along his jaw.

"Bring him in for questioning," he finally replied. "But this isn't an arrest. No cuffs, no theatrics. Play it firm but aboveboard. He has to answer to his fake alibi, and more importantly, he has to answer to where he was the night his son was murdered."

CHAPTER TWENTY-TWO

Courage never came easily to Jack Farney.

The question of nature versus nurture fascinated him. What defines a man? Is it the culture he is raised in? Is it something hereditary, passed down like blond hair or nearsightedness?

He already knew what made him Jack Farney. Whether it was nature or nurture, the answer was always the same: his father, the monolith who stood so tall and unmovable he blocked out the sun.

Jack was never quite sure why he lacked courage. His father certainly had it. Thomas could have had an easy, comfortable life. The Farney family had been in banking out East for ages. They had plenty of loyal customers, old families descended from the *Mayflower* and the *Fortune* families. Banking had set hours. Money multiplied in its coffers like rabbits. Thomas could have been any other wealthy man of leisure. He could have worked easy hours in a sumptuous office, then spent long hours golfing or sailing.

Instead, Thomas struck out on his own. He bought an unproven, bankrupt mine. He hacked out his own empire independent of his family, carved his own mark in the glittering seam of coal he dug out of the earth. That coal went on to fire the furnaces of Pittsburgh, which made the steel that built famous bridges, famous buildings.

Thomas had despaired that his only son lacked the courage he himself had. Jack was born soft, and Thomas had never been able to forge him into tougher stuff. He had signed Jack up for baseball, convinced that shagging fly balls and sliding through the dirt would toughen him up. He forced Jack to join him when he went hunting, where hired men flushed out game for Thomas to gun down.

Jack was too nearsighted for baseball, too timid to make friends with the other boys. He lasted less than a season.

And hunting? The few times Jack got a deer in his sights, he always pulled his shot at the last minute. He couldn't bear to kill anything, let alone a deer, all soft-muzzle and flicking white tail. He always shut his eyes and shot over it, smiled despite his father's furor when the boom of the rifle sent the deer darting away to safety.

*

When the two detectives showed up at Jack's door and requested his presence for further questioning, maybe he wasn't brave, but he faced it with a certain sangfroid.

He stood from where he sat in the parlor with his mother. She thought him her own long-dead brother, but Clara had fond memories of that brother, and Jack never minded playing the part. Everyone else was there too: His wife curled in a chair, her feet tucked underneath her. His mother's nurse nearby in case she was needed. His father staring at the flames in the fireplace.

Jack pressed a kiss to his mother's soft cheek. He asked the detectives if he could get his coat, and his voice didn't tremble at all. He grabbed his wallet and keys and ignored everyone else.

He especially ignored his father. He used to think the old man could read his mind, could see any duplicitous thoughts behind his eyes. Now? He just didn't care anymore.

Jack had guessed they would come for him eventually. In the backseat of the car, he stared at the backs of the detectives' heads and sifted through the unreality of the last few days. The bolt out of the blue when he found out Tommy had been murdered.

The absurdity of it—a small boy tucked away in a huge mansion, slaughtered in the night—still hadn't sunk in with Jack. He knew it was shock; a strange, compelling conviction that it was wrong. That someone with authority would stride in at any moment and proclaim a mistake had been made, that it was being set right. That his son would step out from behind the authority figure and say "ta-da!" and "here I am, Dad!"

The world's best magic trick. The dead returned to life.

Jack knew it was his mind protecting him. He had learned that at Haverhill. The brain judged how much a person could bear and doled out the information accordingly.

The thought of Tommy being dead was unbearable, so Jack's brain did what brains did best. It doled out the information at a minuscule rate, as much as he could bear at any given moment.

When his father had grabbed him by the upper arm and shook him hard, said, *"Junior is dead."*

When he gave his statement at the police precinct.

When he and Abigail went to the funeral home, the rarest of moments where they were together and united, hand in hand at the unbearable task before them.

When they chose which casket would hold the tiny body, when they chose the music and the flowers Tommy liked best, as if the seven-year-old boy ever considered the flowers he wanted at his own funeral.

When the detectives returned and said, "We have some more questions for you."

When any reminder of Tommy's murder was presented to Jack, Jack's brain shifted him elsewhere, kept him coddled in wool batting until he was strong enough to process it.

When the detectives walked him through the police precinct— the eyes of the few police and detectives still on duty boring into him—he kept his composure.

The detectives. The young one and the old one. The former seemed more sympathetic, though his neck and face were splotchy red. He talked softer, and when Jack met his gaze, there was something pleading there.

Tell me you didn't do this, the look said. *Tell me a father didn't kill his son.*

The older one. What adjective to describe him? One question came out tight, the voice wound-up from anger. The next question held a sly lilt, like he hoped to catch Jack in a lie. He gazed at Jack with a knowing look, like he'd seen every cut of man in his career and had Jack's measure immediately.

Jack kept his composure. He sat and let their questions go unanswered. He let them do their good-cop, bad-cop routine. He let the younger detective's face flush more, and he let the older one's words get harsher, crueler. The older one promised him pain in prison. He explained how time in lockup goes poorly for soft rich boys like Jack and doubly hard for kiddie murderers.

"I didn't kill my son," Jack finally said, and he was proud his voice didn't tremble. "But I'm not answering any more questions until I speak with my lawyer."

The two detectives exchanged glances. They left the room. Jack studied his reflection in the mirror. He wondered if his gaze fell on whoever stood on the other side of it. He'd seen plenty of cop shows and movies. He knew the drill.

And he knew the drill in Mariensburg. His father had the police in his pocket for Jack's entire life. He knew he couldn't give away his real alibi until certain details were handled. He guessed that was the crux of this whole affair—his lack of alibi. Henry must have folded under questioning.

The detectives returned with their captain. Jack was informed that he was being held. He was informed they could hold him for up to forty-eight hours without charging him. He'd be booked at the county jail, and perhaps after experiencing those accommodations, he'd be more forthcoming.

The younger one cuffed him, and Jack could have wept at how gentle the man was about it.

"I want to speak with my attorney," Jack said. "*My* attorney. Not my father's."

✳

Jack had failed to protect his son, Tommy.

He had failed to protect him not just from the unknown killer who had crept in during the night, but even earlier than that. He had failed to protect Tommy from his own father.

It was supposed to be a clean start. Jack married to the lovely Abigail, and it didn't matter that she was the daughter of one of Thomas's business associates. He knew of his own parents' unhappy marriage, the chill that pervaded any room they shared before Clara got sick.

Love could grow, Jack thought back then, *if I'm everything my father is not.*

Jack had vowed to be better. A better husband, a better father for the child on the way.

Then came Tommy, born weeks too early. Jack had been terrified of his son, terrified to accidentally hurt him. He could hold the newborn Tommy in both of his cupped hands, could see the pulse through the thin skin of his scalp. Abigail had the baby blues, endless weeping that ceded to stony silence, then disinterest in the baby.

Of course Jack ceded the care of Tommy to Martha. She sat at the right hand of his father and did his bidding.

His courage failed him back then. Jack was the disappointing son, and Tommy—Junior, by then—was the promising future. Jack let it happen. He let himself be pushed out, his wishes overruled at each turn: When Thomas took his namesake to the factory. When Thomas gave the boy his first pellet gun, took him out to the sportsmen's club to teach him how to shoot trap. When he hired the college kid to teach the boy Latin to ease him into the boarding school he'd eventually be shipped off to.

Spineless Jack sat back and let it happen, even though the misery on his young son's face was a mirror to his own lonely boyhood.

I'm going to do better, he thought in the backseat of the squad car that took him to the county jail. He would be held there until Monday morning, but the younger detective promised to call his lawyer.

"I'll have your lawyer meet you there," the detective told him before Jack was loaded into the squad car.

"Thank you," Jack murmured back.

I'm going to do better, he thought as he was processed at the jail, then led to his solitary holding cell. *I failed Tommy, but I'm going to do better.*

＊

Courage never came easily to Jack Farney, but if a man's final thoughts count much in the final tallying of his life's achievements—or failings—then he did find his mettle in the end.

He had failed his son, Tommy.

He had failed himself, too, though he couldn't be faulted much for that. The few times he had stood up to his father, he had been swiftly cowed and pushed back into line.

But he had plans now. He had a path to finding himself, to honoring Tommy, to standing up to his father. His lawyer would meet him at the jail, and they would talk out of earshot of the police who may be in his father's pocket. They would put their plan into motion. The lawyer would go away, spend the rest of the weekend making his moves, and then on Monday, they would clear the whole sorry affair.

I did not kill my son, he would tell the judge. *I can account for exactly where I was when he was killed, and who I was with, what we did and said, and how I felt.*

His father would rage. The detectives would return to the drawing board. His wife would ask for the divorce they both wanted but held off on until their fathers were dead. Abigail's was already dead, so they were already halfway there anyway. The tongues in Mariensburg would wag, doubtless, but Jack would be free.

The wool batting of Jack's brain kept the fact of Tommy's death away from him, and his brain instead let him focus on the future.

When Jack heard footsteps in the hallway of the holding cellblock, when he heard the jingle of keys, he didn't flinch or tremble. He thought it was his lawyer. The guard unlocked the cell door to admit the detective. It wasn't the young or the old one, but the beady-eyed one from the factory, the one asking questions the other day.

Jack's brain stuttered for a moment in its musing on the future because he recognized the guy, not only from the factory but from before. The man had been in his father's office long before Tommy, that pinched ferret face coming and going—

Courage never came easily to Jack, the poor little rich boy, the pathetic man, but when Detective Haney stepped into the cell and wrapped the cord around his neck without a single word uttered, Jack Farney fought for his life.

He failed, in the end. But he fought for it.

CHAPTER TWENTY-THREE

Felix would always look back on the Farney case as the dividing line between the epochs of his life.

In the raw months that followed the case, Felix would think of himself before Junior Farney had been killed as a happy idiot, stupider because he had thought himself so smart. He with his college degree from night classes, his policing seminars, his constant study of new procedures and famous cases.

Then came the Farney case. Once the sting of it wore off, he realized it wasn't a matter of smart or stupid, but innocent or worldly. The Felix from before had been naïve. The Farney case marked the loss of his innocence.

He had been blind to the clues in front of him. Even if they had been circumstantial, the fact of them had been there the whole time. The flimsy alibi had crumbled when pressed even slightly. The presumed ugliness around the family fortune, the passing over of Jack for his own young son. The murder weapon of the quaaludes, even if they never found the knife used to deliver the postmortem injury or the syringe that delivered the hot shot.

The coup de grâce of Jack Farney's suicide in his jail cell. Hanged himself with his own shoelaces, which seemed as much an admission of guilt as a signed letter of confession.

"Innocent men don't off themselves," Adam had explained. His voice had lost any of its fire from earlier that night. He talked to Felix in a gentle tone, as if he were one of the bereaved. Because Felix hadn't believed it. He'd shaken his head in disbelief and tried to come up with another explanation. Even with word fresh from the county jail, Jack's body already cut down, bagged and tagged—

"Hell, kid," Adam had said with a sigh. He had scrubbed his hands over his face, and in that moment, he looked haunted. "A person is usually murdered by someone they know. Family, a lot of times."

Felix had bristled at the primer on murder statistics, said nothing.

"I bet being the son of his old man wasn't easy, and Jack just snapped." Adam had paused, studied Felix closer, his eyes soft with sympathy. "You get along with your old man?"

"Huh?"

"Your dad. You get along with him?"

Felix had nodded, and his temper cooled a few degrees at the thought of his dad. Felix had never known a gentler man. His father, a county worker with calloused hands and a deep tan from working in the weather. The sort of man who moved earthworms off the sidewalk when it stopped raining so they wouldn't fry in the sun. The man who wrangled his household of rowdy sons with humor instead of the belt, like so many other men did.

"Yeah, I got along with him," Felix had finally replied.

"That's your blind spot. You never saw Jack as a suspect because you couldn't fathom a father killing his son."

"I don't—"

"Kid, we all have blind spots." A beat, a moment of hesitation. "I never saw Jack as anything *but* suspect number one. It's my blind spot, too, on the inverse. I just happened to be right in this case." He shook his head. "Could have just as easily been you as the right one and me wrong. There's no shame in it."

✱

They parted soon after. Felix returned to his corner desk under the clock. Adam checked out of the motor court to head home to Harrisburg.

"You've got the makings of a damned fine detective, kid," Adam said, and the nickname didn't goad Felix like it had only days ago. They shook hands. Adam clasped him on the shoulder, told him to stay in touch.

"The state bureau will be hiring in a few years," he said. "Buncha old bastards like me nearing mandatory retirement. Could be a good opportunity for a young buck."

"Maybe." He'd wanted nothing more than that, but now the prospect seemed tinged in bitterness, spoiled by the Farney case not getting a clean closure.

Felix stood outside of the precinct and watched as Adam drove off. He lifted his hand in a wave, stood there until the car was around the corner and out of sight.

It had only been days, but it felt like years ago when he and Captain Krause stood outside the Farney mansion, watching the sunrise. Felix had thought of the case as his ticket out. In the few days that passed, Mariensburg had settled more firmly into its autumn scene. Dried leaves crunched under the soles of his shoes. The coming winter bit stronger. The Farney case was closed, an inglorious ending without any glittering commendation that would launch him into a new career elsewhere.

The days would keep getting shorter and Felix would remain here, exactly where he began.

*

Some things did change.

Captain Krause retired. Officially, he had reached the age where he could enjoy his pension to the fullest. Unofficially, he was railroaded out of the department because someone needed to be blamed for Jack eluding justice. Why not Krause?

He wasn't the only one. A guard, a shift commander at the county jail got axed, too, but Felix only cared about Krause.

"You gonna cry for me, Kosmatka?" Krause asked in his gruff way. Felix stood in the doorway as the captain boxed up his stuff: the photos on his desk, his dispensary of rot-gut liquor from his desk drawer.

"I've learned a lot working with you," Felix answered, and he wasn't embarrassed by how earnest it sounded.

"Coulda done a better job here," Krause replied. He eased himself into his chair and gazed around the half-empty office. "Still, I did better than my predecessor. It's not all a loss. Maybe my successor will do even better."

"He'll stand on the shoulders of giants," Felix murmured, and

Krause said he'd drink to that. He held out a hand, gestured Felix to sit, and poured out generous dollops of whiskey into two Styrofoam cups.

Captain Krause and Felix toasted each other, then sipped their liquor as they cast their thoughts to what came next: Krause with his long days of leisurely retirement, Felix with his future unspooling in front of him as a Mariensburg detective, his career limited to the small-time cases of a small-time town. The Farney case had been his lone shot at escape, the single boost of rocket fuel to help him slip the gravity of his hometown.

But he remained here, still caught in the trap. Another high-profile case would probably never come again.

Winslow was named interim captain. He was promoted to the position permanently a few months later.

It didn't turn out to be the catastrophe Felix thought it would be. Winslow, lazy and uninspired for detective work, was uniquely suited for the boring bureaucracy of running the precinct. He pulled together budgets, sat in meetings, listened to endless bitching from union reps with a zest he never held for actual police work.

Haney retired early, took a bath on his own pension. He declared the Farney case ("a murdered kid, for fuck's sake") took it out of him. Said he was going to soak up the rays on the panhandle of Florida while he was still young enough to enjoy himself.

No one seemed to miss him. Not even his own longtime partner, Winslow, who claimed there wasn't enough money in the budget for a proper going-away party, but who sprung for a cake from the bakery as a cheap nod to the detective's retirement.

In January of 1973, a pair of adventuresome teenagers snowshoed through the old logging trails that crisscrossed the forest surrounding the country club. A glint of pale winter sunlight through the trees, and Jack Farney's Cutlass was discovered under its skeletal branches of camouflage and a melting layer of snow. One teenager told his father, who called in a tip to the police. He thought it might be stolen, boosted by teenagers looking for a joyride and then abandoned.

Officers went out to investigate. They found the car and used a Slim Jim to get into it. They raided the glove box and found the registration, now expired.

Winslow sent Felix out once they realized what they'd found. The case was closed, but it didn't mean a coda couldn't be tacked onto it. Felix found himself in the dripping woods full of snowmelt and early birdsong.

He pulled on a pair of gloves and tossed the car. It made his breath catch in his throat, these last, sad vestiges of Jack Farney. The expired registration, the flashlight and napkins tucked into the glove box. A scatter of coins in the ashtray. A gas station map of Pennsylvania that had been refolded wrong.

And under the driver's seat, nearly missed by Felix's reaching hand: a little brown bottle with red letters on the label.

SOPORAL.

*

A week after they found the car, Rhonda called his desk phone and requested his presence in the waiting room. Her voice lacked its usual teasing quality, and her face was somber when he made his way over to her.

"These finally came," she said. She tapped the lid of a large white box, unmarked. "The phone records from Bell."

Felix had forgotten about them entirely. He'd assumed they'd been boxed up with the rest of the evidence, the case notes and crime scene photos, the coroner's report and the final write-up.

"It's been months," he replied.

"It was a big request."

Felix sighed. It was a waste of time. All of it was, in a way. All his by-the-books crossing off of names, the careful elimination of suspects, the consideration of a serial. All of it just to end up being Jack in the end.

"Toss them," he said.

Rhonda heaved the box off her desk, then set it on the floor. She pushed it under her desk, and when she caught Felix watching her, she shrugged and said she'd leave a note for the night cleaning person to handle them.

"They were a long shot anyway." He felt stupid thinking back to how earnest he'd been, how convinced some clue lay in the phone records, pointing to a bigger conspiracy involving drugs or mafiosos running paper.

She offered him a smile, sympathetic. "Yeah, but a long shot is still a shot worth taking." She paused, glanced at her watch. "I'm off in an hour. Wanna grab a beer?"

A beer sounded damned fantastic, and when he told Rhonda so, she smiled brighter and said she'd meet him in the parking lot in an hour. She said she'd drive, since he seemed to require several beers, and that sounded pretty damned fine too.

✳

The Roadhouse sat outside of the city limits, a throwback to when Farney owned the town and entrepreneurs staked their claim outside of his control. The place had started as a bar that served near beer during Prohibition, then had evolved in the subsequent years as a honky-tonk before it settled into its final form as a certifiable dive bar.

The bar flies and the bartender alike knew Rhonda. They waved at her, called out their hellos. She greeted them each, asked after their families, as gracious as a queen receiving her subjects. She took a corner seat and gestured for Felix to sit, then flagged a passing waitress for a pitcher and two clean glasses.

"Guess the 'Roadhouse' nickname is still fitting," Felix joked.

She hummed at that but didn't reply. The waitress brought their pitcher and poured them each a glass. Felix took a deep swallow of his, the faint burn of the beer against his soft palate. Rhonda sipped at hers, pacing herself as the responsible driver.

"Can I let you in on a little secret?" she said after a long beat. The jukebox switched from Merle Haggard singing about how his mama tried to raise him up right to Albert King lamenting his bad luck. Felix nodded at her.

"My uncle used to own this place. Went to my cousin when he died, but when I was in high school..." She took another sip of her beer. "Well, home was tough."

"So you came here?" Felix guessed.

Rhonda cast an expansive look over the place—from the beer-stained carpet to the pair of pool tables with scuffed-up felt. The expression on her face was one of pure love—a soft smile paired with the obvious memories playing behind her eyelids.

"I used to sit at this table right here and do my homework. The regulars used to try to help me sometimes. I was their little mascot. I felt safer here with a bunch of drunks than I did at home with my dad."

A sting of shame needled him. All those assumptions from back in high school. Had he teased her then too? He doubted he had been as cruel as some of the other kids, but he also doubted he had been gracious. He'd been a quiet kid, but even quiet kids were susceptible to real asshole behavior.

"I'm sorry," he said, and he looked her dead in the eyes when he said it, so she knew he meant it.

Rhonda focused her smile on him, but he could see the old pain behind it, how she tried to cover it up and nearly succeeded, but not entirely. "We seemed like a nice family to everyone who saw us. He was good at hiding it."

Another father, another home full of secrets behind closed doors. Felix sat back in the cracked vinyl of the booth and slumped a little.

"Sometimes things aren't what they appear to be," Rhonda added. She reached for the pitcher and topped off his glass, then clicked the edge of her own against his in a toast.

CHAPTER TWENTY-FOUR

To things not being quite what they appear: Felix had never considered Rhonda Kormos as anyone other than the girl from the neighborhood growing up, then the receptionist at the police station.

What did a receptionist do? She took phone calls. She handled the public when they came through the precinct's doors, indignant with complaints. She handled the precinct's mail and correspondence, and Felix had never once really considered the woman behind the desk in the waiting area, marooned from the rest of the precinct.

Rhonda, he came to find out, was a detective-story junkie. She lived for the stuff. The high-brow British stories, Agatha Christie and Ellery Queen. The gritty American stuff of Dashiell Hammett and Raymond Chandler. She watched all the cop shows with an especial love for *Columbo*. She scoured newspapers—she had the *Pittsburgh Post-Gazette* delivered to her apartment—for real-life stories.

That obsessive love of solving cases alongside Sam Spade or Miss Marple was a natural segue into solving her own puzzles. She had long hours to fill at her desk. There were only so many letters to type or angry citizens to usher back into the bullpen on any given day.

She failed to mark the box of Bell records to be carted out by the cleaning staff. She simply forgot. When she banged her toe against the box the next morning, she looked down thoughtfully, then pulled the first bound stack out of the box. She flipped through it as the day dragged out.

She found a pattern, she explained to Felix later, so she took the box of phone records home and pored over them while she watched TV.

"It was a way to fill the time," she said.

She'd called him at home, breathless with excitement. He'd

played along, drove over to her side of town to humor her. He had found the scene alarming. The spread of marked-up phone records across her tiny living room made her look like a maniac. The minuscule font and numbers were enough to make his eyes ache in sympathy for the long hours she must have spent on a futile task.

"It was just a way to kill time," she repeated, her eyes bright with excitement. "Until it wasn't anymore."

✳

Felix picked his way across the living room floor, around the haphazard spread of papers, and sat on the edge of her sofa. He looked at her, caught obvious zeal in her expression.

"I skimmed the phone records at first," she said. "There's obviously a lot of repeat numbers coming in and out at the country club. You know, calls back and forth with suppliers, food and alcohol deliveries. Normal stuff."

"That makes sense."

"There's a lot of one-time calls in both directions too. I'm guessing those are just, you know, people calling the club to check on hours or availability. Or the club calling out to fundraise or whatever. I don't actually know how the country club works."

Felix leaned back against the couch and smiled up at where she marched in a tight back-and-forth. "Not much of a golfer?"

She ignored the comment, breezed past it. "But I caught this pattern. It was always the same outgoing number to the same incoming number. And it was always on the same days and nearly the same times."

"A pattern doesn't prove anything," he pointed out as gently as possible. "My mother calls my brothers like clockwork every Sunday."

"I thought that too." She walked over to sit beside him. She reached for a legal pad on the coffee table and paged through it, then balanced it on her knee and pointed for Felix to look.

"I pulled your case notes on the Farney murder. I saw your question about there being a mafia link. I wondered about it."

Felix sighed. "That lead was a bust. Obviously."

"Only because Jack killed himself before it could prove out. The threads you and the other guy had got dropped, you know? Nothing was actually proven."

Felix knew she was right. It had been his argument, right after the case was closed. There was no careful tying up of leads. The case had been closed in a rush by the district attorney. Felix had, in his more fervid moments, wondered if the attorney was in Thomas Farney's pocket, too, if the urgency to close the case had been at the old man's insistence. When he had mentioned it to Captain Krause, though—the man only weeks away from his own forced retirement—he'd frowned at Felix and said he was being paranoid.

"The DA thought Jack's suicide was a pretty damning piece of evidence," Felix countered. "And then we found the bottle of Soporal in the woods in his hidden car, months later."

"I'm not saying Jack *didn't* do it. I'm just saying, there's a mighty big *what-if* there."

Felix tapped the notebook on her knee. "Keep going."

"This pattern of numbers. I called the country club one first, the outgoing side of the call. I called on a Thursday night, which was the same day of the week the boy was murdered. A man eventually picked up. He seemed pretty drunk, but when I asked where he was, he said he was in one of the lounges in the club."

"I think I know the one," Felix said. "That's where they play cards."

"Then I called the other number, the side that received the call." Rhonda paused, glanced at him. "I made the call from the pay phone outside of the gas station to be safe. I called on Thursday evening around the same time those calls used to go out."

She stopped. She seemed to be considering her words, and part of him hated the unexpected dip in his stomach—the possibility she was really onto something after all. Rhonda was no dummy, he knew, and even if she was naïve—

"I thought I'd get some gruff guy on the other line. A bookie-type, you know? My dad used to bet on football games, and sometimes rough-looking characters came around looking for him. Used to scare the shit out of my mom."

Felix's gut did that thing: the fluttery feeling people used to describe love at first sight, but for him had always meant that a shift was coming to a case.

"It wasn't a bookie-type?" he guessed.

Rhonda shook her head, and her hands gripped the notebook so hard the pages squeaked against each other. "No, it was a woman. I didn't say anything at all. She kept saying, 'Hello?' and I didn't say anything, but after a moment, she... well, after a moment of neither of us talking, she whispered, 'Is that you, Jack?'"

Felix's throat felt too tight all of a sudden, like he had to push out the words through a pinhole.

"And then?" he asked.

Rhonda looked at him, her face a rictus of pain. "And then she started to cry."

CHAPTER TWENTY-FIVE

The drive to McKean County felt thick with tension. Rhonda had called her buddy at Bell and found the owner of the line from the records, then gotten the address.

They'd argued over it. Felix had wanted to go the house unannounced—perhaps stake it out, perhaps be bold enough to march up to the front door and knock. Rhonda wanted more restraint. She felt guilty for making the woman cry when she called and said nothing.

In the end, Felix won. They carved out a Saturday to go, and Felix drove while Rhonda sulked. It was late February, but spring loomed in the distance, a gossamer thread of warmth on the breeze. Mid-morning, and the sun peeked through the trees, glazed the lingering snow and ice in a lacquer of pale gold.

"What exactly are we going to say if we knock on her door?" Rhonda groused from the passenger seat. "'Hey, sorry to drop in, but did you know the guy who killed his kid and then himself, perchance?'"

"Not in so many words. And I won't say 'perchance.'" He glanced over at her, hoped to tease at least the beginning of a smile out of her, but she scowled deeper.

Felix sighed. "Okay, fine. Maybe we don't even approach, but aren't you curious?"

She made a disgruntled hum, a literal *harumph*, but then added, "Yeah, I am."

"It was your lead. You're the one that found it."

"I *know*. I just don't want to make anyone cry."

Felix's mind had churned so much over the past few days he wouldn't be surprised if smoke curled out of his ears. A million questions without answers, just as before. Would this prove Jack definitely killed his son?

Had he and Adam been close the whole time? Had they only fumbled the motive?

He thought back to Henry Murray, Jack's fake alibi. What had the man said? *"I just always thought he had a side piece tucked away somewhere."* Was that the missing link, a kept woman tucked away an hour north of Mariensburg?

Had Jack, trapped in an unhappy marriage, finally snapped? Had he killed his own son to break away, to be with his mistress? If so, it spoke to the level of Jack's desperation, which would allow his suicide to rest easier on Felix's conscious.

Or would this prove Jack had been innocent all along? Felix's mind boggled at the implications. The fine hairs on the back of his neck stood up when he thought about it, the hinky feeling Krause had chalked up to paranoia.

If it hadn't been Jack, then who was it? If the DA rushed to close the case, what lengths would they—the murky *they* Felix imagined, marshaling their forces against him—go to in order to stop him?

"I'll play it gentle," he promised Rhonda. "I promise. Like Krause used to say, I'll use kid gloves."

The house stood as far north as a person could get in McKean without tipping into New York State, outside of the Bradford city limits, nearer to the Allegheny National Forest. It was set back on a state road, a sweet little Cape Cod in white with deep-blue trim and shutters.

"So much for staking the place out," Rhonda said. Felix piloted his car up the long driveway, aware whoever was inside—a Ford Falcon was parked off to the side—could see and hear them coming.

"We don't say we're police, since we aren't here on police business. We say we were friends with Jack."

She arched an eyebrow. "You think she'll buy it?"

"We can say we knew him from the club."

She took a moment, then nodded. "Yeah, okay. That might work."

Felix parked behind the Falcon, killed the ignition. He turned to face Rhonda, who looked pale in the weak daylight. "You sure you're okay with this?"

"I am. It's my lead. I want to see it through."

He climbed out of the car, and a moment later, Rhonda did too. Together, they made their way along the sidewalk, picked their way around the patches of ice until they were on the front porch.

"Here goes nothing," Felix said, but Rhonda beat him to it, lifted her own gloved fist to rap on the door. Together, they waited and listened to the noise on the other side of them: the quiet roar of a television, murmured voices in conversation, and the tread of footsteps as they approached.

The door cracked open. The woman on the other side peered out, asked if she could help them.

"We're here about Jack," Rhonda said.

The woman shut the door in their faces.

Felix thought it a dead end for an agonizingly long beat. But just as he reached for Rhonda, tugged on her coat sleeve, and gestured toward his car, he heard more murmured conversation, then the rattle of the doorknob again. The woman opened the door and invited them inside with a polite smile and wary eyes.

The phone records listed the woman as Victoria Fortin. She introduced herself as Vicky, bade them to sit, offered them something to drink. She had just brewed a pot of coffee, she said, and she always made too much.

"That would be lovely," Rhonda said, and Vicky disappeared into the kitchen.

Felix studied the living room while they waited. It was cozy. It reminded him of when he was a little kid and one of his friends went on vacation to the shore and brought back a massive conch shell. That shell had been the obsession of the playground for weeks. They took turns pressing it to their ears, convinced they heard the ocean that most of them had never seen.

Felix had been taken with the colors of the shell, the sheen to it, and that's what Vicky's living room reminded him of—the smooth inside of the conch. Everything was rosy pink, pale creams, light-tan accents.

A beat later, he realized that the home was also striking because it was the opposite of the Farney mansion with all its coolly tasteful wealth on display, its untouchable quiet quality that made it seem more museum or mausoleum than domicile.

He pictured Jack lounging here, stretched out across the deep, comfortable couch. He pictured him with his arm around Vicky, the two of them listening to a record together or watching television—

The mansion might have been where he lived, Felix thought, *but this was his home.*

Vicky returned a moment later with a laden tray: coffee, cream, and sugar, and a little plate with sugar cookies arranged on it. She passed them their cups, and Felix looked her over too.

She was pretty in an everyday way, hair tied back and eyes maybe a fraction too close together to be truly beautiful. She had a hectic flush high in her cheeks, and he wasn't sure if she was naturally red-faced or if their visit had caused it. He guessed it was the latter.

Once they settled, Vicky asked, "You knew Jack, then?"

Rhonda sipped at her coffee. "Yes, from the country club."

"He mentioned some friends there. I never supposed he mentioned me."

"We were closer to Jack," Felix interjected. "Maybe more than his other acquaintances."

"We're only trying to piece together what happened. We couldn't believe it when we heard." Rhonda said it so sincerely Felix knew she wasn't lying, even if the cover story was subterfuge.

"It's his father, you know. Jack never could trust anyone—" Here she cast her gaze between them again, studying them closer, and Felix put on what he hoped was a trustworthy face. "But he must have trusted you," she finished.

"We're missing pieces," Felix replied. "We hope you can fill in some of them."

Something about his tone or phrasing set the woman's hackles off. She narrowed her eyes, and her voice grew cold, clipped. "And you're not police?"

Rhonda answered. "No," she said softly. "We were fond of Jack. He told us about you, how he'd call you from the country club..."

Felix watched as the words hit Vicky. Her eyes grew brilliant with tears, but she blinked against them, brushed one away with the back of her hand as it coursed down the side of her nose.

"It was our signal he was on his way. Tuesdays and Thursdays. It was all he could manage."

"We only want the truth," Rhonda said. She reached out a hand to Vicky, and a moment later, the woman took it. She held it and gazed between the two of them, the pain drawing her features into a mask of suffering.

"What's it matter now? He's gone."

"We know a man in the state detective's bureau," Rhonda said. "He's outside of Thomas Farney's influence. If we can fill in some of those gaps, we think we can clear Jack's name. It's not—"

They were interrupted by a childish voice laced with petulance. When Felix glanced over Vicky's shoulder, he saw a small boy standing in the doorway.

Felix knew that family resemblances sometimes skipped a generation or two, but the boy—small, only three or four years old—had the same sandy hair, the same watercolor-blue eyes. The boy walked over to Vicky and tucked himself between her arm and her side. He turned his face against her and peeked out at Felix and Rhonda shyly.

Vicky watched him, then Rhonda, as they studied her son and filled in one massive gap in Jack Farney's story at the same time.

"I guess Jack never mentioned his son," she said.

✶

Felix found his focus shifting between Vicky's face and the boy—Jack's son—as he sat at her feet and nibbled at one of the sugar cookies. He was his father's spitting image. It made him revise everything he knew about the man as Vicky told their story.

They met at Haverhill. She'd taught the art courses the patients were encouraged to take, the thought that painting or sketching could help them make sense of their disordered thinking.

"Of course, there was nothing wrong with Jack," she said. "Not really. He just had a breakdown."

It was strictly verboten, their relationship. Haverhill attracted its rich clients through its reputation, yet Jack and Vicky had fallen into an easy friendship. He took his art lessons seriously, had a natural talent for oil paints. She brought him a monograph of the Ashcan School of painters, and they bonded over their mutual love of Edward Hopper and John Sloan.

The friendship deepened to earnest discussions about their mutual loneliness, their dissatisfaction with their lives. They both had a keen sense of time slipping away from them. They both felt estranged from the world, as if a veil separated them from everyone else lucky enough to experience the full richness of life. Vicky, estranged from her family in Quebec. Jack, defeated by falling short of his father's aspirations for him.

It was a short path from there to love.

Jack was honest about his first family. The unhappy marriage, the longed-for son named after the old man to flatter him. Jack told Vicky how Junior had been snatched from under Jack's and Abigail's noses, Thomas's opinions on the raising of the boy above rebuke. How Abigail, caught in the riptide of the baby blues, didn't resist. How Jack tried to fight back, argue. How he failed.

"Jack tried to set up his own home away from his father. He had a whole plan to move out with his son, and when Thomas found out... well, Jack ended up in Haverhill."

When Jack left Haverhill, he took Vicky with him. Kind of. He drained his savings account—a drop in the ocean, compared to the entirety of his father's fortune—and bought her this house, this car. He put the rest into an account with only her name on it, told her to make the house her own.

Their sole fight sprung up when Vicky discovered she was pregnant. She was tired of hiding, tired of being a kept woman.

"He sat me down and told me what it had been like, growing up with a father like that."

"What was it like?" Rhonda asked, quiet.

Vicky told them the secondhand stories. How Thomas had given Jack certain amounts of money when he was young, an attempt to see what he did with it. Thomas, Vicky said, used to take his own allowance as a boy and see how he could multiply it, the cents turning into dollars, his coffers growing fuller. How Jack lacked that money-making instinct, how he always spent it on the other boys in boarding school—candy and sweets when they were young, then beer and cigarettes when they were older. How he'd been desperate for friends but had also lacked that social skill, too shy and uncertain to win anyone over without paying for it.

"He wanted to protect me and the baby from that. If his father knew there was another Farney in the world, he'd find a way to take him."

She told them the secondhand stories about Thomas then, the rumors that Rhonda and Felix had already heard. Thomas the ruthless businessman. His rough play with the miners, the strikebreaking. How it was common knowledge that he drove a partner to suicide back in the forties when he was closing down the mines and breaking ground on the factory. How that suicide might have been outright murder, but the partner's family was paid off to leave the area and never return.

"Jack thought his father would do just about anything to secure his legacy," Vicky said. "He felt guilty about Tommy. He saw Jackie here as his second chance."

"So he kept you hidden from Thomas," Rhonda said.

"To keep you safe," Felix added.

"To keep both of us safe," Vicky replied. She laid a gentle palm on the top of her son's head and ruffled his hair affectionately. "That's why he never told the police where he was the night of the murder. He was here the whole time. The police would have told Thomas, and then everything would have been for nothing."

*

Outside, Rhonda held her gloved palm out to Felix.

"Give me your keys," she said. "You look like you need time to think."

He obliged. He waited until they were on the highway before he said, "It was ballsy, lying like that. Admitting we knew about the phone calls from the club."

"That's because you nearly lost her." The teasing edge was back in her voice. "Using your 'we have some questions for you, ma'am,' bullshit cop-voice."

"I don't have a cop-voice."

"You absolutely do." They sat for a moment, listened to the sound of the tires on the roads wet with snowmelt. Rhonda's voice turned serious. "We know it wasn't Jack, which means the real murderer is still out there."

"The case is closed. We can't reopen it without solid proof."

"The only proof we have would blow Vicky and Jack Junior's cover. That's exactly what Jack was trying to avoid."

"He wasn't wrong to suspect the police department. Krause's predecessor was in Thomas Farney's back pocket." He thought back to the ledger book of Thomas's sins. It was tucked away in his bedroom. He'd never returned it. He could show it to Rhonda, to get her impressions on it.

The fact of police bribery didn't seem to shock her. "What's next?"

Felix turned to watch as she drove, to see how his two options landed with her.

"One, we leave it. It wouldn't bring Jack or Junior back from the dead anyway."

Rhonda shook her head. "No way. Not a chance. We can't just *leave* it, Felix."

He smiled. If he remembered one thing about their childhood in the neighborhood, it was how Rhonda Kormos never backed down from a challenge. Even if she'd been a scrawny thing, undersized and facing off against bigger kids. Even when the outcome of a fight was already decided with her the loser, she went down swinging. She'd bloodied plenty of noses in her scrappy, hellcat way.

"Then two," he said. "We investigate it together, off the record and off hours. So long as you know I could lose my badge and you could lose your job."

"Fuck my job," she replied, cheerful. "Let's find a goddamned murderer."

CHAPTER TWENTY-SIX

L aura sometimes held imaginary interviews in her head. She pretended she sat primly in a television studio as she was questioned about her life's work.

The interviewer (in her mind, he was a look-alike for Chet Huntley, long-faced with those deep-set eyes) would ask: *"Why did you do it?"*

She would answer: *"Because it was God's plan."*

The interviewer: *"You realize that sounds crazy."*

Gattina: *"If it were not God's plan, wouldn't I have been caught?"*

It was the point she returned to over and over. If she had overstepped the bounds of God's will, wouldn't He have punished her? Wouldn't He have allowed her to be caught?

After all, once one looked past Jack, all the facts of the case pointed to *her*.

The postmortem injury should have been obvious to the coroner. Tests should have been run. A bloodstream full of quaaludes should have pointed at her, the medical professional who was trained to measure medicines, who knew how to deliver an injection quickly and efficiently.

Her obfuscating work had been a bid to buy time. She had wanted to luxuriate in the suffering of Thomas Farney, just for a little bit.

When the detectives had shown up that evening, she thought they were there to arrest her. The older one had settled his gaze on her when they entered the room. They had all been there, keeping a sort of wake even though there was no body present, Thomas and Clara, Jack and Abigail. And Laura, who sat watch nearby in case her patient needed her.

Laura thought herself caught in that moment and was ready to turn to Thomas. She had been turning, in fact—had craned her neck to see the old man, the words bubbling from the innermost chamber of her heart, up the column of her throat. They were right at the tip of her tongue, the last words she ever planned to say in her life now that her life's work was complete—

Instead, they took Jack away.

The detectives said it was for more questioning, but it was so late in the evening, and their tones held no magnanimity. Laura had caught all their expressions: Clara's bafflement, Abigail's surprise. Thomas's disbelief that grew to awareness.

Then Jack died at the jail, and the case was closed.

Laura found herself with a surfeit of time to revel in the suffering she had caused, but she didn't think of it that way. She hadn't *caused* his suffering. She thought of it, for Thomas's benefit, in business terms, which she explained to the imaginary interviewer in her head.

"It wasn't suffering that I caused," Gattina would explain. *"It was suffering Thomas Farney dealt to my family. I only paid him back, with interest."*

Laura's parents used to tell the story of their journey to America. Nicola and Maria DeLuca repeated the well-worn lines, a call and response to the typical immigrant story. The scraping together of enough cash for their tickets after they married, determined to shuck the hard lives of their parents for better opportunities in America. The journey from their *comune* outside of Milan, from Robecco sul Naviglio to Naples where their ship waited.

The miserable ocean crossing, cramped and stinking, packed with a motley assortment of people: Milanese and Lombards, Grecians, a lone Magyar. The fervent prayers in all those disparate tongues as winter storms turned the Atlantic into a frothing grey mass.

"It made for a miserable honeymoon, though we made the best of it," Nicola used to say, making Maria blush, though the insinuation was lost on Little Gattina.

When Laura became a nurse, she did the math herself. She realized her brother had crossed the ocean in a way, tucked within the snug confines of Maria's body, little more than a bean-sized lump that would eventually become Carlo. Her mother had probably chalked up any nausea to the relentless rocking of the ship. They docked at Ellis Island. They were processed and sent to the coalfields of Pennsylvania to meet with a distant cousin of Nicola's who could get them work.

By then, Laura guessed her mother knew of her condition. She'd soon give birth to the first DeLuca born on foreign soil since before memory.

✳

America was supposed to be the land of opportunity, but life in Shale Hollow was just as hand-to-mouth as life in the *comune*. Laura's mother used to lament the fact, said it would have been better to stay poor in their homeland instead of traveling so far to be poor in a foreign land.

At least they had family in Lombardy. There, they could speak the language and share a kind word, a bawdy joke with a neighbor. They could swim in the canal that bisected the *comune*, or revel in the history of the place. Maria's grandfather, she told Laura once, had tilled a field and turned up a cache of ancient coins. Their land had seen the rise and fall of empires.

Shale Hollow? It was an ugly place, only recently hacked out of the wilderness, behind the rest of the country's progress because of its geography on a plateau, the relative difficulty of navigating around the steep valleys that surrounded it. The town proper was little more than a company store, a one-room schoolhouse, and a pair of Catholic churches—one for the Italians, the other for the Slavs and Huns. Most of the roads were dirt. They kicked up a fine dust in the warm months and froze in the cold, with long intermediate periods of mud so heavy it drew the shoes off unwary walkers.

The houses were all owned by the mine, and they were thin-walled and hastily thrown together. There was no hope of heating them in the winter. Maria and Nicola and their new baby Carlo piled together like puppies around the iron stove and clung to the lingering warmth of the banked coals each night that first winter and the ones that followed.

For four, almost five years, it was the three of them. Maria conceived, then lost babies. They failed to take root or slid from her half-formed, malformed, all the pain and work of labor with none of the reward of a healthy, bawling baby at the end.

She blamed the dusty air of the town, blamed the frigid winters and water that stunk like the fumes of hell. She blamed the long hours she spent at the tailings pile with the other women, picking through the shale for overlooked bits of coal she could use to heat their gimcrack home.

She blamed the stress of her husband working underground. Later on, Maria would tell Laura how she used to be afraid to even step too hard on the ground, terrified her foot would create a seismic reaction that would cause a beam to crack, a shelf of coal to sheer off. That she would unwittingly be the cause of her own husband's entombment in the dark underground.

Then came Laura. She turned them into a quartet, rounded the family out into an even number. Laura gave them symmetry: two men, two women. Four sides of their small kitchen table, four points on a compass, four seasons.

When Laura was nearly three, Carlo went into the mines with his father. He was small for his age, but he had a wiry strength and long, nimble fingers. He was perfectly sized to work in the coal breaker, and the extra scrip helped keep the family in food and coal for their stove.

Laura only rarely cracked open that innermost chamber of her heart where she kept the *before* stashed. She undid the locks and let the door creak open on its rusty hinges. When she did, she sifted through her meager memories of her time in Shale Hollow.

She had one good memory of Carlo. It was hazy, as if she viewed it through a frost-laced window: a boy sitting on the faded rag rug in the living room, watching as she played with the little homemade doll her mother had sewn for her. She could remember the shock of his black hair, how it hung in his eyes. She thought she could remember his laugh, but Laura wondered if that was wishful thinking, her own mind's attempt to add color and dimension to the brother she never really knew.

She had more bad memories of Carlo.

Coal breakers staffed with little boys were already going out of fashion back then. Some clever man had found a way to automate the process, but that innovation hadn't reached Shale Hollow yet. Boys still hunched over and sorted through the coal with their bare hands, still went home with fingers chaffed and bleeding and eyes puffy and red from the dust. The shale dug up with the coal sliced them. The sulfuric acid—a byproduct of watering down the coal—burned them.

The coal breaker, if it caught a sleeve or a finger, crushed them.

Laura didn't remember when the Black Maria brought Carlo home to them, crushed and mangled but somehow still alive. If she was there—and she *had* to have been, as young as she was, still clinging to the skirt of her mother's housedress—her mind never processed it into memory. She didn't remember the horse-drawn carriage, painted black as it bore the bodies, both living and dead, from the mines back to their kin. She would remember it from later, but not when it bore Carlo back to them.

She only remembered after Carlo's accident. The house turned quiet, sullen, as if the walls absorbed their misery and insulated them in it. Her mother stopped singing, her father stopped telling his raucous jokes. Her mother experienced long crying jags that left her choking on her own tears. Her father spent more time out of the house.

She remembered how her parents scraped together every spare cent, even borrowed from their neighbors to bring in a doctor from outside of Shale Hollow. Laura remembered the man, a red-nosed vulture of a man who stunk like spilt beer, who took a single glance at her brother and declared him a lost cause.

She remembered how her parents tucked Carlo into the bedroom at the back of the first floor and waited for him to die.

Laura remembered her mother gripping her upper arm so hard her fingertips left smudges of bruising the next day. Maria forced her young daughter onto her knees—bare knees on cold wood floors, the more suffering to offer up for Carlo, the better. Together they prayed the rosary, always the *Mystéria Dolorósa*, the Sorrowful Mysteries, a blunt appeal to the Virgin Mary from one suffering mother to another.

Laura remembered her mother washing her brother's body, turning him when he got bedsores. Changing the sheets that reeked of piss, forever washing them, drying them, washing them again. She remembered her mother feeding Carlo soft foods, spooning broth and polenta into the gaping maw of his mouth, forever slack and drooling thanks to the misshapen dent in the side of his head.

As a nurse, Laura knew human bodies were fragile things, little more than bags of blood so easily broken.

As a nurse, she also knew human bodies could be miracles. They could survive a bullet to the brain, a head-on collision with a car, a fall from a building. Carlo's body survived being crushed in the machinery of Thomas Farney's mines for one year, three months, and eleven days before it finally released the boy from his suffering.

Maria told Laura she hoped Carlo's soul found its way back over the Atlantic, over the Alps, and across the Po River where it could be at rest in his homeland. That's where she intended to go when she died. Not this wretched place with these wretched Americans who used little boys' bodies and then tossed them away like refuse on a slag heap.

The mine foreman hadn't even stopped the coal breaker when Carlo was pulled into the great chewing gears. The foreman kept the machinery running at the owner's order. At Thomas Farney's order. Turning the breaker off would cost money, so they had only retrieved Carlo's mangled body at the end of the shift.

CHAPTER TWENTY-SEVEN

The second time around, the investigation's nerve center was Rhonda's living room. Rhonda found an old corkboard and propped it against the wall. She laid out the notes from the first case she had copied on the sly over the past few days.

"We have to pretend we are starting from scratch," Felix said as he wrote out fresh cards naming everyone—people with access to the Farney home, people who Thomas considered enemies.

Rhonda shook her head. "No, we have so much more to go off of now. We know for a fact it wasn't Jack."

Felix snorted. "You wanna run lead on this one, Kormos?"

Rhonda leaned back against the couch, crossed her arms over her chest and smiled. "Maybe I should. And I like that better than *Roadhouse*, you calling me by my last name."

"Yeah?"

"Maybe you should deputize me. *Detective Kormos*. Has a nice ring to it."

"That would make you *Deputy* Kormos, though."

She heaved a heavy sigh, exaggerated. "You always were a pedantic little shit, Felix. Even back in school."

Felix smiled and turned back to the board. He pinned the last name onto it, then propped it back against the wall. He walked over to the sofa and plopped down beside her. They studied the artifacts of the first case spread out in front of them. After a moment, Rhonda shifted, tucked a leg underneath her to face him. Her mouth curved into a frown.

"We have to be careful. If we get caught..." She let the implied threat hang in the air. It wasn't just their jobs on the line, though Felix found his desire to land in a bigger precinct had faded away. It used to gnaw at his gut like hunger, but the edge of it had grown dull in the face of the rot within Mariensburg. His ambition had shifted.

He also found himself growing more paranoid, constantly

wondering if someone was watching him. Winslow—Captain Winslow, now—had promoted one of the more senior cops to detective rank to replace his own and Haney's positions. While Felix was cordial with the new Detective Beck, the man still huddled around with his officer buddies, their voices low but their laughter cutting. They seemed to look Felix's way more than he liked. He *knew* they weren't talking about him. He knew it was paranoia, but it still made his skin crawl.

Who could he trust? He trusted Krause, but he was loath to bother his former captain in his leisure. He supposed he trusted Adam, but he also knew if he reached out to the man, he'd sigh and tell him to leave it. Felix wouldn't even be able to get the punch line out: that he found Jack Farney's alibi, it was airtight, and the murderer still walked among them.

He had Rhonda, which was a blessing and a curse. Blessing: She was clever, she was discreet, and she knew police work from being at the periphery. She could offer fresh eyes.

Curse: She wasn't a cop, and they toed a dangerous line now.

"If you want out, I wouldn't blame you," he said.

Rhonda glowered at him. "No way. I'm in this until the end." A beat. "So tell me where we start."

Felix walked her through his original theories.

"The gambling angle is dead," he said. "Jack Farney only used the club as a cover for driving north to visit his second family."

"That leaves the other two theories."

"Serial killer, or person known to the Farney family seeking revenge."

Rhonda twirled the pen in her fingers. "If it's a serial killer, there should be other murders of the same kind, right?"

"Usually, yes. Krause polled some nearby jurisdictions and found nothing." He pointed to the list of enemies Thomas had provided in the nascent beginnings of the case. "Which is why I'm leaning toward option three."

"Revenge."

They sat in silence and considered it. The radiator clicked on, air hissing in the lines, and broke the reverie.

"We keep hearing stories about his ruthlessness. Vicky told us about a partner who might have been driven to suicide but might have been murdered. Back in the forties, she said. That wasn't that awful long ago."

"I get it," Rhonda said. "My cousin works at the factory, you know. He has all sorts of stories about the guy."

Felix leaned over the side of the couch and snagged his satchel, undid the buckle, and reached inside. The ancient ledger shed dust motes of crumbling yellow paper as he handed it to Rhonda.

"Captain Krause showed me this. His predecessor received regular payoffs from Thomas Farney, but he obviously didn't trust him. He kept records of all of it."

Rhonda paged through it, turned the pages gingerly between her pinched forefinger and thumb. "It's full, Felix. Damned near."

"It's an accounting of Thomas Farney's bad behavior. You could read through it and see if anything stands out. Krause and Adam thought it was a long shot, but now I'm not so sure. Thinking back on the crime scene, it feels intentional. The overkill of the slashed throat feels like it was sending a message."

She offered a little mock salute but didn't look up. She turned back to the first page and started reading, already engrossed.

"What are you going to do?" she asked, half-distracted.

Felix stood and grabbed his coat from where it was slung across the back of an armchair. He pulled it on, buttoned it, dug in his pockets for his gloves.

"I'm going to go talk to Jack Farney's lawyer. The night Jack died, he was adamant we call *his* lawyer and not his father's. I wonder if the man has anything for us."

"Good luck." She glanced up from the book and smiled at him, then settled deeper into the sofa and returned to the book.

"Happy reading," he replied.

*

The law offices of George Hines were right over the county line in downtown Brockway. The name seemed familiar to Felix, but he chalked it up to the oblique way he learned the lawyerly landscape through his police work.

The offices were neat but run-down. The carpeting was threadbare from foot traffic, and everything seemed a bit dented or chipped. Felix expected the usual lawyer template in Esquire Hines—older white male, greying hair, wire-rimmed glasses.

Instead, the man who greeted him looked like a recovering hippie. His brown hair curled against the collar of his shirt. He didn't wear a suit jacket. Deep lines etched his tanned face and spoke of a love of the outdoors. Felix could almost picture him at Golden Gate Park, stoned out of his gourd and listening to Big Brother and the Holding Company.

"C'mon back," George said, and he led him into his office.

This was Jack Farney's lawyer? Felix thought as he settled into a chair across from George. He wondered if he'd gotten the name wrong. Maybe George Hines was a junior, and Jack had been working with his father.

"What can I help you with?" the lawyer asked. He leaned back in his chair, the definition of casual.

Felix had fibbed on the phone when he set up the appointment. Kinda. It wasn't enough to qualify as a straight-out falsehood, but he'd hedged and said he needed legal advice, which was near enough to the truth.

"I'm here about Jack Farney."

If George felt any specific way about that, he hid it well. His face didn't change except for the barest twitch at one corner of his mouth. He remained casual, leaned back.

"Go on."

It was Felix's one chance to make his pitch. He had to trust that Jack had trusted George. It meant *Felix* could trust George, so long as he got George to trust *him.*

He walked the man through it. He admitted the closure of the case didn't sit right with him. He thought Jack may have been innocent. He didn't admit to knowing about Vicky or her son. He wanted to keep that secret for Jack's sake.

George watched him without a single visible emotion. When Felix hit a stopping point, the lawyer said, "So you're the one honest cop, and you're here to set things right." His tone held a slight tinge of disdain.

"Yes."

Another long moment passed while the man studied him, his eyes boring into Felix until he had to fight the urge to squirm in his seat.

"You know client privilege extends even beyond death," he finally said. "Even if I wanted to help you, I couldn't."

"You could provide me with your impressions of the man. Any impressions you may have had on the case."

"Why should I trust you?"

"I suppose you shouldn't. All I can offer is my word."

"Which isn't worth anything to me." George moved quickly—sat up, stood up. He was around his desk and at his door before Felix could even blink. The lawyer held the door open for him, swept his arm over the threshold in case Felix missed the message. He was dismissed.

Felix swallowed his disappointment. He stood and offered George a polite smile and a nod. As he stepped past him, George must have thought better of his brusqueness because he reached out and touched Felix's arm, held him back for a moment.

"My impression of the man," he said, his voice low, "is that he was not in any way suicidal."

Felix turned his head, looked into the man's eyes. He nodded, but George tightened his grip on his arm.

"Do you know what it means for a man who wasn't suicidal to hang himself in jail?"

Felix nodded again. "It means it wasn't a suicide."

CHAPTER TWENTY-EIGHT

"I'm asking you again. Are you sure you're in?"

Sunday evening. Felix paced Rhonda's small living room, back and forth, over and over until she said he was wearing a groove in the floor and forced him to sit.

"What did the lawyer say?" she asked. She got him seated, then went into the kitchenette to snag a couple of beers. She cracked the top on one and handed it to him, sat beside him with her own bottle.

Felix took a deep swallow before answering. He stifled a burp against his fist, the sour yeast heavy against the back of his throat.

"He didn't have much. Very distrustful of the police." He shifted his gaze from the shag carpeting to Rhonda. She watched him with those bright eyes of hers, the slight tilt of the head that made him think of the sparrows who frequented his mother's feeders.

"But?"

"But he didn't think Jack was suicidal."

She furrowed her brow in confusion before the implication hit her a moment later and she widened her eyes.

Felix ran his thumbnail under the edge of the label. "You told me on the drive back from Vicky's. You said, 'Let's find a goddamned murderer.'"

"I remember." Her voice was quiet, edged against timid, and it sounded so unlike her that he lifted his head and watched her. It had been fun, pairing up and paling around. The visit to George Hines sobered him up. It reminded him there were stakes beyond his badge and her job.

"We have to find two murderers now." He peered at her closer, tried to judge her feelings by her expression. He caught the way she swallowed at his words, the quiet gulp as she considered it. The way she squared her shoulders, an infinitely small movement. The way her eyes met his, like she was trying to read him in turn.

"Then we have to find two," she replied. "It's a good thing there's two of us."

*

While Felix and Adam perhaps grated against each other, they never really had an actual argument. He'd known the state detective... what? A handful of days? The irritation had been forgivable, given how they had been two strangers tossed together on a stressful case.

Maybe if the case had stretched on, they would've had a fight. Insulting words tossed over the conference room table, perhaps. Maybe they would have come to blows. Adam was bigger than Felix, and he probably packed a wallop of a punch with all that weight behind his fist. But Felix was quicker, lighter on his feet. He guessed he could have landed a stinging punch or two before he got his ass beat.

Felix would never, ever hit Rhonda, but he wondered if she held the same consideration for him. She certainly *looked* like she wanted to hit him, her fists clenching and unclenching at her sides and her eyes narrowed to slits while they argued.

There was no easy way to split the workload of two cases. Two off-hours, off-the-record cases. The first, a murderer still at-large who was possibly a professional. The second, a possible murder entangled with corruption. Felix wanted Rhonda safe. If he thought that bought him any goodwill for being so chivalrous, he had the wrong girl.

"I'm not made of glass," she spat out.

"I never said you were."

She took the few steps to bridge the distance between them. She jabbed him with her forefinger in the sternum, hard enough to leave a crescent-shaped bruise from her lacquered fingernail.

"I chose to be here, so get over it." She drove the point home with another hard jab to his chest. He caught her hand in his, gripped her wrist to still her before she could poke him again.

"Fine," he grumbled. "Just stop poking me, alright? We can come up with a plan."

*

They assembled their plan over a greasy pepperoni pizza and a six-pack of Straub. The food and beer mellowed them out enough they could argue without coming to blows.

Case one: the unsolved murder of Junior Farney. Felix would focus most of his time on it. He'd start over with the notes Rhonda pilfered. He'd pull her in for a fresh perspective, but he planned on going slowly, carefully. He had the luxury of time now.

Case two: the potential murder of Jack Farney. Rhonda would focus on teasing out the facts from the murk of that night. Rhonda could make quiet inquiries. Her role as a member of the precinct's support staff gave her some coverage. Few people took her seriously, either because she was the receptionist or because she was a woman or both.

"You wouldn't believe the shit people tell you when they think you aren't smart enough to understand them," she said. "I play the dumb broad routine all the time to get the dirt."

"Oh, you *play* at being dumb?" he joked. It earned him a stinging punch to his arm that he rubbed with his free hand. He added, his tone rueful, "You hit really hard."

"Asshole."

He felt more than a little ashamed he'd fallen for the dumb broad routine too. Had he ever considered her as anything more than the receptionist and the precinct's lone woman? He cast his memory back. It was easy to come up with instances when she'd batted her eyelashes, looked coy. Moments when she'd couched her questions in a kittenish "gee, I don't understand all this confusing police work" sort of way.

"I am an asshole," he replied, and he meant it. "What are you thinking for your case?"

She sat her bottle of beer on the table. "*My* case. I like the sounds of that." She reached onto the table for her small notebook. She flipped it open with the ease of a seasoned detective—a consequence of all those cop shows and movies, Felix assumed— and walked him through her plan.

"First, I want to talk to Doctor Miller."

"The coroner?"

"Yes. I assume he would have signed off on Jack's death certificate." A beat. "He's safe, and we get along. If I ask him questions on the hush-hush, he'll keep our confidence."

"That's a good place to start."

"After that?" She shrugged. "We can see where best to focus. I could run through the phone records again to see if I missed anything. I could take a run at Jack's lawyer. He might be more forthcoming with me, since you come across"—she waved her hand vaguely in front of Felix—"like such a cop-like cop."

"What makes a cop cop-like?"

"You know. Short haircut like a G-man. Never smiles. Beady little eyes always staring, like you're waiting for someone to slip."

"My eyes aren't beady," he replied, a little stung at the insult.

"They are when you narrow them. You know, when you're staring a suspect down."

He grumbled that she was rude, but she only laughed and said he was a big boy and could take the criticism.

"Fine," he said. "Keep me updated on what you find out. I'll do the same."

"It's Sunday now. You want to meet back here, say Friday evening after work?"

Felix nodded. He snagged another slice of pizza and turned back to his case notes. "The House Eight," as Adam had called them. Everyone who wasn't family who had access to the Farney home. That's where he would start again.

CHAPTER TWENTY-NINE

C lara's sharp decline never slowed, not even after the funerals. They were one right after the other, son and then father, two mounds of fresh-dug dirt side by side in the family plot. Laura watched Thomas from under the veil of her funeral hat.

This was her reward. She was Thomas Farney's great sea change, the agent that had changed the arc and sweep of his life. At the gravesite, standing over the graves of his son and grandson, realizing his hard work and empire building had been for naught.

The man looked haunted.

Laura went home after the funerals and assumed the familiar position: bare knees on the cold wood floor. She took out her mother's rosary beads, cheap green Bakelite made to look like jade. She rolled each bead in the decade between her fingertips, but she allowed herself to recite the *Mystéria Gloriósa*. The Glorious Mysteries, just this once.

Thomas Farney approached her the month after the funerals with the offer to move into the mansion to care for Clara full-time. She pretended to consider it before agreeing. Of course she'd move in, she told him. Anything you need.

The house fell silent again. The staff was reduced. Thomas kept shorter hours at the factory, so his driver was fired. He drove himself to and from work like any other person.

The gardener was let go. When late winter storms brought down dead branches from the sugar maples, they were left to rot where they lay. One crushed the trellis where Clara's prize-winning Lamarque roses climbed each year. It felt like a portent to Laura, seeing the crushed vines in the dirty snow, the trellis a heap of twisted, rusting metal. The hidden decay and rot brought out into the light.

Thomas fired the two maids. He closed off most of the rooms on the second and third floors. Laura helped Martha with the task, shook out the large drop cloths to cover the furniture. The housekeeper cried to whole time, quiet sniffles and loud, red-faced bawling that ebbed and flowed as they worked.

When Laura cast a backward glance over her shoulder, before the doors were shut tight, the covered furniture looked like ghosts.

The Farney family dwindled. The son and grandson, the heirs of the family, lay in their graves. Abigail had been brought in as part of a business deal between Thomas and her father, as if she and Jack were the children of medieval lords maneuvering for mutual power. An unhappy marriage paired with a foray into motherhood that never took, whether from her own cool character or Thomas's interfering. Widowed and childless, she packed her belongings and returned to New York.

Laura wondered how quickly she put her years in Pennsylvania behind her, and if they would eventually seem like just a bad dream.

✱

The question Laura kept circling in the months that followed: *Why did Jack kill himself?*

Jack's suicide perplexed her. If there were any two people on earth who were certain of who killed the boy, it was her and Jack. He still chose to hang himself before he faced a judge or jury. What did it mean?

Laura gnawed over the question as the autumn turned cold, ceded to winter. She pondered it as the leaves fell, as the sky spat snow and ice that stung the face when one went out in it.

Laura worried at the mystery of Jack's suicide as the tree limbs grew dark with ice, then snowmelt. As the days grew short, scant hours of weak sunlight, the sky swathed in its low grey clouds, she still considered what it meant that Jack Farney killed himself.

Was it God's judgment on her? Laura rarely had crises of conscience, almost always moved with the certainty of her life's work. And yet, when she moved into the mansion and found herself sleepless in her narrow bed, she wondered if her ceaseless ruminating was her conscience.

She'd gotten away with it. She should have felt complete. She prayed each night to the cadence of Clara's shallow breathing in the other room. She prayed until her knees ached, until she felt every single year of her life heavy in her bones when she tried to stand hours later.

"Please," she muttered into her folded hands, though she wasn't sure what her plea was. An answer to the riddle of Jack's suicide? A revelation to what her next step might be? Was her life's work really done now?

She'd always steadily worked her way back to Mariensburg, back to the old patch town of Shale Hollow, back to Thomas Farney, but now that she was here and done, what came next? She couldn't imagine a life without this purpose.

What was she going to do now, if her work was done?

"Please," she begged God on her aching knees. "Please."

The year turned over. Laura marked the time by the world events she saw on the news. Kissinger in Paris to talk about ending the war in Vietnam. Ireland and their interminable troubles, which Martha held numerous opinions about and shared with Laura whenever she wandered into the woman's orbit.

March came. Clara's crushed roses put out a hopeful scattering of green buds, then thought better of it and died. The mansion filled with the sounds of ice-melt dripping from the eaves, the trees around them groaning to life. Storms blew through, sometimes icy rain, sometimes warmer showers that soaked the bare ground and left curling tendrils of grass shoots in their wake.

The town shook off its winter solemnity, but the mansion remained wrapped in its grief, its inhabitants moving in silence. Clara spent more time locked in the past. She chattered about time spent on Long Island with the Phipps, a dinner party in Rhinebeck on the Astor family estate.

Thomas spent fewer hours at the factory. Martha hissed at Laura one afternoon that there were rumors he planned to sell to a Japanese outfit. A disgrace, Martha said, barely thirty years out from the war and the old man was willing to give them a foothold here in their town.

Laura shook her head in outrage along with the woman. She studied the housekeeper closer and saw the disgust on her face, realized Thomas had lost some of his hold on his most loyal soldier.

A small sign, maybe. Not the big answer she had been hoping for from God, but a small one: Thomas Farney still had much to lose, even in the face of so much loss already.

*

Maybe Laura would have puzzled over Jack forever. Maybe the bloom of conscience would have turned to guilt. Maybe her questions about her purpose would have remained unanswered, save for the tiny realization about how far Thomas still had to fall.

She should have never doubted Him. God always answered her, just in His own good time. She had to cultivate more patience.

Laura hadn't been snooping. Late one morning, she needed to use the phone to call in a prescription refill for Clara, so she crept into Thomas's study instead of the kitchen. Martha and Susan had made the kitchen their home base. Martha had far less to manage now that large swathes of the house were closed up, and Susan had fewer people to feed. From late morning to early afternoon, the two women claimed the kitchen as theirs and talked as freely as girls gossiping at recess.

Laura didn't want to get pulled into another tedious discussion about the troubles in Ireland or the potential sale of the factory to the Japanese. She skipped the kitchen phone and ducked into Thomas's study. The old man was at work and wasn't due back for hours. What was the harm?

The few times she had been in his study before the deaths—when he had interviewed her for the nursing position, for example—his desk had been immaculate. A single notepad in front of him, no detritus strewn about.

Now? Snowdrifts of paper covered the desk, loose pages and notebooks and folders with their contents spilled out. A pen leaked onto the expensive wood of the desk and left a sticky pool of ink like an oil slick. An overflowing ashtray with a nub of cigar curled its ghostly scent against Laura's nose.

She pulled the phone toward her. She reached for a blank piece of paper and a pen, and as she sifted through the mound of paperwork, she read what she saw.

Production reports from the factory. A drafted memo to a second-shift supervisor. A receipt for the funeral home, crumpled as if it had been gripped in a fist.

Laura almost missed the notation written on the margin of a time-clock report from August of last year. Thomas had scribbled out the words, sloppy, as if he'd taken a call and reached for the first scrap of paper to take down the notation.

SH. 9/10. 11 pm, wgt stat. 100$ cash.

It was followed by a phone number.

What did it mean? September 10th was the day after Jack killed himself. Why would Thomas have a meeting? *Was* it a meeting, the day after his son died? A meeting near midnight? What did "wgt stat" mean?

Instead of calling the pharmacy, Laura dialed the phone number written in the margins. It rang three times before someone on the other end picked up.

"Detective Beck," the voice said.

Laura's heart stuttered in her chest. "Ah, sorry," she stammered. "I have the wrong number. I was, uh, trying to reach someone else—"

"You looking for Detective Haney?" the voice said, cutting her off. "He retired, ma'am. Is there something I can help you with?"

SH.

Detective Something-or-other Haney.

Laura cast her memory back to the two detectives she'd met with, the Laurel and Hardy pair. Neither of them had that name.

One was Shaffer and the other had some bohunk name full of clashing consonants, started with a *K*.

Laura was no detective, but she pieced together the few clues and came up with a theory: A detective not on the case who had a direct line to Thomas Farney. The day after Jack died in his cell, a late-night meeting somewhere. One hundred dollars, but that was probably just note-taking shorthand. If Laura was guessing correctly, it was probably more like one hundred thousand.

A cool one hundred thousand dollars to murder Jack.

It was speculation. She couldn't prove it, but she *knew* Thomas. She knew his wrath, easily roused. She knew how he used others, especially the police, to do his dirty work.

It was the police who killed her own father, all those years ago.

Nicola lost himself in his grief while Carlo languished in that back bedroom. When the boy finally died and was laid to rest in a cheap pine coffin, Nicola's grief found its purpose.

Laura's father had always been a gregarious man. On the ship over to America, he'd been the unifying force between all those disparate people. He had cobbled together a makeshift deck of cards from torn-up cardboard and taught everyone how to play *Scopa*, led sing-alongs and story-telling contests to pass the time.

That gregarious nature turned to sharp focus after the death of his son. Nicola spent his evenings leading small meetings with other miners, their wrists still ringed with black coal dust, their eyes swollen and red-rimmed from digging in the dark all day.

They could band together, Nicola told them. They could demand safer conditions, better hours. They could demand cash money for their work, not the near-useless scrip that was only good in the company store.

If there was one man who could bring the coal miners together—all those men from disparate places, not a common language among them—it was Nicola DeLuca.

If there was one man who could crush any burgeoning unionizing attempts with a single blow, it was Thomas Farney.

All told, the strike lasted little more than a week. The miners barricaded themselves in their homes, refused to pick up their tools. The constant beehive humming of the mines fell silent for the first time in years. Laura's papa came and went. He held meetings with fellow miners, with representatives of the mining company, but he was home far more than he'd ever been before.

"Things will be better," he promised his wife and his young daughter. He swept his Little Gattina into a tight hug, and for the first time she could remember, he smelled only like himself: the faint scent of homemade soap, the earthy smell of his woolen shirt. The dusty, gritty smell of coal dust was gone.

On the eighth day, Nicola and the striking miners marched through Shale Hollow toward the mining complex as a show of strength. They were unarmed. Nicola, for all his genial nature and his ability to unify, had been tragically naïve about who his opponent really was.

The men—and some of their wives and children alongside them—marched. Past the company store and tailings piles, past the weigh station that stood idle for a week and hadn't weighed a single pound of coal. Up to the gate that led to the entrance to the mine shafts, where men waited for them.

The waiting men wore plain clothing, but Shale Hollow was a small place. Everyone recognized the policemen, even without their uniforms. Their meager numbers had been buttressed by Pinkertons armed with Tommy guns.

Thomas Farney was nowhere near the fight, they'd later find out. He was in New York, courting the woman who would become his wife. The owner of the mines, the one whose word drove the carnage, had been dining at Delmonico's when the bullets tore through the crowd.

The massacre left five dead, nineteen injured. The Black Maria had a busy evening, carting the dead and dying back to their homes. Nicola's body was the last to be returned, late into the night. Laura had been awake, and if she didn't remember when her brother returned to them, the memory of her father's body was seared impossibly deep in that innermost chamber of her heart.

His body wasn't riddled with bullets like some of the other men. He had been returned to them with a deep wound on his neck, the thick line purpled from where the garrote had crushed veins and capillaries before his life had been choked from him.

His body had been the last one removed from the blood-soaked ground, then parked in front of the company store for a long while in the open wagon of the Black Maria. His body had been left as a clear message to the survivors, a testament to what it meant to cross Thomas Farney.

CHAPTER THIRTY

Rhonda always wanted to be a detective.

Well, that wasn't entirely true. She'd originally wanted to be a deep-sea explorer, but with the dearth of oceanic coastline in the middle of Pennsylvania, she had switched her career aspirations to the law.

It seemed possible when she was younger. The receptionist role was supposed to be temporary, a way to learn the ropes on the sly before she approached the captain about taking night classes for her degree. There were women in Congress now. Women ran for the presidency. Surely a lone woman in the ranks wasn't asking too much?

Mariensburg, Rhonda had forgotten, ran a solid decade behind the rest of the country. When she approached Captain Krause with her plan, he'd only stared at her, thought she was joking. She hadn't even tried to approach Captain Winslow yet, but there was a small kernel of optimism in her, bright and hard. She hoped helping Felix wouldn't boomerang around and get her fired, of course... but that bit of optimism flared vivid, made her hope that the consequences would skew the other way and land her a job as a detective instead.

Rhonda knew the coroner. She talked to him when she handled the paperwork that helped usher a newly dead person out of the rolls of the living. She'd always found the man polite. He never tried to look down her blouse, anyway.

He also was no one's fool. He saw right through her when she turned up at the morgue during her lunch break on Monday. She had the flimsiest of stories, a missing form on a recent death. She tried to segue into death in general, and then broached the subject of Jack Farney.

Doctor Miller gave her a long look, tried to peer past her bubbly chattiness to see the real motive behind her visit. "That was months ago."

Rhonda shrugged, hoped it looked nonchalant. "It's strange a boy was murdered, his father killed himself, and there wasn't more about it. Even the paper didn't say much."

He stared a beat longer. Said nothing.

The palms of her hands grew clammy with sweat. She felt her chest prickle with uncomfortable heat, like she straddled the line of trouble. She'd insisted to Felix that she wanted this, that she was all in. Aside from her desire to do this sort of work full-time, she hated to appear weak or scared. She stared back at the doctor, willed herself to keep a neutral face.

"Did you see Jack Farney's body?" she asked. She didn't bother to play it dumb. The doctor was too savvy. "You signed off on the death certificate."

"No," he replied. "I didn't."

She swiped her hands along her thighs, swallowed despite her dry mouth. "What do you mean? You didn't see the body, or you didn't sign the certificate?"

He looked past her, over her shoulder at the closed door of the morgue. There was no one there, but he dropped his voice anyway, took a half step until he stood inches from her.

"Both. I sign off on every death in this county." His eyes bore into hers. "Except one."

"What do you mean?" she repeated it almost mindlessly. The heat prickled further up her neck, underneath her chin and onto her cheeks, and she knew she looked flushed.

The look he gave her was one of pity—not that she was too stupid to understand, but perhaps too naïve.

"I mean I never got to examine the body. I only heard about it after the jail had already released the body to the funeral home. I wasn't involved at all."

"Then who signed off on it?" Rhonda knew of a few instances, rare in her career, where Doctor Miller had been indisposed and an acting coroner—usually another physician from the hospital—filled in.

He shook his head. "No idea. I pulled the certificate after it was filed out of professional curiosity. I didn't recognize the signature. It was a scrawl smeared to illegibility."

Rhonda could piece together most of it. It might seem paranoid in any other case. Signatures were illegible, ink got smeared. Honest mistakes, sloppy filing practices. But it seemed too coincidental, especially given the general deference around Thomas and his family. She thought Jack's death would have been handled carefully, everything aboveboard, but instead it seemed rushed, slipshod.

Like they, whoever *they* were, were hiding something.

Rhonda stopped at the precinct long enough to gather up her things, then marched into Captain Winslow's office.

"I need to take the rest of the day off," she said. "I'm not feeling well."

The man frowned. "We don't have anyone to cover the front desk."

She laid a palm across her belly. "Cramps. Awful ones. My monthly is a few days late, and—"

The captain's forlorn face twisted into a look of disgust. "Stop. Fine. Go. I'll get one of the officers to fill in."

She thanked him, apologized for the inconvenience. As she walked through the bullpen, she glanced over at Felix. He sat at his desk, reading through a folder half-tucked under the blotter. It was probably the notes on the Junior Farney case, studied on the sly.

He must have felt her eyes on him because he glanced up, caught her look. Neither of them said a word, but the message was clear.

They were both on the case.

Rhonda drove back to her apartment, but when she killed the ignition, she sat. The engine cooled and stopped its rhythmic ticking, and the warmth bled off until she could see her breath plume in front of her.

She barely noticed the cold. She ran through the hypothesis she was teasing out.

She knew all about Thomas Farney. Her cousin worked in his factory, and both of her grandfathers had gone into the mines for him. She knew all the stories rehashed around holiday dinners, told like boogeyman tales meant to keep recalcitrant children in line. The darkness of the mine shafts, the low-ceiling rooms that could fill with black damp or afterdamp in an instant. The factory where safety inspectors signed off on leaky furnaces, where the punch clock shaved time off everyone's timecards.

All of it lorded over by Thomas Farney. King Coal himself, back then. Now an indomitable bastard who stood in his office overlooking the production floor, a waning liege lord overseeing his kingdom.

Those boogeyman tales informed her hypothesis. She knew the man was ruthless. She knew he had people in his pocket, police and politicians he slid fat envelopes on the sly. She knew he had people killed without compunction. Some distant great-uncle had been injured by a flying bullet loosed at Thomas's command, back during the miner's strike.

But how did that translate to Jack? Was Jack a victim of the same drive for revenge as the boy had been? Or did Thomas, who held such little regard for human life, have his own son murdered? If he really believed Jack capable of murdering Junior, Rhonda thought he might. If the boy had been poised to be Thomas's heir, she thought the man wouldn't have even blinked to have Jack killed.

Or maybe none of it was right. Maybe Jack, in a jail cell and despairing at the thought of Vicky and his second son being discovered by Thomas, had hung himself. It certainly took pressure off the investigation. Rhonda had to believe that if the case had been allowed to progress, Vicky and Jack Junior would have been discovered.

When she looked at any of those theories in the right light, they seemed plausible.

Jack murdered in his cell as revenge against Thomas.

Jack murdered in his cell at Thomas's order.

Jack dead by his own hand, a desperate attempt to protect the family he had tucked away from the world.

There was one man who might be able to help. Felix had already taken a run at him, but Felix lacked the charm and finesse that Rhonda had. Maybe she could get further with George Hines.

✳

Rhonda arrived in Brockway just as the sun moved past its apex and started its slide into the west. She parked, took a steadying breath. She climbed out of her car and entered the law office of George Hines.

The receptionist's desk was unmanned, so she strode down the hallway—past an empty conference room, a pair of bathrooms—until she reached the man's office. She rapped on the door, and when he called out, she stepped inside.

He looked up, and she forestalled any small talk by saying, "I'm here to talk about Jack Farney, and I'm not leaving until we do."

The man blinked in surprise, blew out a sigh between his pursed lips, but then swept his arm in front of him. He gestured for her to sit down, so she closed the door behind her and did just that.

She told him almost everything, but she kept Jack's second family out of it. Everything else? She spilled it to George. Hers and Felix's hunch that Jack hadn't been suicidal. Her discussion with the coroner and the rushed death certificate signed by an unknown person. How suspicious it was that a man of Jack Farney's stature could die in prison without a single inquiry, a single investigation. Even if it was suicide, there should have been an inquiry, she thought. Guards should have been questioned as to why a man left in their care had been able to hang himself.

"I don't disagree with you, but this is all speculation," he replied when she was done.

"It is. We're hoping to find solid evidence, though."

George narrowed his eyes. "Who's *we*?"

"My partner, Felix."

The lawyer sat back, but he gazed at her in frank appraisal. "You're a detective?"

"No." *Not yet*, she wanted to add. "We're working this off the books."

"Were you friends with Jack?"

"No."

George made a *hmm* noise but didn't add anything.

"You told Felix that Jack wasn't suicidal," Rhonda continued.

"That was just my impression." He gazed at her a beat longer. "You could get into a lot of trouble for this. Why do you care?"

"A child was murdered, and the original case was never solved. Jack died under at least mysterious circumstances. Seems like someone should care," she replied, and it came out sarcastic.

"Of course I care. I liked Jack." George tipped back in his seat again. "Attorney–client privilege extends into death. I'm not sure how much I can help."

She sagged in her seat, muttered she understood. There was nothing here after all.

"I can't tell you what Jack and I spoke about," he continued. He stood up. She thought he was going to dismiss her, but he went to a filing cabinet instead. He opened a drawer, rifled through the folders, then pulled one out. It was thick, and he dropped it on his desk with a loud *thunk*.

"I realized I haven't offered you any coffee," he said. His voice had a casual tone that rang false to Rhonda's ear. "I like to have a cup after lunch. You?"

"I guess." She usually had a pop from the machine in the afternoon to bolster her flagging attention. She didn't care much for coffee but didn't say so.

"Unfortunately, my coffee maker is broken. There's a little café down the street. I'll go get us a coffee, yeah? I'll probably be gone for ten minutes or more."

Rhonda glanced at the thick folder. *Farney, Jack* the label said.

She glanced back at George, took in his unblinking stare.

"I understand you," she said, her voice the same strain of faux casual. "Thank you for the coffee."

CHAPTER THIRTY-ONE

Felix considered his next steps.

He had to reinterview everyone from the first time around, but doing so would spark a maelstrom of gossip. He was especially impatient to track down the housekeeper and dig into her thoughts without the formalities of his detective's shield.

He also guessed Martha couldn't hold a secret to save her life. The minute he talked to her, it'd be like a signal fire burning on a hill: something's afoot with the Farney murder case.

He ran through his list of people to interview and struck on the easiest name. Mr. Castaldo had served as the nurse's alibi. A shut-in with few surviving friends and fewer family members, it seemed a safe bet to start with him. Anyway, hadn't Felix promised to drop in? The man lived only a few streets over from him.

It gave Felix plausible deniability, should anyone ask.

It seemed impossible Mr. Castaldo could look any older in such a short span of time, but his stoop was more pronounced, his cough phlegmier. He got winded as he led Felix into his kitchen. His hands shook more when he poured their instant coffee.

Felix let him talk. Why not? Old people had the best gossip, and gossip was sometimes grounded in fact.

The nurse's alibi was the same. Mr. Castaldo went through his notebook stack (the one from last September was several notebooks ago) and found the page from that night. He slid the book over to Felix who confirmed the man's shaky handwriting. Laura Lucas arrived home the night of the murders around 8:30 and hadn't left until the next morning.

"I thought the case was closed," Mr. Castaldo said as he lifted the cup, trembling, to his lips.

"It's protocol. Paperwork."

Mr. Castaldo took another sip of his coffee. "Tell you something rotten."

"Go ahead."

The man fixed his eyes where his gnarled hands lay on the kitchen table. "I feel bad about that boy, but Old Man Farney had it comin'. The boy, then his son." He glanced up from under his wildly overgrown eyebrows. "That make me a bad person?"

Felix chuckled. "You can take it up with the priest. That's beyond my pay grade."

"Farney had the *malocchio* on him."

"What's that?"

Mr. Castaldo tapped a forefinger under his left eye. "*Maloccchio.* Evil eye. Someone gives you the evil eye, it can curse generations. Not just you but the ones who come after you." He reached under his shirt and pulled out a silver chain. A saint's medal and a small silver cross clinked together faintly. His trembling hands sorted through the pendants, found a small gold twist that looked like a chili pepper.

"*Cornicello,*" he explained. "Protection from *malocchio.*" He stroked the pad of his thumb over the charm, then tucked the entire cluster of pendants back into his shirt, gave it a little pat as it settled over his heart.

"You think Thomas Farney was cursed?" Felix was fascinated by Old World folklore. His mother made the same lentil stew each New Year's Day because it was apparently good luck in Hungary, but none of their holdover traditions extended into curses.

Mr. Castaldo nodded. "Oh, yes. Could be any sort of curse. Not only *malocchio.* People give him the evil eye, but spirits can follow a person. Torment them."

"The miner's strike?" Felix guessed.

"I guess it was '25. No, '26. I remember the man who tried to form the union. A Lombard, northerner, but good folk. He had a boy killed in the mines. Awful business, so he organized the workers. They marched and got fired on by police. The Black Maria was ran damned near to glue, she was so busy those days."

"Who's Black Maria?" Felix asked, bewildered by the history

spilling from the old man's mouth. The further into the past Mr. Castaldo sank, the thicker his accent got. His impeccable English, usually only threaded through with a faintly vague European accent, ceded to a thicker, Latinate one.

"Black Maria was the horse wagon. Ambulance, hearse, whatever. It carted bodies from the mines." He took a shaky sip of his coffee, coughed to clear some phlegm in his throat. "I worked at the weigh station, right at the entrance of the mines. Saw the Black Maria coming and going all the time."

Felix chanced a surreptitious glance at his watch, and he considered making a graceful exit from the old man. For all his time in Mariensburg, though, he only knew a little about its beginnings. His own family had emigrated while the coal mines had been at their peak, but they never worked them. His grandfathers had been well-educated in Hungary, spoke fluent English, so they'd been able to slot themselves into a marginally higher economic class than most of the other immigrants. Working-poor instead of miserable-poor.

And the old man was lonely. Felix could spare the time. There was only one official case on his docket anyway, a missing person case. Felix had a hunch the missing girl had taken off for New York City. He had calls in to the police there and didn't have much else to do.

"Tell me about the mining days," Felix said, and Mr. Castaldo's eyes lit up at the invitation. He got up from his seat, tottered over to a cabinet, and pulled out a package of Fig Newtons. He brought them back to the table and opened them, slid them across the table to Felix.

"Well, back then, the place was just a little town called Shale Hollow," he started. "And me and mine came here from Campania."

By the time he had brought Felix up to the near present, they'd polished off the Fig Newtons and downed more cups of coffee. Felix left with a heady little buzz, the caffeine and the sugar fizzing in his veins.

*

Felix hadn't missed much back at the precinct. He hadn't been missed either. He slipped into the bullpen, and no one seemed to notice him. He sat at his desk and saw the few messages that Rhonda had left for him.

The top one was from a sergeant in the 33rd precinct in New York City. Felix's missing girl had been located, had moved there with friends to make it big in the big city. Felix sighed, called the girl's mother. He informed her that her daughter wasn't dead in a ditch. She was just a victim to the lethal combination of stars in her eyes and the gullible optimism of the young.

The second note was from Rhonda herself. *Stop by tonight* it said. *Mother made dinner.*

Felix started to crumple the note, thought better of it. He smoothed it out, folded it neatly, and tucked it into his pocket. It was a code Rhonda had devised.

Mother made dinner meant she had information she wanted to discuss. *Mother isn't feeling well* meant they should lay low until further notice. It was as far as the secret code went, those two phrases, but if it made her happy, what did it hurt?

CHAPTER THIRTY-TWO

"My mother thinks I'm seeing someone," Felix told Rhonda when he showed up at her door that evening. "I've spent enough nights out she's been calling my brothers to see if they know anything."

He held out a six-pack of beer and a bag of Chinese food like a bouquet. Rhonda relieved him of his armful, then ushered him inside.

"You *are* seeing someone, technically."

"She made a comment about needing more grandchildren."

"Your mom was always a handful," she called from her kitchenette as she heaped two plates with chop suey and egg rolls. "Wasn't she one of the women who protested that movie a while back?"

Felix sank down into her sofa. "*Billy Jack*. And yes."

"What's wrong with *Billy Jack?*" She handed him his plate and a bottle of beer, settled beside him.

"It was a forbidden film according to the Catholic League of Decency," he replied. He flapped a hand at her to dismiss the topic. They could spend a lifetime sorting through Irina Kosmatka's general temperament of being a busybody, of combing through the pop culture landscape for anything ready to corrupt the youth of Mariensburg.

"*Mother made dinner.* Tell me what you've found out," he continued. He took a bite of egg roll, breathed through his mouth as he chewed because it was scalding hot.

"I think Jack Farney was murdered," she said without preamble, and Felix inhaled sharply, choked on a shred of cabbage. He coughed, wheezed out, "What?"

She walked him through it as well as any seasoned detective. As well as she could. She told him about her talk with Doctor Miller, the fact of the compromised death certificate. She told him about her visit with George Hines

"He talked to you?"

The corners of her mouth twitched into a smirk. "Yeah, turns out when you smile at people and don't treat them like they're perps, they're friendly back to you."

Felix started to lift his middle finger, a reflex to all the times his brothers made a joke at his expense. He caught himself, lowered his hand to hide the motion.

"What'd he tell you?" he asked instead.

Rhonda with her easy smiles, her friendly nature. Felix was ashamed he ever doubted her.

She gave him the rundown on George Hines: how they had chatted; how he accidentally, on purpose left his file on Jack behind while he went to run an errand; how Rhonda had ten minutes ("They flew by so fast like you wouldn't believe," she told him) to glean whatever she could.

Ten minutes turned out to be plenty to realize that Jack Farney—mediocre, middling Jack, disappointment to his leonine father—was not as inept as everyone thought. Not quite as spineless, either.

"He was helping George build this massive case against his father," Rhonda said. "He fed him information for months. Memos about mine runoff in the groundwater. Stuff that proved Thomas knew how bad it was and did nothing. Evidence about payoffs to state officials to keep it under wraps."

Felix scooted forward on the sofa and said, "Wait, a case about water contamination?"

"Yes. Those farmers. George took their case, and Jack fed him all this evidence behind the scenes."

"Holy shit." He sat back again, raked a hand through his hair. That's where he knew George Hines from. The farmers had listed him as their alibi, another attendee of their charity dinner the night Junior Farney was killed.

"You and Adam had been circling around it. You just didn't have enough time to get all the way there."

"Did Thomas know about this?"

Rhonda reached for her beer, took a drink. She stifled a

delicate little burp against the back of her hand. "After George got back with our coffee, he admitted that he'd been getting a lot of hang-up phone calls at home and in his office. He said Jack thought someone was following him."

"But why didn't George go to the authorities? Poisoned water, bribery... that's criminal."

The look she shot him was a blend of incredulity and pity. Perhaps he still had a shred of innocence left to lose.

"A criminal investigation would have been buried. Come on, Felix. Farney paid off politicians all the way in Washington. A civil case was the best route, Jack and George thought. They have the cancer cluster of those families near Stinking Creek. George had notes. He thought the case would get bigger once they got into the discovery phase. The entire city is built on top of those mines. We've all been drinking from the same reservoir, breathing the same air."

"Mariensburg as a cancer cluster." Felix thought of his grandparents and their battles with cancer, all those miserable visits to the hospital when he was a child. Mr. Castaldo and his wet gasping, each inhale a battle in his narrow chest.

Rhonda snorted, a bitter sound. "Thomas Farney as a cancer." She took another sip of her beer, added, "That's not all."

"Tell me."

"George knew about Vicky and Jack Junior. Jack told him everything. They had a... well, I guess you could call it a nuclear option. Jack was always paranoid about Thomas finding out about Jack Junior. An heir and a spare, I guess."

"We have to be very careful now. If Thomas finds out he has a grandson out there..."

"Exactly." Rhonda nodded her head, vehement. "Jack built this nuclear option with George, basically. If Thomas ever found out about Jack's second family, he had a plan to get them over the border into Canada. Vicky's from Quebec, so it would have been easy enough. There was money set aside in offshore accounts, a restraining order... a whole thing."

"To protect them." Felix shook his head. "Poor man."

He missed the punchline; Rhonda elbowed him, jostled him to keep him from sinking into a fit of ruminating.

"Hence what I told you. I think Jack was murdered. Think about it. He had this whole master plan in case things went toes up. He probably thought he'd have to get Vicky and Jack Junior out of harm's way because he was feeding evidence to George. Junior being murdered threw a wrench in that, but only for a bit. My guess, Jack didn't give up his real alibi because he wanted to buy a little time to see Vicky and Jack Junior safe."

Felix set his plate down, his appetite gone. "That's why he was adamant about getting his lawyer to the jail."

"If he was trying to put his plan in motion, I'm certain he wasn't suicidal."

"So, what then?" He ran a hand through his hair again. "Someone murdered him in his jail cell. Who? And at whose orders?"

Rhonda's expression was somber. "You can probably guess the latter." She pointed at the ledger book on her coffee table. "And I have a theory about the former."

"At Thomas's orders," Felix replied. "But who did the deed?"

She sat her own plate down, and the grave cast to her face spoke to a similarly vanished appetite. She turned her beer bottle around and around in her hands, didn't look him in the eyes when she asked, "Don't you think it's strange that Haney left right after the case was closed?"

It took Felix's mind a long moment to catch what she implied. He never liked Haney, always thought him a lazy asshole. It didn't jibe, though, a lazy asshole going to the trouble of murdering Jack Farney. He told Rhonda so.

She didn't argue. She only toyed with her beer bottle, a nervous tic of restless energy as Felix let the theory percolate.

Haney the lazy asshole, but also Haney the gossip. Haney skulking in the shadows. Felix thought back to that final evening. Sweating Jack's false alibi, picking Jack up and putting him on a hold when he refused to speak. Haney creeping around the perimeter that whole day, the whole evening. He'd even been in the conference room at one point, chatting up Adam.

Probably more too. The conference room had never been locked down, only set apart. Who could say the weasel-faced little fuck hadn't been in there, studied their board?

Their board always pointed to Jack Farney. The shaky alibi. The speculations about possible MOs. Him and Adam spitballing about greed, about Jack being jealous of his own son, about the fortune at stake. All of it written down for anyone to study and report back to Thomas.

Hell, did Haney even need to study their board? They'd sent him out as their errand boy, had him running down the shit-work. He'd been at the edge of the investigation the whole time.

A bead of sweat trickled between Felix's shoulder blades. Of course it made sense. Haney and his fun-guy, goofy fucking routine. No one ever took him seriously. Haney and his low-level grifting. Always cheating his timecard by five minutes for the few extra bucks, always taking advantage of free coffee, free meals from businesses who supported the boys in blue.

"I know damned well he didn't get his full pension," he muttered. "It's all he ever talked about. Counting down until he could retire."

"He probably got a payoff. I mean, he obviously did. Why else would he do it?"

Felix grunted in agreement.

Rhonda retrieved the ledger book of Thomas Farney's sins. She set it on her lap and tapped it with one pink-painted fingernail.

"I read through it," she said. Her soft voice turned angry, too, her words shaky. "It's awful stuff, Felix. If Thomas thought Jack really killed that little boy, his heir, of *course* he'd have him murdered before anything could go to trial."

"We have to think about how to approach this," Felix replied.

He felt a sudden wave of guilt at the guileless way she gazed back at him. She was a civilian—more than just the receptionist, and a damned fine investigator in her own right—but she wasn't trained for trouble. Best case, she earned a suspension from Winslow for tampering in police business.

Worst case? Maybe Winslow was in Farney's pocket too. Felix had grossly underestimated Haney. Perhaps he underestimated Winslow, too, failed to see malice or greed behind that long, doleful face. If Winslow was on Farney's payroll, Rhonda could be in danger. Would her brakes get cut some night? Would she get run off the road, or would some rough trade hired by Thomas follow her home?

Felix could try to cut her loose, but she was stubborn. She wouldn't go quietly. No, it was better to keep her close where he could protect her.

They sat in silence for a long stretch until Rhonda stood up. She took away their half-full plates and empty bottles, tidied up as they talked.

"That covers Jack Farney," she called over her shoulder. She stood in the kitchenette, scraping the plates into the garbage before setting them aside. "What about your case?"

He slumped against the sofa and groaned. He had far less progress to share. "I reinterviewed one single alibi, and most of that was old town history."

The sound of running water, the clatter of cutlery. "What do you mean?"

"The nurse's alibi is this lonely old man. I felt bad because he doesn't have many people, so I sat and talked with him."

The running water cut off, and Rhonda walked back into his line of sight. She held a damp sponge in one hand, dish soap bubbles frothing down her forearm. "That's sweet. Sitting with him, I mean."

"He thought Thomas had it coming to him. Thought he had the evil eye placed on him."

Rhonda nodded sagely and pointed one soapy finger at the ledger book. "There's a whole book's worth of evil eyes there."

"He told me about the miner's strike."

"Yeah, Krause's predecessor noted it. It's about halfway through the book. Three whole pages of notes and amounts for the payoffs."

"Mr. Castaldo told me Thomas hired the police to break the strike."

Rhonda shifted her hand to rest on her hip. She made a disgusted noise in the back of her throat, a guttural *tsch* sound. "Yeah, he strangled the union organizer guy to send a message to the other miners. Garroted him." She mimed the motion across her own slender neck, pantomimed choking herself with a taut wire while she made harsh death rattle in her throat.

"What?" The words *send a message*, her pretending to be strangled dislodged something in his head. A ghostly finger traced down the knobs of his spine until the hair on the back of his neck stood up.

She turned back toward her sink of dirty dishes and called out, "It's in the book. Halfway through. The police captain kept impeccable notes."

Felix swallowed down a greasy, sesame-flavored burp. He opened the ledger, paged through. He saw the familiar names as he flipped past—names of his neighbors, names of people he went to school with—until he found Captain Fontaine's notes.

It was too similar to be coincidence. What had he said, those long months ago in Krause's office? *The past may illuminate the present.* Hadn't one of his theories hinged around the staging of the body? The deep-sliced throat once the boy was dead. He himself had called it overkill...

"But it was a message," he said. He read Captain Fontaine's spidery cursive, the once-black ink faded to brown after damned near fifty years.

N. DeLuca it said. *Labor organizer. Garroted. Left in wagon outside co. store for miners to see, then returned to family.*

The man strangled and left with a gruesome wound for all to see, a message for other miners.

The boy poisoned and left with a gruesome wound for all to see, a message for Thomas Farney.

✱

Part of the problem had been the speed with which the original case had unraveled. Felix and Adam only had those handful of days back in September. Jack had been killed, the scene had been staged as a suicide, and the district attorney had closed the case suspiciously fast.

They could prove exactly none of it.

"I bet the district attorney is in Thomas Farney's back pocket," Rhonda said. "He's got political aspirations. Everyone knows that."

"Which rules out going to him to reopen the case." Felix's mood swiveled wildly. One moment, he felt as though he and Rhonda were cornered. They made solid connections that would go nowhere, would die in the darkness without ever being dragged into the light.

But the next moment, he felt electrified. The original spark of hope when he caught the case, and how it might be his ticket out of Mariensburg. That spark was tempered now by something less selfish.

It was the names in the ledger book. The miners from before, the factory workers now. The farmers with their spaghetti dinners to raise money for one of their own. The good people like the barflies at the Roadhouse who helped a teenaged girl with her homework when her home was too dangerous. The good people like Mr. Castaldo, like his mother's church friends. His brothers. Rhonda. Krause with his rot-gut whiskey and generous use of the word *fuck*.

Underneath the virtuous flush of feeling, an icy-cold rage simmered. These were his friends and family, his neighbors. Thomas Farney had lorded over them for so long, had poisoned their town to make his fortune. He twisted and poisoned his own family, and the violence had spilled outward, corrupted others.

Aside from how quickly the original case had spiraled out of control, the fact remained that neither he nor Adam had considered revenge as a real possibility. They had toyed with the idea of a message being sent, touched on it but never really explored it. They thought of the mafia and their paper game, debts due to gambling. They thought of drug dealers at the country club.

They never considered the entire population of Mariensburg,

formerly Shale Hollow. The ledger book spoke to how many families Farney had hurt, irrevocably altered.

The past always felt further away than it actually was. Felix thought of the past as sepia-tinted antiquity, but many of the miners were still alive. Mr. Castaldo remembered the strike firsthand. Others probably did too. And their children were only in their forties or fifties, not much older than him.

Still young enough to do harm to a child. Old enough to let their vengeance cool and refine for decades before they unleashed it.

"I think we have to track down what happened to the DeLuca family, as a start," Felix said.

Rhonda finished washing up and joined him on the sofa, her hands damp and faintly scented from the lemon dish soap. "I can dig into it," she said.

"What's your plan?"

"Easiest place is the phone book. Even if they were evicted, maybe someone else took them in. Family, you know. If that's the case, maybe they stayed local this whole time."

"I doubt Farney would be sympathetic to anyone housing them, but it's worth a shot."

"I planned to go to the county courthouse for work anyway. Maybe I can poke around old property records or something."

Felix liked that plan. It got Rhonda farther away from George Hines and his case-building against Thomas, away from Jack's murder. Away from corruption within the police. But a second later, his brain replayed her words, singled out *courthouse*.

"Wait." He held up a palm. "What's your cover story if you start poking through old records?"

Rhonda shot him that irreverent smile she used to have when she called him *Puss*. "Have a little faith in me. Didn't I find the pattern in the phone records that kicked this whole thing off again?"

She had, and Felix did. He had faith in her, more than anyone else, but when he told her so, she chucked him hard on the shoulder and accused him of going soft on her.

CHAPTER THIRTY-THREE

The phone book was a bust. Rhonda checked hers that night and didn't find a single *DeLuca* listed. The list went straight from *Delonge* to *DeMarco*.

The courthouse was a bust too.

The regular clerk, the one Rhonda held a friendly rapport with, was off for the day. The woman filling in was less than helpful, bordering on outright suspicious.

"What do you need?" she asked. She examined Rhonda over the rims of her glasses, a blatant scan from the soles of her pumps to the top of her hair. The sour expression on her face made it clear she found Rhonda lacking.

She fumbled her way through her planned story, an accounting of her father and disputed property lines, which was near enough to the truth, considering how often her father had tried to twist the law to his favor. The clerk sighed, gave her a baleful glare in return, and said there were no walk-ins for the recorder of deeds. She'd have to make an appointment.

Rhonda thanked her. She left as quickly as she dared, slow enough to not seem suspicious but fast enough to get away. Her armpits were slick with nervous sweat. The feeling of being watched crept over her. It took all her strength not to break into a dead run back to her car.

Back at the precinct, she sat at her desk and let her racing pulse calm.

She contemplated the question more rationally.

The county records would likely be a bust anyway. The ledger book implied the DeLuca family—what had remained of them, anyway—had been evicted after the miner's strike. Rhonda knew enough about the bad old days. Everything in the South Side had been owned by the mines, so property records were useless. The DeLuca's never owned their home.

Likewise with most other records at the courthouse. She could probably track down birth certificates for any children, and death certificates for the man and the boy, but both forms were staid, useless bits of information. They gave no intel on the survivors' movements after their eviction.

She gnawed at her thumbnail. A filthy habit, one she usually could abstain from, but when she felt anxious, she fell back into it. She bit too far and tore the nail to the quick. She hissed out a curse before she put the tip of her thumb back into her mouth to soothe the sting.

What next? She knew the library had telephone directories of the towns surrounding Mariensburg. Maybe she could try that. She also had her contact at Bell, though she didn't want to burn too many favors. There were census records, more uniform and reliable since the federal government ran them. They were only released to the public after an outrageous amount of time, though. She doubted any records from 1930 or 1940 were available yet.

Her mind drifted. The DeLuca family, faceless in her mind's eye, transformed into her own family. They had migrated here, too, worked the same mines. It could have just as easily been her family evicted, thrown out into the cold. Where would they have gone? Back to Hungary, their American sojourn chalked up as an ill-advised adventure? Even if they wanted to, they probably wouldn't have. They had been desperately poor. They wouldn't have been able to afford the fare.

Not to another mine. Little outfits littered the area, though most ended up owned by Thomas Farney. A widow with an indeterminate number of children wouldn't go to another patch town anyway. She'd move to where there was work for women, where there were houses to keep or clothing to take in for laundry or sewing. Piece-work at a factory. Hell, even prostitution.

"Pittsburgh or Philadelphia," she muttered. "If she stayed in the state. If not, it's anyone's guess."

An option dawned on her slowly, bit by bit as she imagined the fortitude of a woman alone in the world. A woman packing her meager belongings and her children. Striking out on her own in an unfriendly country where she likely didn't speak the language.

A woman so dangerously close to the precipice would find solace in her church. Didn't parishes keep rolls of their congregants? Not just the births and deaths, but the baptisms and marriages?

When a congregant joined the parish. When they moved away.

It was worth a try. Saint Boniface was the Italian and Irish church in town and had been there as long as the patch town had existed. They might have something useful for her.

✱

Rhonda visited Saint Boniface during her lunch break the next day. The historically Italian and Irish Catholic church sat on one end of the South Side while Saint Callistus—the church of the Poles and Hungarians—sat on the other end. Rhonda had been a semi-regular at Saint Callistus as a child. Her mother went through periods of abject guilt and used to drag Rhonda to Mass in the hopes that some time with the Lord could cure all that ailed her.

This marked the first time Rhonda had stepped foot in a church since her mother passed. She half expected some flood of emotion, lingering guilt or sadness, but she only felt the slightest uptick in her pulse as her heels clicked across the floor of the office building.

The church secretary was cut from the template of church ladies everywhere. She wore a tightly permed helmet of blue-rinsed curls, thick-framed glasses, and a distrusting scowl as Rhonda approached.

The scowl, at least, faded away by degrees as Rhonda laid out her story about researching long-lost family. It was as near the truth as any lie could be. She felt a kinship with the DeLuca family. She felt a kinship with everyone listed in that damned ledger book, all the grandparents and great-grandparents and long-lost family of people she'd known her whole life.

"I wish I could help you, honey," the woman replied once Rhonda finished her spiel. "But all the records from back then got ruined when a pipe burst in the rectory basement." She shook her head, rueful, then added, "You could always reach out to the diocese, you know. They keep immaculate records in Erie."

Rhonda's heart sank, but she kept her smile etched on her face. The last thing she wanted to fuss with was the diocese. She pictured a hive of priests bustling about in some dark, cavernous building full of old books. She doubted they'd take time out of their ecumenical duties to help a lapsed Catholic like her on a snipe hunt to find a long-lost family—though she wryly thought shepherds finding lost lambs was sort of their whole deal.

"I appreciate your help," she told the secretary. She wished her a good afternoon, then left.

She didn't return to her car. The weather was still cool, but the sun hung in the sky like a pale gold coin. When she tilted her face, she felt the warmth of it on her cheeks, her forehead. It was difficult to lose heart when the hope of summer was right in front of her.

She had time to kill. She didn't want to go back to work yet, where her sad ham sandwich and can of Fresca waited for her. Instead, she walked around the side of the church and strolled through the cemetery.

Cemeteries never creeped her out. She always found them tranquil, their occupants far more peaceable than their still-breathing counterparts. Even if she was a lapsed Catholic now, she tried to visit her mom's grave to keep it clean.

The cemetery at Saint Boniface was serene too. The trees lining the path dampened the noise from the road. Rhonda walked, read the inscriptions on the stones. The farther she walked, the deeper back in time she went. From the recently buried, the dirt still mounded on the graves, to the older plots with worn stones and slight depressions in the grass. The war dead with their faded flags rippling in the breeze. The tiny stones that marked the infants, the heartbreaking inscriptions where their birth and death dates were the same.

Farther back, the graves became lonelier. They had a derelict, neglected air, as if no one stopped by anymore to weed them or to stop the lichen from taking hold. Rhonda read the names, the dates, and saw the deeper she walked into the cemetery, the closer she came to those bad old days of Shale Hollow.

These were the graves of those immigrants, the ones who settled the area. They weren't marked by granite or polished marble. It was a motley assortment of cheaper stuff—flat bits of slate with names carved by careful hands. Sandstone with their legends fully eroded. A family of wooden crosses, four in a row, the wood grey and splintered with age.

She would have missed it if it weren't for the flowers. The cemetery was still dun and grey from the winter. Only a few green shoots poked aboveground. Rhonda turned to head back to her car—her grumbling stomach reminding her of her missed lunch—but a bit of color flashed in the corner of her eye. She stopped, turned, looked closer.

A bright purple bouquet lay incongruous among the dead grass, wrapped in matching cellophane. A clutch of hyacinths, tight clusters of curling little flowers, and at first, she felt a wash of love for whoever left them. It lightened her heart to see the long dead remembered, still loved by the living, even in this forlorn part of the cemetery.

Her eyes shifted upward to see the name etched on the stone—a far more modern stone than its neighbors. A far nicer stone of polished grey marble. *DE LUCA*, it said.

"Holy shit," she blurted out, and she took the handful of steps from the path to the gravestone, her heels sinking into the thawing ground. "Holy *shit*," she repeated, louder, when she read the rest of it.

NICOLA PADRE NATO A 1893 MORTO A 1926
MARIA MADRE NATO A 1894 MORTO A 1936
CARLO FIGLIO NATO A 1914 MORTO A 1925

They were right here, the names in the ledger book.

"Holy shit," she whispered a third time, and even though she was out of practice for several years now, she crossed herself and mumbled a prayer over the graves of the DeLuca family.

CHAPTER THIRTY-FOUR

Felix knew Rhonda struck on something when she called his desk. She told him to meet her outside in the narrow alley where some of the cops smoked in the warmer months.

If she was dispensing with her coded notes, it meant something big. He played it as cool as he could, gathered his coat, and walked at an easy saunter through the bullpen and outside.

Whatever she'd found, she practically vibrated with excitement. Or anxiety. Or both. She shifted on her feet, back and forth, back and forth. She looked like a boxer dancing in the ring, ready to dole out some of her stinging punches.

"You found them?" he asked, his voice low. He kept his head on a swivel, scanned the alley and the adjacent street for anyone who might be watching. There was no one.

"Yes and no." Rhonda's voice held the faintest tremor, like she was edging against some stronger emotion. Like she might be on the verge of tears or laughter.

Felix lifted his hand and rolled it in a circle, gestured *go ahead.*

"I found where they're buried," she said. "I stood at their graves."

The buoyancy of hope for a brief second, then the crashing disappointment a second later when her words sunk in. "I'm not sure how that helps," he replied. He tried to keep his tone level, gentle. "We guessed at least the father and the son were buried here."

"And the woman, the mother. She's buried here too." Rhonda paused. Her eyes swept along the perimeter of the narrow alley before they found Felix's. "She died in 1936, so they maybe stayed in the area after the massacre. Or came back."

Nineteen thirty-six was closer, at least. Nineteen thirty-six put them less than forty years away from the DeLuca's last known whereabouts. Marginally better than almost fifty years, he guessed. But it didn't help them with any living DeLucas, the obliquely mentioned *family* in the ledger book.

Did Nicola and Maria have more sons who held the score all these years? Felix knew families immigrated in clumps, cousins and grandparents and even neighbors clustered into little clans. Were they even looking for a DeLuca or some other relative with a different surname? Or a neighbor?

"How about the courthouse?" he asked.

"It was a no-go. My friend wasn't there today." She shrugged. "Anyway, everything was owned by the mine back then. Property records wouldn't help."

"There's birth records. It would help us figure out if the DeLucas had more children who—"

"Stop." Rhonda shot her hand out and grabbed his wrist, squeezed him into silence. "Listen. I found their grave plot."

"I know, but—"

The pressure on his wrist tightened, like a steel band cutting off his circulation. "They're buried in the old section of the cemetery," she said, and she stared at him hard. "It's nothing but old stones, worn down and neglected. But not theirs. Theirs is nice, polished marble. Clean."

"Okay..." He felt the gears in his head engage. He picked up her line of reasoning. "You think someone put a nicer stone there later on?"

"Happens all the time, right? Someone dies and the family is poor, so they leave that little metal one the funeral home gives out. Years later, they have the money, so they put in a proper stone."

"It could confirm there was another DeLuca child who survived. Once he grew up and got a job, he put a real stone in for his family."

Rhonda released her hold on him. "Exactly."

"There's only one place in Mariensburg to get gravestones," he mused. He thought back to when his father died. He remembered signing forms in triplicate, a subtle panic he might have spelled his own father's name wrong—

"There were fresh flowers on the grave," Rhonda said, interrupting his thoughts.

His heart knocked uncomfortably against the inside of his chest at her words. His mouth gaped open like a trout, but Rhonda didn't tease him for it. Her own eyes shone as she gazed back at him, her head nodding faintly as she watched her intel sink in.

"Fresh flowers," she repeated. "Or fresh-ish. I don't know about Saint Boniface, but at Saint Callistus, the sexton cleans the graves once a week. Puts new candles into the votives—"

"Throws out the old flowers," Felix finished. He knew that. His mother complained about it. She had a conspiracy theory that the sexton took the nicer arrangements home before they wilted. She'd put a poinsettia on Felix's father's grave that had turned up missing—a mystery her church friends chewed over for months.

"If there's fresh flowers on their grave," she started, and her faint nodding got stronger as he put it together too.

"Then whoever is leaving them is local."

"And he'll leave them again," she added. Her hand, chilled from the March weather and her lack of gloves, reached out and grasped his wrist again. "We're close, Felix. I bet he leaves them every week. We need to catch him."

His heart rate sped up until he felt the hot flush creeping over him, adrenaline being dumped into his system. He and Adam had never been this close. The case had spiraled out of their control, but they'd been pointed in the wrong direction the whole time. How long would it have taken them to get turned this way—not toward the future the slain boy had represented, the heir skipping over his father, but instead back to the past where revenge had cooled and refined over decades?

"It's your lead again," he said, and his own voice held the same tremor of excitement Rhonda's did. "Ever want to do a stakeout, Detective Kormos?"

✱

It was as easy as an anonymous call to Saint Boniface, asking when their sexton cleared away the detritus in the cemetery. The answer? Every Thursday, unless there were an inordinate number of graves to dig any particular week.

"I bet he leaves fresh flowers on Sundays," Rhonda said. "Before or after Mass."

Felix hedged against his flaring optimism. He tried to dampen it by pointing out that maybe their suspect wasn't a local. Maybe it was a one-time thing. He remembered their church did a thing each Memorial Day where they took a second collection to put flowers on everyone's grave, regardless of age or lack of living relatives.

He warned Rhonda not to get her hopes up, that this was a long shot anyway. It was the flimsiest of hunches, a decades-old grudge they assumed came home to roost. Even if it was revenge for the massacre, it could be a different family. Others had been killed. Plenty more had been injured. It could even be someone who hadn't been in the fracas at all. Perhaps it was a child who had lived through it, seen the bodies and blood-soaked ground. Perhaps time had warped and twisted their mind.

Adam had called it psychopathic. Wasn't psychopathy rooted in traumatizing childhoods? Felix had read a write-up on Charles Manson, how his childhood had been rife with abuse and neglect.

Hell, he knew his own tame childhood had molded some of his neuroses. Thanks to that intense period when he was a boy, visiting his dying grandparents, he now felt a near-irrational fear of hospitals: his stomach churned, and his skin got clammy with fearful sweat each time he had to visit the morgue.

He told Rhonda all of this. He wanted to hedge *her* optimism too. He didn't want her disappointed if a lead went up in smoke, though he supposed if she were serious about this sort of work, she'd have to get used to it.

"No way," she replied with a shake of her head so hard her hair whipped her in the face. "I can feel it in my gut."

Now he knew how Adam felt with a green investigator making an assured claim about the infallibility of their so-called gut. Felix rolled his eyes.

"Calm down, Columbo," he said, and it earned him another surprisingly hard jab to the bicep as she punched him. He rubbed his arm and considered if the nickname "Roadhouse" didn't quite apply anymore, he could call her "Right Hook" instead.

*

They took turns staking out the cemetery, though the bulk of it fell to Rhonda. With the weather improving every day, she spent her lunch hours perched on one of the splintering park benches that lined the path. She spent swaths of her weekend there, too, tucked into her coat with a Len Deighton paperback clutched in her hands.

"I sit near a guy named Mancini. He died in the First World War at the age of nineteen. I keep him company."

"I'm sure he appreciates it," Felix replied. It earned him a withering glare, which stung as much as her mean little punches and jabs.

"It's important to honor the dead," she chided. "You'll want someone to tend your grave when you're gone."

Felix doubted it. He had a suspicion he wouldn't much care once he was dead.

Rhonda bore most of the cemetery surveillance, and Felix chipped away at reinterviewing everyone who had access to the Farney mansion. The DeLuca's were a long shot. The revenge angle could be a long shot. It didn't hurt to keep other irons in the fire.

He went slow, kept it methodical and under the radar. He couched it as boring paperwork, necessary red tape to officially close a case. No one seemed to question it. He found that many of the employees at the mansion were former employees now, months later. None of the ones he managed to reinterview had much love for Thomas Farney. Their alibis stood, but there was added bitterness.

Fresh flowers turned up on the graves a week later, but they missed whoever left them. The purple hyacinths were gone, replaced by cheery yellow daffodils.

"I was wrong," Rhonda whispered over the phone to him at work that Monday afternoon. "I don't think he leaves them on

Sundays after Mass. I think he leaves them on Fridays, after the sexton sweeps through."

"I guess that makes sense," Felix replied. He kept his words carefully bland. The new detective, Beck, sat across from him. He was engrossed in a handful of cold cases he'd pulled to keep himself busy, but Felix felt the familiar prickle of anxiety. Who knew if Beck was trustworthy? He barely knew the man at all. He only knew he played second base for the barrack's softball team, which didn't speak to where his loyalties may lie.

"Take off next Friday. I'll take off too. We can stake it out together and finally catch him."

Felix leaned back in his chair and considered it. He did have plenty of sick days banked, and his current caseload was appallingly light.

"I can handle that." He hung up and saw Beck watching him.

"Lawyers, right?" Felix said, and he made a jacking-off motion that startled a laugh out of the other detective before he turned back to his cold case file.

✷

The Friday stakeout began in Felix's car. He backed it into a space near the cemetery. He reasoned they'd see anyone coming in or out.

The morning of the stakeout, and though the sun had risen, the sky remained dark. Fleecy grey clouds hung low and pregnant with spring rain. It cast the entire scene—the cemetery, the church off to the side with its elderly congregants doddering in for early services—in a depressing light.

"It's Good Friday," Rhonda reminded him. She had an honest-to-god picnic hamper at her feet, and she reached down and pulled out a thermos. She poured something into the metal cap and handed it to him. He took a sip. It was too sweet, heavy-laced with sugar, but she brewed her coffee strong the way he liked it.

Felix knew what day it was. His mother had been on her usual Lenten oppression campaign for the past weeks. She stunk up the house with fish fries from Saint Callistus, harped on him for not accompanying her to Stations of the Cross. Clucked her tongue in disappointment because he hadn't given anything up for Lent. When she had pressed him, he tried to joke and say he gave up Catholicism, which sent her into a paroxysm of sputtering outrage.

They settled in for the stakeout. Felix offered to turn the car on, maybe play the radio, but Rhonda waved him off. She said she liked the quiet sometimes.

"Helps me think," she said.

She reached back into her hamper and pulled out a box of doughnuts, a half dozen they polished off between them in no time at all. They finished the coffee too. Felix ratcheted his seat back and stretched until his back popped.

They watched some more.

The skies cleared without a drop of rain spilled. The clouds scudded away, pushed by a stiff breeze. They were replaced by white ones high in the atmosphere, wispy and feathery as brush strokes. The sun turned his car into a hot box, so they climbed out, dusted off the powdered sugar from the doughnuts, and made their way through the cemetery. They kept their pace casual, a friendly stroll, and Rhonda linked her arm through Felix's to make them seem cozier.

"Stop being such a cop," she said.

"What am I doing wrong this time?"

"You're too stiff. And you have your head on a swivel. Act *normal*."

She led him to the bench she now considered hers, and he saw she'd been savvy about it. The path curved around the cemetery in a rough oval, and Rhonda's bench sat right on a curve, tucked back behind a gnarled old oak. It was the perfect vantage point to keep an eye on the DeLuca plot, which stood a ways away, without being obvious about it.

"This is George." She swept her hand at the grave to the left of them. "He keeps me company on my lunch hours."

Felix turned and looked at the stone. Private George Mancini, died in 1918 in the last year of the war. The little metal stake holding the American flag was tarnished, but the stone was clean, and a fresh candle flickered in the red votive.

The sight sent a wave of some indefinable emotion through him. Melancholy, maybe, at the paltry memorial for such a young man, a boy who'd died before he'd ever really lived. Love, maybe, for whoever cleaned his grave and left a candle burning for him. He could guess who it was.

"This your doing?" he asked, pointing at the candle.

She lifted her shoulders in an embarrassed shrug, turned her head away. "No one seems to remember him." A beat. "I know that sounds stupid."

"Nah." It was sweet, but he'd never admit it to her. She'd chuck him in the arm and call him a sap, and his arm was already bruised from her abuse.

They sat. Neither of them spoke. Felix found he liked it, how the two of them could sit in companionable silence and neither felt the need to fill the quiet with mindless chatter. It was half of the battle with dating, when he had the time for it: the struggle to keep the conversation moving, the sweaty palms and flush of embarrassment when he ran out of things to say.

The cemetery was peaceful in the late morning. The sun cast everything in a soft light. Spring had arrived quick and fierce in the past few days. The budding green of the trees, the snowdrops and crocuses pushing through the ground gave the place a hopeful feel despite it being a resting place for the dead.

Rhonda jostled him after a long stretch, nudged him with her elbow. "Church let out."

"That was a damned long service." He turned his head and hoped it looked natural. Not like a cop. He saw the same parishioners from earlier, mostly the old. They dawdled by the entrance and in the parking lot, chatting in their somber coats and hats.

"Well, it's Good Friday," she replied. "Of course it's..." She saw something he didn't see yet. She nudged him again.

"Here," she breathed out. "Look."

He wasn't sure how they missed her before. They'd nearly

missed her again when she left the church because she didn't dawdle like the other parishioners. She returned to her car—but she didn't leave. She only went to retrieve a fresh bouquet of flowers.

She took the farther portion of the looping path toward the old section of the cemetery, away from where Felix and Rhonda sat. She walked with purpose, her arms full of white lilies, and the sight of her seized Felix's brain to a grinding halt that only released when Rhonda dug her fingers into his arm.

"A woman?" she whispered. Her voice sounded incredulous. "Wait, do I know her?"

Of course she did. They all knew her. She'd been at the police precinct, had given her statement. All this fucking time, Felix and Adam, then Felix and Rhonda, fussing with the corners and edge pieces of the puzzle, just for everything to fall into place all at once.

It made no sense. Did it? Felix reached back, tried to remember her statement at the precinct. Nothing sinister pinged, but Christ almighty, they'd never once suspected a *woman*, it had always been Jack or surly farmers or a presumed vengeful DeLuca son—

Never a woman. Never a *nurse*.

Never the person with access to the house. Never the person who knew Junior, who could have plied him with laced chocolate milk because the boy knew her, trusted her.

He watched as Laura reached the graves and laid the flowers at the marker of the DeLuca family. Another puzzle piece, far too late to do much good. *DeLuca, Lucas*. The last name scrubbed of its subtle ethnic flavoring. He watched as she stood there with her head bowed. He watched as she turned back toward the path that led to her car.

"Felix, she looks familiar," Rhonda whispered, jostling him from the cold fury at how far off base he and Adam had been. He remembered Laura pulling them aside at the Farney mansion, her brows knit together in concern over missing pills—

"It's the nurse," he replied, his voice flat.

And he watched as the wind either carried his words to Laura's ears, or perhaps she felt a pair of living eyes on her when she was so used to communing with only the dead. The woman paused in her stride, turned her head. She peered in their direction, and for a split second, Felix thought they might have escaped her gaze since they were partially hidden by the oak.

All of their collective luck over the past months—Rhonda's find in the telephone records, the break in George Hines's work with Jack, the discovery of the DeLuca grave plot—was spent. Laura's eyes found his. They stared at each other. Laura's gaze flickered over to Rhonda for a second, and Felix watched as recognition dawned on her face.

Hindsight was always cruel. Retrospection often led to revisionist history, recasting the past to fit the narrative now that he knew the truth. Everything became clear. All the pieces fell into place, but Felix marveled as he and Laura stared across the cemetery at each other.

How did he never notice before how crazed her eyes were, how they seemed to shine, to glitter with fervor?

CHAPTER THIRTY-FIVE

L aura had waited for a sign.

For the entire season of Lent, she waited. She prayed. She kept the Liturgy of the Hours. She knelt on the hard floor of her bedroom and prayed to the cadence of Clara's wheezing snores in the next room.

Laura fasted. When she had to eat, she only ate foods which gave her no pleasure. Dry toast and saltines that glazed the back of her throat like a layer of dust. Half a grapefruit for breakfast, so sour that her tongue folded in on itself. A single boiled egg, lukewarm water from the tap that tasted faintly of metal. The first few days, her stomach cramped in hunger, but she pushed through it until the desire for food faded.

Already trim, she shed more weight until she could see the ladder of her ribs when she showered. She swore she could see the divots in her forearms, the space between her ulna and radius bones where the flesh had fallen away. As Good Friday approached, she felt something akin to euphoria. Sparks of light crackled in her peripherals. Crystalline notes rang high and clear in her ears.

She took the euphoria, the sparks and pure notes of angelic singing as signs. Small ones. It was nothing big, nothing observed by anyone but her. No sun dancing in the sky or stigmata weeping blood on her palms.

Small signs were still something. It proved God heard her prayers. Laura could feel something coming: an ending to these forty days in her own sort of wilderness, an end to her long years in His service.

She lived at the mansion now as part of the reduced staff. Only she and Martha remained. Susan had been let go in February, and the housekeeper took over her duties. Martha's low-simmering anger at Thomas manifested in the meals she cooked for him: overcooked chicken without an ounce of moisture left to it, gravy so heavily salted it glittered with undissolved crystals. Everyone had heard the rumors by then, that Thomas was selling the factory to Japanese investors.

"My Paul served in the Pacific," Martha reminded Laura more than once. "The disgrace of it, selling to those beasts."

Laura's days settled into a routine. She left the mansion in the morning to run errands and to stop at her house to bring in the mail. She made sure the doors and windows were locked. She swiped a cloth over the layer of dust, ran her fingertip over the spines of her journals that held the sum of her life's work.

She returned to the mansion and dealt with her patient. Clara was almost completely gone now, replaced by an amalgam of younger versions of herself drifting through time. Some days, she was a young woman about to make her debut, her gnarled hands stroking her robe as if it were the white chiffon gown she'd worn a lifetime ago. Other days she was a child, chattering away with Laura about people and places she didn't know.

Through it all, Thomas was in decline too. He spent more time at the mansion. He sat in his study and brooded. He sat in the parlor and brooded. His thick white eyebrows furrowed as he stared out the window or into the flames crackling in the fireplace. He said very little.

Laura considered how much it had to hurt him. She'd lost everything when she was so young: her brother and father when she was a girl, her mother when she was a young woman. That loss struck her when she was still malleable, able to bend to the sorrow without breaking.

Thomas, though, had lived a charmed life. He'd lost nothing until now. His character was set, so the sorrow broke him. It left him frangible, brittle.

✳

Something coming.

It came on Good Friday. Laura always found God had a sense of symbolic timing.

There was no Communion at services that morning. The bell of Saint Boniface hung silent as Laura and the other congregants knelt, stood, knelt, prayed. Each movement made golden sparks of light shimmer across her eyes before they trailed away and faded like fireworks fizzling into the night sky.

After the service ended, she stepped outside to find the storm clouds gone, washed away clean by a stiff breeze that tousled her hair and flipped the collar of her coat against her face. She walked back to her Buick to retrieve the bundle of lilies she'd left there. White lilies felt apt for the coming Easter, a sign of resurrection and sins forgiven. She cradled the flowers in her arms, and the heady perfume of them tickled against her nose.

The fasting hollowed her, like all the heaviness of her innards had been scooped out by the sharp blade of hunger. It left her empty, ready to be filled by better things. The dial on her senses was turned up, made everything brighter and exquisite: the cold wind burnishing the planes of her face to ruddiness, the thick yellow pollen dusting her thumb when she ran it over the stamens, the grit of the crumbling path under her shoes, the heavy wool of her coat against her shoulders.

At the graves of her family, she knelt and placed the flowers. It occurred to her that she couldn't recall their faces anymore, couldn't conjure them up in her mind's eye. Nothing remained but impressions: her father sweeping her into the air in their game as Little Gattina, the bite of her mother's fingers in her arm as she forced her to kneel on the floor, the sick-bed odors of Carlo's room. Her family was just memories now, but even the memories were degraded, a daguerreotype left out in the sun to fade beyond repair.

Laura's head swam when she stood. She braced herself against the stone until she regained her balance. She took a deep breath of the cool air, then turned back toward the parking lot.

She took the path carefully, mindful of the cracks and loose chunks of macadam that could trip her. She thought of the day ahead of her, the weekend ahead of her, the endless stretch of time. She had things to do—a call to the doctor, laundry to do— but her mind couldn't fasten on a plan for any of it. She usually ordered her days, but her thoughts slipped past her, darting silver fish in a stream, and she couldn't grasp any single one long enough to matter.

Laura felt eyes on her, the sudden weight of being observed. Her scalp prickled at the sensation. It was probably nothing. It was *always* nothing when she had this feeling, but she turned and looked anyway, for peace of mind—

It wasn't nothing this time. She saw the pair of them after a long beat. They blended in with the tree they sat halfway behind, the man's khaki-colored coat camouflaging him. It was only the woman in blue who drew Laura's eye for a closer look, and then she recognized them.

The woman first—the chippie from the police station. What was she doing at Saint Boniface's cemetery? Did she have family buried here?

Then Laura recognized her companion. The detective, the young one with the bohunk name. Both sitting, staring at her. The chippie's mouth gaped open, but the detective's mouth was a grim-set line. His eyes telegraphed to Laura as clear as the chiming bells in her head that he knew, he understood now, that it had been underneath his nose the entire time.

Laura rushed back to her car. A handful of quick steps, then an outright sprint. The crumbling asphalt under her shoes felt like a dream she always had: of running, of struggling to get any speed, of needing to run but not being fast enough. The cold air burned in her throat. Sparks fell in her peripherals, black spots floated in front of her.

No sense in playing it off. This was the end. The long path had wound from Shale Hollow, around the East Coast, then back to Mariensburg, and it ended now. She only needed a little more time, the barest bit. She heard the scuff of shoes on the path near her, heard the detective yell something at the woman and the woman's answering shout.

Laura sent one final plea to God and found it answered. She should be weak from fasting, but she felt a surge of energy, a burst of speed. Her feet found surer footing, and her legs pumped harder. The cold air burned past the notch of her throat and filled her lungs, filled every cell of her to the brim.

She got to her Buick a beat before the detective reached her—she could feel him closing in on her, the brush of wind as his fingertips snagged against her coat but found no purchase. She flung open the door, flung herself into the car. She locked the door and looked out at him. His face was ruddy from the wind, from the footrace, but his eyebrows were knit together in fury. He yelled something, but she couldn't make it out over the ringing in her ears.

She smiled, nodded. *In a moment,* the nod said. *Just need to do a few things.*

She turned the ignition and glanced in the rearview mirror. She saw the detective turn away from her. She saw the car he sprinted toward, a nondescript sedan backed into its spot and parked away from the few remaining cars in the lot. Laura threw the Buick in reverse, lifted her arm over the back of the passenger seat, and swiveled her head to look out the back window. She jammed on the gas, felt the sick thrilling dip in her stomach as the Buick lurched backward toward the detective and his car.

She didn't hit him. She didn't *think* she hit him. There was a terrific crunch as she hit his car, a squeal of metal on metal, glass breaking. It jolted her in her seat, threw her head against the headrest so hard her vision turned fuzzy for a second.

No time. No time to waste. She pushed through the dizziness and threw the car into drive. Jammed the gas again, and the Buick leapt forward. When she checked her rearview mirror, she saw the detective on the ground, but she couldn't tell if he was moving.

A cluck of the tongue, a shake of the head. Collateral damage, she supposed. Even God sacrificed the innocent to make a point sometimes. She'd say a prayer for the detective when she could, she promised herself. It was the least she could do.

*

She sped the entire way back. The handful of traffic lights stayed green for her—her path still kept clear.

At the mansion, she forced herself to slow down. She took a breath, kept herself steady. Rushing could ruin everything. She parked, walked into the mansion with steady, even steps.

To the kitchen, then to the bedroom. She gathered the kit she'd pulled together months ago, back when Jack still lived and the house stood stunned in its fresh grief. She had put everything she needed into a small purse, and she carried it now to the parlor where Clara lazed in front of the fire.

Thomas remained in his study.

Laura knelt beside her patient, one ear tuned to the noises outside the door. No sirens. No ringing telephone. She had time, but not much.

"How are you feeling, dearie?" she asked the old woman. Clara blinked at her, but no spark of recognition or intelligent thought seemed to drift through her mind. Whatever had made her Clara for the course of her life had been swept away. This would be a mercy.

"Here," Laura said. She handed the woman a glass of water and five tablets that Clara swallowed without question. She was just as trusting as the boy had been. Laura took back the glass and set it on the side table.

Clara folded her gnarled hands in her lap while Laura performed the same ritual she'd used on the boy. She watched, mindless, as Laura ground a handful of the pills, made a runny paste with a dribble of water in the spoon, then sparked the flint of the lighter under it.

The junkie method. She'd learned it at the veteran's hospital when patients would slip their morphine pills under their tongues, then store them to shoot up later for a bigger high.

Laura filled the syringe as far as it would go. This was a mercy. She ended suffering. It was what nurses did, what angels did. They ushered the suffering away from their world of pain to the great hereafter. Laura laid one hand on Clara's head, smoothed back the white candy-floss hair. She leaned forward and pressed a kiss to the old woman's forehead, then pushed the needle into Clara's neck, right into the carotid.

"You're going to sleep now," she told her.

The Soporal acted fast. Already the woman's purplish eyelids drooped. The pills dissolving in her stomach were insurance, but she wouldn't need them. Laura always did an excellent job the first time around.

"Go with God," she added, and she gathered her kit, put everything away, and tucked it under the chaise. Behind the chiming bells in her ears, she could now hear sirens. Time was running out. The final few grains of sand were ticking through the glass.

Laura reached over the woman's body and snagged the blanket from the back of the chaise. She shook it out and covered her, then went to find Thomas.

*

She didn't bother to knock on his study's door. They were past the point of her deference.

Thomas looked up, startled. Laura shut the door behind her, locked it, and she caught the flare of irritation in his expression. He wasn't a man used to having actions foisted on him—people waited on his orders. Laura's sudden appearance and uninvited settling into the chair across the desk from him likely chafed.

The sirens grew louder. She wasn't hallucinating them.

"Jack didn't commit suicide," she said without preamble.

Thomas narrowed his eyes at her. He shook his head, opened his mouth to respond, but she didn't let him.

"I know you had him killed." A beat to see how the admission hit, and Thomas flinched. It was barely perceptible, but Laura's senses were dialed up to a thousand. She could practically see his heart rate speeding up, the dilation of his blood vessels, the minute flex of his hands along his chair's armrest.

"Detective Haney," she continued. "Your lackey. A cool little sum to have your only son murdered."

The old man gained a semblance of control over himself. He leaned forward. "You don't—"

"I wanted you to know." The sirens were louder still, and Thomas cocked his head at the sound of them. His eyes snapped back to Laura as she continued.

"I wanted you to know that you ended your own bloodline. *You* did. You will pass nothing on when you die."

Thomas gaped at her, the realization perhaps dawning on him slowly, but she only smiled back at him. This delicious moment, almost fifty years in the making. Her journey from here, then back. Guided in her steps by God, protected the whole way so she could have this moment.

This delicious moment. Like manna on her tongue.

The sirens grew closer, then cut off. They were here.

"Have you ever read the Bible?" she asked. "Deuteronomy has a verse I've always liked. It goes, 'Vengeance is mine, and recompense. Their foot shall slip in due time, for the day of their calamity is at hand.'"

"I don't—" Thomas tried to cut in, but Laura didn't let him finish. She heard distant pounding at the door of the mansion, muffled shouts.

"Your foot slipped, Thomas Farney. The day of your calamity is at hand. I am God's own instrument of vengeance. You formed the mold, but God sharpened me for this moment. You killed your own son, but I killed the boy."

The man's face turned grey at her words. He fell back in his chair, his mouth gumming uselessly as he tried to say something in reply. Laura thought he might be having a cardiac event, and the thought saddened her. She wanted Thomas to live to be a hundred. She wanted him to face decades alone, in penance for his mountain of sins.

Banging now at the study's door. Thomas looked past her, said nothing. His gaze returned to hers, and she stood, leaned across the desk so she could stare into his eyes.

"Carlo DeLuca. Nicola DeLuca. An eye for an eye, Thomas. Your family for mine. Now we're square, you and I."

Everything that came afterward—the sound of the study door splintering, the rough hands jostling her, the cool handcuffs on her wrists—happened dimly to Laura. She observed herself as if she were perched from above. She felt everything that lingered in her fall away, sloughed off by the warm golden light that enveloped her.

CHAPTER THIRTY-SIX

The phone rang shrill that morning.

Adam was already awake. His insomnia always ebbed and flowed, but he was at a high-water mark for sleepless nights lately. His stomach bothered him, churned away full of acid that bubbled up his throat when he tried to lie down. His head often hurt, too, a dull band of aching that ran from ear to ear and seemed to settle behind his eyes as the day progressed.

When his sergeant called, he was already awake. He had been for hours. He sat in his kitchen with a half-empty glass of milk and the previous day's newspaper in the harsh yellow circle thrown by the overhead light.

Adam answered the phone. It was always bad news when it rang that early. He dreaded the new case waiting for him: some bad person had done a bad thing, and Adam would gain a new ghost.

The drive back to Mariensburg was déjà vu. Adam had the sense of being caught in a loop, a Möbius strip twisted to repeat on itself. The drive last year before winter started in earnest; the drive now as winter faded. An entire season come and gone, but the same scrubby outskirts as he approached the city. The same church, the same auto repair shop. The same factory with its smokestacks reaching up into the blue-grey sky to skate across the thin clouds that raced high up in the atmosphere.

He and Felix had gotten it wrong. His sergeant had given him the broad strokes over the phone, though he didn't know much. He only knew the captain—the new one, not Krause—had called. He sent up the signal flare for help, and Adam answered the call.

It hadn't been the father at all. Jack Farney was no killer. The entire case had been a string of errors, of rushing against the clock. They had been led, sure, but Adam's own perceptions had clouded his judgment and made the leading easy. The goddamned nurse—a woman, for Christ's sake—had led him by the nose.

He had never even considered the possibility that the killer could be a woman. He guessed he had more than one blind spot after all.

He should have seen it. He was the seasoned detective. He had worked that murder years ago where the mother killed her own child—he knew it was possible. But he'd missed it by a mile, and Felix had kept teasing at the case even after it was closed.

No, scratch that—Felix and his new partner. Off the books, after hours, the two of them had started over.

And they solved it, he thought.

The realization that Felix and the receptionist had cracked the code left him a little bitter, and more than a little melancholy. He was the old guard. Felix, still young enough to be optimistic, was the new. And women, too, the cute little receptionist with the bright painted nails and the eagle eyes. Adam's world was changing—the world always changed—but this time he wasn't swept up in the change but instead was being left behind.

His time was coming to an end. He could feel it in his bones. Jack Farney was another ghost he'd have to drag around, but maybe he wouldn't have to drag many more after this.

Back to the barracks, then. Déjà vu all over again.

Captain Winslow greeted him near the receptionist's desk, currently unmanned. Winslow shook his hand. He cast his doleful eyes at Adam and thanked him for coming. He reiterated some of what Adam's sergeant had told him. He said they'd all gather and talk after Felix took him to the scene.

He led Adam into the barracks, and there sat Felix: the chipper asshole with the grin on his face, then a grimace as he struggled to stand. Adam looked down and saw the thick plaster cast that encased the man's ankle, and Felix caught his glance.

"My first field injuries," he said. He tapped his temple, and Adam saw a nasty scrape there that looked fresh.

Felix held out a hand, shook with Adam. He said it was good to see him again, and Adam didn't detect even a hint of lying. Felix plopped down into his seat, but only long enough to retrieve his crutches from where they lay on the ground. He stood back up, got himself situated with his coat, his crutches. He hobbled toward the exit.

"C'mon," he said. "I'll bring you up to speed while we head over. You're driving. My car is toast."

In the Bonneville, Felix directed him not toward the mansion, but instead toward an older part of town where the houses stood in neat, cramped rows. His sergeant had given him the broad strokes, and Felix filled in a bit more.

"Jack's suicide didn't sit well with me, so we kept digging into it. Off the clock."

"Risky," Adam replied. "That's a good way to lose your shield, kid."

"It didn't sit right." His tone was firm, but not petulant. "We found evidence Jack wasn't in Mariensburg the night of Junior's murder, and we went from there. It turns out the revenge angle had been the right one."

Adam shook his head. "The nurse. She had an alibi, though."

"Faulty alibi. Turns out she had a second car parked in the alley behind her house. Mr. Castaldo across the street had no idea."

"Christ above. She was right in front of us the whole time."

Felix glanced at him, and Adam caught his expression. His mouth twisted into a sympathetic frown.

"It would have come to light eventually," he said. "Things deteriorated beyond our control."

Felix pointed out the turns to Adam, and he filled in the rest: The work on the ledger book, the chat with Mr. Castaldo. How it had been a hunch, a guess, and how it had paid off. The stakeouts at the cemetery that culminated with his own near brush with death when Laura rammed his car. How Rhonda had set off running toward the rectory, banging on the door until a bewildered deacon let her in to use the phone. How Felix had hobbled to his mangled car, each step an agony, and drove toward the mansion in a car smoking and leaking oil in big, shiny puddles.

How the cavalry beat him there, but just barely: a handful of officers, Winslow, Krause. How Rhonda, in her distrust of the authority around her, had called everyone and hoped for the best.

Then the scene inside the mansion. Thomas Farney in shock, gaping at them as they arrested Laura. The nurse didn't say a word, had only smiled a small, secret smile like the statue of a saint.

How they found Clara Farney when they secured the scene, still warm but long gone.

"That's a hell of a story," Adam said. "But you solved it."

"It was good luck and better timing," Felix said.

"After bad luck and worse timing the first time around." It sounded acerbic, so he tacked on a weak chuckle to soften it.

The younger man pointed out a house, told him to park against the curb. The house looked like its neighbors, save for the bright police tape that marked it off. The giant yellow seal across the door.

"Here. The nurse's house." Felix opened his door, swung his unwieldy broken leg out of the car. "You're gonna want to see this. This is why we called you."

✱

Laura Lucas's house reminded Adam of a monk's cell. There was little in the way of homeyness. Everything was sparse, simple: no family photos, no whimsical bric-à-brac. The only nod to decor was a single framed print hanging on the wall, a reproduction of an old painting. Adam studied it.

It was dark, creepy. He recognized Jesus, circled by the lone bit of light in the upper part of the painting, but the lower half showed a crush of people trapped underground, harried by angels and tormented by twisted black demons.

"Nice, right?" Felix clumped over on his crutches. "At least my mom just hangs pictures of Jesus with fluffy white sheep."

"It's creepy."

"It's the Last Judgment."

"That doesn't make it less creepy."

Felix snorted. "Come on."

Adam followed him through the living room into the back of the house. It was just as sparse—a small desk, a single chair, a tall lamp in the corner. And a bookshelf neatly lined with bound books that bore no titles along their spines.

"Here." Felix leaned on his crutches and nodded toward the bookcase. "Pick one. Just put it back where you found it. Library rules, old man. We're still cataloguing the scene."

Adam furrowed his brow but did as Felix said. He reached out and plucked a book from the shelf. When he opened it, he found it wasn't a book but a notebook. A diary. The pages were filled with neat cursive, each entry dated.

"She kept a diary?" he asked. He thumbed through the pages and glanced at Felix. The man's face was somber, a touch pale. The nasty scrape on his head peeked blue and purple from under the bandage.

Felix balanced himself and held his hand out, and Adam gave him the diary. He watched as Felix paged through, his lips moving a little as he read. When he found what he was looking for, he handed it back to Adam.

"Read it." He tapped at the entry marked as July 12, 1953.

Adam cleared his throat and squinted at the handwriting. "'I have prayed for the girl. She has lost the grace that made her a human being. I prayed over her tonight. When she calmed, I released her from her pain and prayed for her soul.'"

Adam paused, and his stomach twisted in his gut and sent a wave of acid marching up the line of his chest toward his throat. He glanced at Felix again. "Is this—"

"She notes the names and the dates."

He looked down at the entry and saw it. Yes, the date and then the words *Katherine Kimbark*.

Adam took the few steps over to the chair and sank into it. He clutched the journal in his hands, then paged through more.

There were other entries, bizarre and disjointed. The nurse had documented her dreams. She documented visions she had, shafts of sudden sunlight or peals of thunder in the clear blue sky. She wrote about someone named Gattina. She documented her prayers, the conversations she had with God.

She documented his responses to her.

But there were other entries like the one for Katherine Kimbark. Dates, names. *Charlie Murray. Josiah Washington. Sarah Bauer. Mary McVie. Infant Dominguez. William Novak.* A perverse echo of the old ledger book of Farney's sins, only Laura Lucas—Laura DeLuca, rather—had kept track of herself.

Adam's stomach twisted again, and he swallowed against the hot bile at the back of his throat. The bookshelf was full of these notebooks.

Adam couldn't even bear to meet Felix's eyes when he asked, "Are all of those like this?" All those books, pages and pages full of neat, small handwriting. Felix had floated the idea of a serial killer all along and Adam had thought it ludicrous—

"They seem to be. The ones we've gone through, at least."

"Jesus Christ, kid." Adam closed his eyes, felt the press of his ghosts crowding around him. "I thought you'd call someday to grab a beer or something."

He heard the younger man chuckle, heard him move closer on his clumsy crutches. A beat later, and he felt the man's hand on his shoulder, a friendly clasping but with a deeper undercurrent. Bracing him, maybe. Letting him know he wasn't alone.

"We're cataloguing the scene now, but there's a lot to unravel here. Here and elsewhere." He fell silent a moment. "Laura worked all along the Eastern Seaboard for decades. There's Jack's suspicious-looking suicide. And there's Thomas Farney knowing about the impact of his mines on the soil, the water here. There's malfeasance. He paid off elected officials."

"Goddamned," Adam groaned.

"Captain Winslow's already been in contact with other agencies."

"Interstate crime will fall to the FBI."

"True. He talked to them too. They're sending someone on Monday." A breath. "But this is huge, Adam. Winslow thinks they'll pull together a task force. They can't even estimate the potential victims yet. She worked in hospitals and clinics. How many times did a coroner sign off on a natural death that was anything but?"

"Kid—"

Another squeeze on his shoulder, cutting him off. "They'll need all the help they can get to unravel it all. At least in Pennsylvania. Who knows with the other states?"

Adam kept his eyes closed. He willed his hammering heart to slow a bit. Maybe this would be his swan song. This would be his final case, the case that spawned other cases, the rabbit's warren that led to more and more evil the deeper they went.

He tried to shift his perspective. He tried not to focus on the work ahead, the long nights and bad meals and poor sleep in motel beds that reeked of mildew. Instead, he tried to imagine the victims. How many? Could they even know for sure? Laura had worked with the sick and vulnerable for decades. These voiceless victims rested uneasy in their graves. Could Adam be their advocate?

That's why he got into this work, wasn't it? Speaking for those who couldn't.

The thought buoyed him. He felt his pulse slowing back to normal. He laid a hand over his stomach to calm the churning there. He felt his old resolve return, the bright burning filament—naïve, he knew—of justice served, bad guys locked away. He opened his eyes and looked up at where Felix stood over him, patiently balanced on his crutches and his remaining good foot.

"Alright, kid," he said. "Tell me where I'm going and I'm on my way."

ABOUT THE AUTHOR

Christine Boyer's writing has been honored in both the *Best American Mystery and Suspense* anthology (Distinguished Mystery and Suspense of 2022) and the *Best American Essays* anthology (Notable Essays of 2020). Her work has been published in numerous anthologies and literary journals, including *Jacked: A Crime Fiction Anthology, Weren't Another Other Way to Be: Outlaw Fiction Inspired by the Songs of Waylon Jennings, FOLIO, Little Patuxent Review*, and *Tahoma Literary Review. Black Maria* is her first novel. Originally from Pennsylvania, Christine now lives in Massachusetts.